ADVANCE PRAISE FOR *WHEN DEATH DRAWS NEAR*

"I've always known Carrie as someone devoted to mastering her craft, be it forensics, fine art, public speaking, kick-butt dinners (but please, no more zucchini!), or writing suspenseful mystery novels with just the right touch of her characteristic wit. *When Death Draws Near* reflects Carrie's way with all things creative: it's engaging, tightly woven, painstakingly researched, and a just plain fun read. Dive in!"

—FRANK PERETTI, *NEW YORK TIMES* BESTSELLING AUTHOR

"Carrie Stuart Parks is a riveting storyteller, and every book about forensic artist Gwen Marcey shines with authenticity from this real-life forensic artist. Her books are an automatic buy for me and stay on my keeper shelf. *When Death Draws Near* and every other Parks novel is highly recommended!"

—COLLEEN COBLE, *USA TODAY* BESTSELLING AUTHOR OF
MERMAID MOON AND THE ROCK HARBOR NOVELS

"Thank you so very much, Carrie Stuart Parks, for giving me a reading hangover! Carrie injected this story with so much tension, suspense, and superb characterization that I lost hours of sleep and ignored my own work because I simply HAD to finish the book. I highly recommend [*When Death Draws Near*], but only when you have several hours of uninterrupted time to read because you will NOT want to put it down. Fabulous job! Eagerly waiting the next Gwen Marcey story!"

—LYNETTE EASON, AWARD-WINNING, BESTSELLING
AUTHOR OF THE HIDDEN IDENTITY SERIES

A race from the first chapter to the end, *When Death Draws Near* is a delight for suspense lovers of all types."

—CARA PUTMAN, AWARD-WINNING AUTHOR OF *SHADOWED*
BY GRACE AND *WHERE TREETOPS GLISTEN*

"Christian fiction lovers will devour this new work by Carrie Stuart Parks because it delivers on so many fronts. It's not only a page-turning murder mystery, but a gripping and compassionate story about personal trial."

—CRESTON MAPES, BESTSELLING AUTHOR OF *THE CRITTENDON FILES*

PRAISE FOR THE GWEN MARCEY NOVELS

"Once again, Parks has written a top-notch forensic thriller . . . The details are rich but not overpowering, and Parks writes with an excellent balance of science, forensics, action, and comfort. This second Gwen Marcey novel will create a following for Parks, with readers anxiously awaiting the next installment."

—*RT Book Reviews*, 4½ stars, on *The Bones Will Speak*

"This book holds the reader's attention from the first page with a riveting mystery that will keep them guessing until the final chapter."

—*CBA Retailer + Resources*, on *The Bones Will Speak*

"Parks, in her debut novel, has clearly done her research and never disappoints when it comes to crisp dialogue, characterization, or surprising twists and turns."

—*Publishers Weekly*, on *A Cry from the Dust*

"Besides having a resourceful and likable heroine, the book also features that rarest of characters: a villain you don't see coming, but whom you hate with relish . . . *A Cry from the Dust* will keep you hoping, praying and guessing till the end."

—*BookPage*

"Renowned forensic and fine artist Parks's action-packed and compelling tale of suspense is haunting in its intensity. Well researched and written in an almost journalistic style, this emotionally charged story is recommended for fans of Ted Dekker, Mary Higgins Clark, and historical suspense."

—*Library Journal*, on *A Cry from the Dust*

"Parks's fast-paced and suspenseful debut novel is an entertaining addition to the inspirational genre. Her writing is polished, and the research behind the novel brings credibility to the story . . . an excellent book that is sure to put Carrie Stuart Parks on readers' radars."

—*RT Book Reviews*, 4 stars, on *A Cry from the Dust*

"A unique novel of forensics and fanaticism. A good story on timely subjects well told. For me, these are the ingredients of a successful novel today and Carrie Stuart Parks has done just that."

—Carter Cornick, FBI Counterterrorism and Forensic Science Research (Ret.), on *A Cry from the Dust*

WHEN DEATH DRAWS NEAR

A Gwen Marcey Novel

CARRIE STUART PARKS

Thomas Nelson
Since 1798

Published in Nashville, Tennessee, by Thomas Nelson. Thomas Nelson is a registered trademark of HarperCollins Christian Publishing, Inc.

Thomas Nelson titles may be purchased in bulk for educational, business, fund-raising, or sales promotional use. For information, please e-mail SpecialMarkets@ ThomasNelson.com.

Scripture quotations are from the King James Version of the Bible and the New King James Version®. © 1982 by Thomas Nelson. Used by permission. All rights reserved.

Publisher's Note: This novel is a work of fiction. Names, characters, places, and incidents are either products of the author's imagination or used fictitiously. All characters are fictional, and any similarity to people living or dead is purely coincidental.

Library of Congress Cataloging-in-Publication Data

Names: Parks, Carrie Stuart, author.
Title: When death draws near: a Gwen Marcey novel / Carrie Stuart Parks.
Description: Nashville: Thomas Nelson, [2016] | Series: Gwen Marcey; 3
Identifiers: LCCN 2016006263 | ISBN 9781401690472 (softcover)
Subjects: LCSH: Facial reconstruction (Anthropology)--Fiction. | Forensic pathologists--Fiction. | Cold cases (Criminal investigation)--Fiction. | GSAFD: Suspense fiction. | Mystery fiction. | Christian fiction.
Classification: LCC PS3616.A75535 W48 2016 | DDC 813/.6--dc23 LC record available at http://lccn.loc.gov/2016006263

Printed in the United States of America
16 17 18 19 20 21 RRD 6 5 4 3 2 1

To Frank,
the master storyteller.
Once again, thank you.
—Grasshopper

PROLOGUE

MIRIAM KNEW, SHE *KNEW* TONIGHT WOULD BE the night the Holy Spirit would anoint her. The tingling filled her chest and ran down her arms. "Shananamamascaca," she whispered in prayer language, spinning to the pounding, driving music.

The Spirit was powerful in the church tonight. Around her, the congregation, led by Pastor Grady Maynard, danced, twirled, and praised the Lord in tongues. The bare lightbulbs hanging from the ceiling cast a harsh yellow light on the worshipers. The odor of candles, sweat, and musty carpet rose like incense. Arms were raised, voices lifted, eyes closed.

The burning power of the Holy Spirit rushed through Miriam's body. An indescribable sense of joy and peace filled her to overflowing. Time was meaningless. The music faded, singing muffled, shouts muted. Her lips moved in a prayer she could barely hear. "Shaaaanaamaascaca." Tears slid down her face, pooling on her chin.

Pastor Maynard placed his microphone on the pulpit and

reached under the pew in the front of the church. Sweat soaked his green dress shirt and streamed down his face.

Several men moved closer, arms raised and waving or hands clapping.

Pulling out a wooden box with a Plexiglas lid, Maynard reached inside. Louder shouts of praise erupted around him. Tambourines and cymbals joined the cacophony of sound.

Miriam took her place in the circle surrounding Maynard.

From the box came a slow *chchch* speeding to a continuous *cheeeeeheeeee*.

The pastor drew the giant timber rattler from the serpent box. The snake twisted and coiled in his hand, its flat, gray-black head darting from side to side. He draped the serpent around his neck and reached for more from the box.

Miriam moved closer.

Pastor Maynard raised several serpents overhead before handing them to the next man. Keeping the timber rattler around his neck, he lifted his voice in jubilant tongues.

The snakes passed around the circle. Worshipers would drape the snakes on their heads or cuddle them in their arms while spinning or dancing.

Miriam moved out of the circle and slipped next to Maynard. This would be the serpent she would handle. She reached for the rattler.

Pastor Maynard slipped the snake from his neck and into her hands. She lifted it over her head and closed her eyes. The Spirit's power over the serpent charged up her arm. She stomped her feet and whirled, the serpent held high. The Holy Spirit claimed overwhelming victory.

She lowered the serpent.

The snake whipped around and struck her wrist, sinking its fangs deep into her flesh.

Pain like a million bee stings coursed up her arm. Someone snatched the serpent from her hands as she doubled over in agony and dropped to her knees.

The drumming music stopped. A chorus of voices rose, then faded.

Miriam gasped. Blackness lapped around her mind. The world retreated into velvet nothingness.

CHAPTER ONE

"MA'AM. SHERIFF REED TOLD ME TO COME AND get you. He said he was sorry you had to wait so long. The body's here. I mean, it was here before . . . downstairs. In the morgue."

I craned my head backward to see the young, lean-faced deputy standing over me. He had to be six foot four or taller, very slender, with wispy brown hair. His eyes were blue with heavy lids and his mouth red, probably from chewing his lips. Sure enough, his cheeks flushed at my studying him and he started gnawing his lower lip.

Sitting outside the Pikeville Community Hospital, I'd been enjoying the late-October sunshine and waiting for someone to remember I was here. I picked up my forensic art kit and followed the officer through a set of doors to an elevator next to the nurses' station. "I'm sorry. I didn't catch your name."

"Junior Reed." He nodded at his answer. "Sheriff Reed is my father."

I did a double take. He didn't look anything like Clayton Reed, the sheriff of Pike County, Kentucky, who'd picked me up from the Lexington airport yesterday. "Nice to meet you, Junior." I stuck out my hand. "I'm Gwen Marcey."

He hesitated for a moment, staring at my hand, then awkwardly shook it. His hand was wet.

The elevator door opened. As we entered, I surreptitiously wiped my hand on my slacks. The elevator seemed to think about moving, then quietly closed and slipped to the floor below, taking much longer than simply running down the stairs. The elevator finally opened. The smell hit me immediately.

I swallowed hard and took a firmer grip on my kit.

Several deputies had gathered in the middle of the hall, talking softly. They turned and stared at us. I couldn't quite decipher the expressions on their faces. They parted as we approached, revealing a closed door inscribed with the word *Morgue*.

Junior entered the room and moved to the body bag resting on a stainless steel table. Sheriff Clayton Reed—a large man with a thick chest, buzz-cut hair, and gray-blond mustache, stood next to a man in navy blue scrubs. I nodded at the man. "Hello. I'm Gwen Marcey, the forensic artist."

"Ma'am. I'm Dr. Billy Graham." He noted my raised eyebrows and grinned. "My parents had high hopes for a particular career direction."

I grinned back, then slowed as I approached the table. I'd seen bodies before. Too many times before, but I still had a moment of hesitation when I knew what was coming. This was once someone's son or daughter, parent or friend. And no one knew of the death. Then the analytical part of my brain would take over, and I could concentrate on drawing the face of the unknown remains.

I just had to get past the *ick* moment.

"Here you go," Sheriff Clay Reed said in a deep Appalachian

accent. My brain was still trying to translate his comments for my western Montana ears. "So far, no one has recognized . . . what was left." He unzipped the body bag. Several flies made an angry exit. The odor was like a solid wall.

Junior spun and made it to a bucket near the door before losing his lunch.

I fought the urge to join him.

The sheriff frowned at Junior, then caught my gaze. "He never had much of a stomach for smells."

I could relate to that. "What . . . um . . . what can you tell me about the body?"

"According to the doc here"—Clay nodded at the man— "he's been dead for at least a month, but hard to say exactly at this time . . . critters and all . . . in his late teens or early twenties. Slender. Teeth in pretty good shape, but obviously never been to a dentist. No help there."

Pulling out a small sketchbook and pencil, I jotted down the sheriff's information. "No one reported him missing?"

The sheriff shook his head. "But that's not surprising. A lot of folks around here steer clear of the law."

"Cause of death?"

"Can't be sure just yet," the doctor said. "But I'd guess . . . snakebite."

I stopped writing and looked up. "I thought, I mean, didn't you say he was murdered?"

"In a sense, he was." Clay nodded toward a counter beside him. "We found those with the body."

A white cotton bag, badly stained; a golf club with a bend at the end; a long clamping tool; a revolver; and a moldy Bible all lay spread out.

"Okay. What does that tell you?" I asked.

"I'd say he was snake hunting," the sheriff said.

"I still don't understand."

"The golf club with the metal hook on the end is a home-made snake hook. They cut the club off the end, then bend a piece of metal to form a U."

"Can't you just buy one?"

"That can cost a bit. But folks are always throwing away golf clubs." Clay chuckled. "I've tossed more than my fair share after a bad round of golf."

He stopped chuckling at my expression. "Well then, those are snake tongs, and the bag is to put the snake into. The revolver is loaded with snake-shot ammunition."

"But that doesn't mean—"

He unzipped the body bag farther. Lying across the man's stomach was what was left of a very dead snake.

I dropped my pencil and paper. "Ohmigosh!"

"That's a big 'un." Junior had stopped throwing up and had moved next to me. He wiped his mouth with the back of his hand, then started twiddling his fingers as if playing a trumpet.

Resisting the urge to bolt from the room, I bent down and snatched up my materials, then reached into my forensic kit and tugged out my digital camera. I stayed bent over until I felt some blood returning to my face. "What kind of snake is that?"

"I put in a call to Jason Morrow with animal control to identify—"

"Rattler," Junior said. "*Crotalus horridus*, also known as a canebrake or timber rattler—"

"That's enough, Junior," Clay said.

When I heard the zipper close on the body bag, I stood. Only the man's ravaged face was now exposed.

"Now, Sheriff," Dr. Graham said, "we don't know for sure yet that he died of snakebite. I only said he *may* have—"

"Come on, Billy," Clay said. "The snake's head was full of bird shot from that pistol. Obviously he got bit while trying to catch a snake. He didn't even try to go for help."

I felt at a loss as to what the men were talking about. Snakes in general gave me the creeps, and a stinky body with a snake on top really was pushing my heebie-jeebies meter. "Gentlemen, my knowledge and experience with snakes is very limited." I resisted the urge to add, *Thank the Lord.* "I still don't get why you consider this a murder."

"Oh, not an out-and-out murder," the sheriff said. "I mentioned he didn't even try to go for help. He shot the snake, then sat down, read his Bible, and prayed."

Before I could say anything, the sheriff held up a finger. "I'm not done. That Bible falls open to Mark 16. I think he was catching snakes to handle in church."

"Church?" My creeped-out meter ratcheted up a notch. "Uh, regardless of how he died, you did still want me to draw him for identification, right? Or are you just planning to go to his church and ask around?"

All the men exchanged glances. "Not that simple," the sheriff finally said. "We'll need that drawing."

I took a deep breath, instantly regretting it as the stench of the body filled my lungs. "Here's how this works. I'm going to photograph him from all angles with this evidence scale." I held up what looked like a small ruler. "I'll be ready to work on this drawing when I return to my hotel. You said the rape victim is upstairs, so I'll interview her—"

"Well now, Miz Marcey." Clay rubbed his chin. "Seems you have a lot to do with this here sketch. You can maybe meet with Shelby Lee tomorrow—"

"Why not now?"

"There's just no sense in overloading you with work."

I blinked at him. "I'm hardly overloaded. I'm here. Although I'm glad to help you with the unknown remains." I nodded at the body bag. "You did fly me out all the way from Montana to work on your serial rapist cases."

"Well now . . ."

"Is something wrong, Sheriff?" I asked.

"No. No. No. Nothing. Nothing's wrong." He shook his head, then turned and headed for the door. "Follow me."

I stared at his retreating back. *He's lying.*

CHAPTER TWO

SHELBY LEE *REALLY* LOOKED DEAD.

Only the minuscule rising and falling of the blanket pulled up to her chest revealed a hint of life.

"Shelby Lee?" The sheriff touched her arm. "Shelby Lee, the artist lady is here. Wake up, honey."

I placed my forensic art kit, a small roller bag, on the floor. After pulling out a notepad and two pencils, tucking one behind my ear as backup, I moved closer to her bed.

Her porcelain skin blended with the hospital sheets. Delicate lavender veins tinted her eyelids while deep smudges of violet underscored her eyes. Her parted lips were raw and cracked. A line of cigarette burns marched up her arm, and the stitches on her temple stood out like a black centipede.

I snapped the pencil in two. *Oh, Lord, I need to catch this guy.*

The infusion pump above her head *click-click-click*ed away and cool, antiseptic-smelling air wheezed from the wall vent, gently fluffing my hair.

"She drifts in and out," Clay said. "Well, we tried—"

"Sheriff?" The question was an exhale of air from the girl.

"Ah, Shelby Lee, honey, this is the lady I told you about. Remember?" Clay moved slightly so she could see me. "Her name is Miz Marcey. She's going to draw a sketch of the man who did this to you."

"Call me Gwen." I kept my voice soft.

Shelby Lee looked from Clay's face to mine, then back to his. Her gaze slid down to his gold watch, then his left hand. Tears pooled in her eyes before trickling down her cheeks. She bit her lower lip and shook her head slightly.

Crimson welts circled her thin wrists and round bruises punctuated her throat.

"I can come back later if you want," I said.

She turned her head and stared at the wall.

"I was afraid of this." Clay touched my elbow and pointed to the door.

I picked up my kit and we stepped into the hallway. A hot flash, a reminder of my battle with breast cancer over a year ago, slipped up my neck and across my face. I waited until it passed.

"Well." Clay sighed. "Like I said, we tried. I can't thank you enough, Miz Marcey, for flying out here to help us—"

"Whoa, wait a minute." I placed the kit on the floor and held up my hands. "I didn't say I couldn't develop a composite sketch. I said I can come back when she's ready."

Clay ran a hand through his hair. "But what if she's never ready? I mean, I don't know anything about the stuff you do—"

"Forensic art."

"Yeah, that forensic art. Now, I'm just a country boy here, but isn't it true some folks can *never* remember?"

"Yeees." I half shrugged my shoulder. "Sometimes. We won't

know until I try again. Or, since this is a serial rapist, I could work with other victims. Most rape victims will never forget the face of their attacker."

"That might be hard. The other victims skedaddled. In some cases, the whole family left town. No forwarding address."

"Why?"

"Don't know. Maybe the shame—"

"Shame? They're victims!"

"Now, Miz Marcey, don't get all riled."

"Please call me Gwen."

"Okay, Miz Gwen. That's not what I think. We have some small minds here." He shrugged. "I really don't know where they are. I had hoped that Shelby Lee—" Clay's cell phone jangled from his pocket. He tugged it out. "Sheriff Reed." He listened a moment. "We're getting busier than a stump-tailed cow in fly time." He dry-washed his face with one hand. "Get Junior on it. Okay then, who is on duty? Get her. No, I . . . hang it, I'll come over myself." He dropped the phone into his pocket and frowned at me. "I gotta run." He swiftly strolled down the hall. "I'll get someone to give you a ride to the hotel," he called over his shoulder.

"But, Sheriff—"

I was alone. A prickling of unease touched me between the shoulder blades. I slowly wandered to the waiting area near the front doors of the hospital and slid onto an ultramodern black sofa. Sheriff Clay Reed seemed to give up pretty easily on using a forensic artist on that rape case. I thought for a moment, then pulled out my phone.

Dave answered on the first ring. "Ravalli County Sheriff's Department. Sheriff Moore."

"Dave—"

"Ah. Gwen. In trouble already?"

"No—"

"Good. I don't have time to spring you from jail. I'm on my way out the door to the Law Enforcement Torch Run in Seattle."

"About this temporary job you found for me—"

"You've been fired already? That didn't take long. Less than twenty-four hours."

"Dave, stop interrupting me."

A family of six poured into the waiting room. Two of the youngest seemed to be having a competition as to who could scream louder. "Hang on." I stood, grabbed my kit, and headed outside. Once there, I made sure no one was in earshot. "I thought you told me the sheriff here needed a forensic artist on a serial rapist case. I'm now working on an unknown remains."

"Hey, work is work."

"But this guy has no clue as to what to do with me!"

"I should welcome him to the club—"

"Dave! I just need to know what the deal is about this sheriff."

"Look, you told me you were broke."

"Well—"

"And you needed work. If I remember, you said you'd flip hamburgers if necessary."

I squeezed the phone tighter. "That's a figure of speech. About Clay . . . ?"

"I'm getting there," Dave said. "I made a few calls to former classmates from National Academy. One sheriff, from the next county over from you, mentioned the serial rapist. I called Sheriff Reed and told him about you."

"And?"

"He initially wasn't interested, but called the next day and requested you."

"What made him change his mind?"

"I don't know, and I don't care. I'm late. If you don't like the job, just come home."

"I will. But something bothers me—"

"Fine. Be bothered. Talk to you later." He hung up.

Before I could call him back, a deputy drove up, parked, and signaled to me. I put my kit in the backseat, then slid into the front. "Ma'am." He drove me over to the hotel.

I suddenly felt exhausted. My plane had been delayed getting into Lexington the previous day, and even though Clay picked me up, the drive from Lexington to Pikeville was another two hours over a winding road. At the hotel, I'd only slept a short amount of time. I wasn't used to street sounds and lights outside my window.

The deputy dropped me off in front of the hotel and I crossed to the front desk. The clerk was a woman in her twenties with short black hair, a purple streak on the left side. Five earrings marched up each ear and a small silver loop pierced her eyebrow. Her name badge said Ina Jo.

"Hi." I grinned at her. "Do you have a list of places to eat? Either walking distance or delivery."

Ina Jo opened a drawer and pulled out a handful of menus. I was about to ask about recommendations when a woman arrived with an adorable baby. "She had a good nap." The woman handed the baby over to Ina Jo. The clerk took her and automatically started rocking back and forth and rubbing the baby's back.

"What a cutie," I said.

Ina Jo beamed, then said to the other woman, "Can you take her tomorrow? I have to work."

I grabbed up the menus and left the two women working out babysitting details. Crossing the marble-and-wood-lined lobby to the first-floor hall, I made my way down to my corner room. Windows faced the front of the hotel and a parking lot on the side. An exit door to my left led to the back parking area. During the day, the staff routinely propped the door open with a large rock to facilitate frequent smoking breaks, a security violation that fell on deaf ears when I pointed it out.

The hotel had been remodeled recently, and my suite featured a kitchenette and a separate bedroom, all decorated in neutral, earth-toned colors. The space allowed me to spread my forensic art materials across the kitchen and living area. After turning off my cell, I kicked off my black pumps and strolled to the bedroom. Then I pulled the drapes to block the view of the parking lot. I took off the claret-colored Burberry jacket and matching slacks and hung them up. My fingers lingered on the expensive fabric. Fortunately I was the right size to benefit from a barely worn, designer wardrobe dumped at a Missoula second-hand shop.

I unsnapped my specially made bra containing a pair of heavy breast prostheses and draped it over a chair. The breast forms were a necessary evil until I decided what I would do about the double mastectomy I'd had over a year and a half ago. I hadn't been able to recover the last prostheses, dubbed Lucy and Ethel, buried somewhere in Utah. It had been my first case after finishing up my cancer treatments, a little more than a year ago. I'd almost lost my life. I was grateful that the only thing buried was a couple of synthetic boobs. The current pair I'd christened Thelma and Louise.

The phone rang. I picked it up, but all I heard was a dial tone.

Slipping into a charcoal-colored lounge outfit, I walked to the kitchen where someone had thoughtfully stocked my refrigerator with cold drinks. I sat at the kitchen table, which I'd already set up with an LED light box, portable drafting board, scanner, and printer.

I should have made a bigger deal about talking to Shelby Lee. Maybe made Clay leave the room. He might have been the reason she didn't want to talk.

After downloading the digital images of the body from my camera to my laptop, I selected the best angle, scaled it, and sent it to the printer.

He'd tied her wrists. She'd struggled, rubbing them raw.

Once the enlarged image emerged, I taped it to the light box and placed a piece of Clearprint drafting velum over it. I traced the image exactly, simplifying the remaining facial features, then removed the photograph and worked with the tracing. The lips were gone, so I drew a line where the teeth came together, ending it between the canine and first premolar. The lips would go roughly from gum line to gum line and cover the first six teeth.

Tomorrow I'll insist Clay leave Shelby Lee's room. And if he fights me . . . Well, that girl deserves a mama bear on her side.

Once I roughed in the outline of the features, I opened a catalog of faces I'd created using old booking photos. I found the nearest feature to the one I'd sketched and used the shading and fine detail to create a more lifelike sketch. This always kept my drawings from looking too generic or flat.

His eyes appeared to have been slightly shallow set, with level eyebrows hovering just above the eye socket. I thickened the brows with short strokes, rotating my pencil to keep the tip sharp.

17

The phone rang.

I jumped. Reaching the phone on the second ring, I picked up the handset. "Hello?"

Silence, then a dial tone.

I stared at the phone a minute, then walked to the door and threw the dead bolt. Returning to my work, I checked the photograph against my sketch. Fortunately the coroner hadn't washed the body before I had time to photograph it, and I could see the rough outline of the hair style and color. Once the body was rinsed, the hair appeared darker and any style disappeared.

I need to talk to Shelby Lee pretty soon or I'll be out of time. I fly out the day after tomorrow.

Two hours later, I was finishing up. The ravaged face had turned into a rather handsome young man under my moving pencil.

After photographing the drawing, I uploaded the digital image to my printer and printed out several copies. I backed up the image on a flash drive. The copies and flash drive went into a plastic file folder for the sheriff. As I tucked the original sketch into a small portfolio, my stomach grumbled, reminding me I'd managed to miss lunch. When I stood and stretched, my muscles joined the protest.

"Food, then a long bath," I informed the empty room, then pulled out the various dinner menus I'd picked up. Several looked promising. I turned my cell back on. It showed a missed call and a voice message. *Click,* then a woman's voice: "Gwen Marcey? This is Dr. West's office calling from the Cancer Center. Dr. West would like you to make an appointment for some additional tests as soon as possible." A phone number followed.

My throat dried, and I wrote down the number with a trembling hand. After hanging up, I covered my mouth to hold back the groan.

I glanced at my watch. I was on eastern time, but the Cancer Center was on mountain. They'd still be open. I dialed.

"Five Valley Cancer Center. How may I direct your call?"

"I received a message from Dr. West. This is Gwen Marcey."

"Just a moment."

Another *click*, then the same woman's voice came on the line. "Hi, Mrs. Marcey. Dr. West wanted me to—"

"What is it?"

A pause. "Well, the doctor would be the one—"

"I'm in Kentucky working on a case. I won't be home for . . . um . . . weeks. I . . . I need to know if this is an emergency."

There was a pause. "This is in reference to your routine tests a week ago. Dr. West just returned from vacation and has had a chance to go over the results. They're . . . not within the normal range."

"Okay." I made an effort to stop squeezing the phone. "So. You're saying my cancer has returned."

"You'll need to see the doctor. As soon as possible."

CHAPTER THREE

AFTER DISCONNECTING, I STARED AT THE DESKTOP.
God, how can You do this to me?

God didn't answer.

I dialed Beth's number. The answering machine picked up after four rings. I hung up without leaving a message.

Cancer. Again.

A call to my fifteen-year-old daughter, Aynslee, was next. The call went to voice mail.

I sold my house to pay for the last of the doctor bills. And the new place is delayed because I'm out of money.

Dave had left for the Torch Run in Seattle.

Robert, my ex-husband, would hardly be someone I'd want to talk to. He'd divorced me because of my cancer and was now involved with his new wife and writing career.

I found myself pacing and stopped.

How would I pay for cancer treatments this time? Insurance would kick in with the new job. But would I still have a job if I was battling cancer?

Shaking my head, I picked up the phone and dialed. Sheriff

Reed's recorded voice greeted me. I disconnected without leaving a message.

I wandered to the kitchen and stared at the sketch I'd completed. I'd drawn one iris darker than the other. I picked up a pencil and adjusted the drawing. *Someone needs to know you are never coming home.*

Those dark spots on Shelby Lee's neck were from his fingers squeezing her throat.

Still holding the pencil, I moved to the middle of the room, slowly sank to my knees, and bowed my head. "God, I know You have a reason and a purpose for what You do. I also know that doesn't always make life easy. I just pray . . ." What? God knew everything, even that I would pray right now. So if He already knew the cancer would return, what good was prayer? God knew the outcome. How could anything I prayed for make a difference?

A cloak of lead settled over my shoulders.

If your cancer returned so soon after treatment, it's bound to be a very aggressive cancer. As in metastasized. Stage IV. Eventually—and inevitably—fatal.

Let's face it, Gwen. Time isn't on your side.

I stayed on my knees until the room was dark. I had to crawl to the sofa to stand again. Slowly rolling the pencil I held between my fingers, I wandered to the window, leaned against the side, and gazed at the street outside. A woman hurried up the sidewalk, occasionally peering over her shoulder. Across the street, two women clutched each other as they scurried past a dark alley. A car parked and a man got out, walked around the vehicle, then helped a woman out. He kept his arm around her shoulders until they reached the well-lit store.

Pulling the curtains closed, I returned to the table and put the pencil next to the drawing of the John Doe. I needed to get out of this room. Go for a walk. I snatched up my purse and a jacket.

Ina Jo was still at the front desk.

"I thought you were about to get off work," I said.

"I was," she whispered, then pointed behind the counter. I leaned over to see her baby sleeping in a car seat on the floor. "My replacement didn't show. And the sitter isn't answering her phone. I left word, but it's just my luck." She noticed my jacket. "Going out for dinner?"

"Going out for a walk."

"Um, I'm not so sure that's safe. What with all the . . . you know."

I knew all too well. "I need the exercise. Don't worry. I'm armed." Even though it wasn't a pistol, but pepper spray and deadly accuracy at kicking men where it counted. *And I just might enjoy using that pepper spray, and kick, on someone right now. Give that rapist a whupping.*

I shoved down the thought.

"Oh, that's right, you're that expert art lady with Sheriff Reed."

The entire town seemed to know the sheriff had brought me here. Again the prickle of unease tapped me on the neck. *Why did the sheriff bring me all the way from Montana to Kentucky, then want to send me right back?*

"Well, if you decide to eat," Ina Jo said, "up yonder you'll find a good place. Go out the front door, turn right, another right at the corner, two blocks up, and turn left. Can't miss it."

I thanked her and left.

The late-October evening breeze had an apple-crisp snap. Amber and rust leaves rustled underfoot, with streetlights spotlighting the sidewalk. I focused on the sights and smells, pushing down thoughts of the earlier phone calls. I walked over to the suggested eatery, but the smell of fried food made me gag. Turning to the empty street heading back to the hotel, I tucked my hands into the pockets of my jacket.

A car engine revved and tires squealed on the pavement behind me. I glanced back.

A pair of blinding headlights barreled straight toward me.

I hurdled my body left, rolled, and smashed against the brick storefront.

The black truck roared past, missing me by inches, and raced around the corner.

I lay on the sidewalk, heart pounding, unable to move for a moment. The smell of the spinning tires burned my nose. The street was empty. No witnesses.

Shaking, I shoved off the ground and leaned against the building. I'd scraped my hands and knees and ripped my pants. The contents of my purse had spilled across the sidewalk. I slowly gathered everything up.

Limping, I made my way back to the hotel. I could phone Clay and tell him someone had attempted to run me down. Or was it a drunk driver?

The lobby was empty of people but echoed with a screaming baby. I raced to the front desk and peered over. The wailing sobs came from Ina Jo's baby, still in the car seat on the floor. Her fists waved in the air, eyes were closed, and face scrunched up and red. Hurrying around the counter, I checked the office behind the registration desk. A series of small television screens flashed black-and-white views of the hallways, elevators, pool, workout room, and breakfast area. Even though the quality was poor, I could see no sign of Ina Jo.

Returning to the baby, I picked her up and hugged her, gently rocking. Her squalls turned to whimpers. The smell coming from her diaper gave some of the reason for her howling. I went back to the security screens and checked again for signs of the woman. They flickered, would go blank, then kick back on. Ina Jo didn't appear.

The baby's whimpers grew, and I looked around for a diaper bag. This time I noted a jacket and car keys on the small desk, a purse resting on an office chair, and an overturned garbage container.

The automatic doors hissed as they opened.

I ran to the front desk.

The babysitter rushed over to the counter. "I came when I got the message—" She froze when she saw me. "Where's Ina Jo?" She reached for the baby.

I handed her over. "I was hoping you knew. Her baby was screaming when I came in."

Motioning her behind the registration desk, I pointed to the keys, jacket, and purse. She started to reach for them, but I stopped her. "Do you recognize them?"

She nodded, eyes wide open. "She would never leave her baby alone. Ever."

Ushering us both into the lobby, I called the police department. "I'd like to have a welfare check on a crying baby and possible missing person." I gave them the facts I knew, then hung up.

"You don't suppose *he* kidnapped her?" the sitter asked.

"Let's not speculate." I did anyway. Ina Jo was about the same age as Shelby Lee. If the rapist kidnapped her from a public place like this hotel, he'd grown incredibly bold.

Shortly, a female officer arrived and I gave her the information I knew. I left out the black pickup that tried to run me down. I wasn't sure why.

Once back in my room, I dropped my jacket on the sofa and returned to the sketch of the John Doe. Closing my eyes, in my mind I superimposed Ina Jo's face over that of Shelby Lee in the hospital.

Tomorrow I'll get a copy of the police report on Shelby Lee.

The screech of bus brakes and chatter from a large number of people came through the window at the front of the hotel. The noise grew as they reached the lobby, turning into a chant for some team.

I thought of Ina Jo.

"Attention, attention," someone spoke through a megaphone. "Please retrieve your luggage before going to your rooms. Pick up your room assignment from Doris. We'll assemble here in the lobby at 0600."

Trying to ignore the laughing, joking, door-slamming, luggage-squealing commotion in the hall, I turned on the hot water in the bathtub. While the tub filled, I tended to my scrapes. The room phone rang just as I settled in. I jumped from the tub, but the ringing stopped before I could get out. I lay back in the hot water. I could still feel the baby in my arms. It had been close to fifteen years since I held my own daughter like that.

I'm scheduled to fly home in less than forty-eight hours.

I'd placed my cell on the shelf by the tub. Picking it up, I dialed. "Welcome to Delta Airlines," the recorded voice said. "Please choose from the following menu items—"

"Cancel a flight."

CHAPTER FOUR

THE NOISE LEVEL HAD DROPPED BY THE TIME I'd finished my bath, but before I could drift off, the *thump-thump-thump* of people in the room above me began. It sounded like they were playing basketball.

I fell asleep with a pillow over my head.

The phone rang.

I groped for it, but whoever called had disconnected by the time I answered. The digital alarm clock read 3:17 a.m.

Bullhorn returned at 6:00 a.m., reminding the partygoers of details of the event that day. I turned off my alarm, set for seven. Dialing the front desk, I felt my heart sink when Ina Jo didn't answer. "How may I direct your call?"

"Did they find her yet?"

A pause. "Um . . . no."

I hung up. My knees and palms were still sore from the near miss the night before. Limping slightly to the television, I turned it on and made a concerted effort to focus on the day and not on the report from the doctor or missing mother. News came on the local station, and the lead story was the rapist. I prepared a cup of coffee from the coffeemaker while I listened.

A bland-faced man seated next to an attractive younger woman was speaking. "Another woman was reported missing and is feared to be the latest victim of the Pikeville rapist." A photo of Ina Jo appeared on the screen. "Ina Jo Cummings, a front desk clerk at the Craftsman's Hotel, was reported missing last night. If anyone has seen her, please call police immediately."

"The sheriff's department reports no leads in the investigation," the woman read off a teleprompter, "in capturing the man responsible for the rape of young women in the Pikeville area. Nicknamed the Hillbilly Rapist, he allegedly tortures the woman for days. Police are unsure of the exact number of his victims."

The man spoke again. "A forensic artist has been brought in to draw a composite sketch of the suspect, and we will bring you the latest information as it comes in. Crime Stoppers is now offering a five-thousand-dollar reward in the case. If you have any information, you are asked to call—"

I turned off the set. Considering Sheriff Reed didn't want me here, I was sure getting news coverage.

The thought stopped me in my tracks. Would Sheriff Reed have wanted me to leave so badly that . . . No. All he had to do was fire me. Not run over me.

Maybe the only reason Reed brought me in was because of pressure from the news outlets. Some way to visibly show that the police were doing everything possible to solve the case. It wouldn't be the first time I'd been in that situation.

I dressed, packed up my forensic kit with the file for the sheriff, and headed to the hotel lobby. The bus crowd had pretty much emptied the coffee on the stand by the door, and I had just enough for one cup by tilting the carafe. I tried not to hover around the reception desk and pepper the clerk with questions on what she knew about Ina Jo.

Promptly at eight thirty, Junior pulled up in front of the hotel. He didn't say anything when he saw me, just jerked his head, signaling me to follow him to the squad car.

"Good morning," I said to his retreating back.

He muttered something in return.

I struggled to open the car door, juggling my purse, kit, and coffee. Junior didn't seem to notice. He slid into the driver's seat and waited while I loaded my things.

He pulled out as soon as I sat beside him. "Junior," I said. "Did we somehow get off on the wrong foot?"

He glanced at me. "I don't know what you're talking about."

"Well—"

Ignoring me, he focused on driving, though the fingers of his right hand tapped out a rhythm on the steering wheel.

We drove in a different direction from the hospital. "Where are we going, Junior?"

"Department."

"Why?"

He didn't answer. We soon pulled up in front of the sheriff's department. The entrance featured a pleasantly laid out entrance with landscaped foliage, a small fountain, and walnut-colored, stamped concrete. Several bronze metal benches rested against the sides. Junior jerked a thumb at the front door. I took the not-so-subtle hint and jumped out, barely retrieving my things from the backseat before he took off.

The gray-tiled lobby led to a bullet-resistant, glassed-in

reception area. The officer looked up as I approached. "I'm here to see Sheriff Reed. My name is Gwen Marcey."

"Identification?"

I removed my driver's license and slid it through the scooped-out opening under the glass.

After reading it carefully, comparing it with my face, then writing my name on a clipboard, he dialed a number. A short time later I was admitted into a bewildering series of hallways, all looking alike, to Clay's office.

He was on the phone but waved me in and pointed to a chair. "Okay, okay, yeah, got it."

I sat and checked out the décor. A walnut-colored bookshelf on my right held a set of *Reader's Digest* condensed books. Above were several framed photographs of Clay enjoying different activities: on a boat holding up a nice-sized fish, gripping a rifle and standing over a ten-point buck, and waving from the back of a decorated convertible with a sign on the side saying *Vote for Clay Reed, Sheriff.* No photos showed Junior or anyone who resembled family. On the opposite wall was a corkboard with his collection of law enforcement patches.

He hung up and ran his hand through his hair.

Pulling out the file and flash drive, I handed them to him. "Here's the drawing I did on the unknown remains. I usually keep the original. Is that okay?"

Clay took the material without looking at it. "Yeah, yeah, sure. You heard about the woman last night."

"I called it in. I thought you knew that and wanted me to make a report."

"No. But since you're here . . ." He pulled out a form and placed it in front of me.

I looked at the form. "Um, Clay, why *am* I here and not at the hospital? With Ina Jo missing, and presumed taken by the rapist, we're in a time crunch. I'd like to talk to Shelby Lee as soon—"

"She's gone. Left town. Just like the others."

CHAPTER FIVE

"I DON'T UNDERSTAND," I SAID TO CLAY. "SHE WAS really hurt. How could she leave—?"

"The nurses told me she slipped out late last night." Clay rubbed his neck. "I drove to her apartment, but the door was open and the place empty. As in a hurry-to-leave type empty. Just like the others."

"You commented about that before, but I'm not sure I know what you mean." I pulled a pencil out of my pocket and twirled it. *The rape victims and their families all leave town without a trace?* "Was there any sign of foul play?"

"No."

"If all your witnesses are leaving town, why didn't you post an officer outside Shelby Lee's door?"

"I did. She must have waited until he took a restroom break—"

"Why did it take so long to see if she'd packed up? You said *you* checked this morning. Why didn't the officer go to her place immediately?"

"He wasn't looking in her hospital room. When the nurse discovered her gone, the officer called me—"

"Why didn't you have her apartment under surveillance?"

Clay shifted in his chair. "I had patrols beefed up, but—"

"Does the press know about the previous victims leaving town?"

"No."

I stood. "The news media know I'm here. They're going to wonder why I didn't get a composite drawing, especially with Ina Jo missing." I held my breath. If Clay brought me in as a token gesture for the press, sending me right back would look bad for him.

With Clay's handling of the case, my drawing skills might be the only way to identify the rapist. And I wasn't leaving town until that mother was reunited with her baby.

Clay absently stroked his gold watch while he stared off in the distance.

I didn't move.

His head nodded slightly, as if he'd just come to some agreement with himself. His gaze returned to me and his eyes narrowed. "Well now, seeing as how we've been as busy as a moth in a mitten, I haven't had time to bring you up to speed on these cases."

Relaxing slightly, I pulled out a sketchbook and pencil, then nodded encouragement.

"We thought the first rape, earlier this year, was a single incident. Found a beat-up prostitute. We weren't surprised when she took off. A month later a second victim, another prostitute, did the same thing. It wasn't until the next two victims that we saw a pattern. Both were taken in the same month."

"The slimebag was accelerating."

"Yeah."

"Did he have a victim type?"

The sheriff pulled a file from a drawer on his left, opened it, and read. "Classic low self-esteem, un- or underemployed, late teens to late twenties, often homeless, in a shelter, or high-risk prostitute. The two women taken that month were living at home in poorer, single-parent households." He looked at me. "Now, not only did the victims scoot out of town, so did their families."

"You mentioned that you thought it might be from shame."

"There was a lot of talk."

I refrained from commenting about that kind of thinking. "Why do the newscasters call him the Hillbilly Rapist?"

"The newspapers nicknamed him. You're smack-dab in the middle of Hatfield and McCoy country, the country's most famous feud. We celebrate Hillbilly Days in April. And his choice of victims is, shall we say, from country stock. I suspect the Hillbilly name came from all that."

"So outside of the victims, no one's actually seen him?"

"Nope." He opened and closed his hands. "Now—"

"Did you call in the FBI or State Crime Lab profiler?" I asked.

"We did, but didn't get much more than what we already had."

"Which was?"

He looked down at the file and shuffled through a few pages. "The Hillbilly Rapist is motivated by the victim's suffering. Needs to control and inflict psychological and physical pain over hours or days. They call him an—"

"Anger excitation rapist."

Clay's eyes shot up. "Impressive."

I grimaced. "Not so much. Some of the stuff you need to learn to be a forensic artist. I worked on a serial killing case recently where one victim was held for hours. And two of Ted Bundy's earlier victims were captured and held before he killed them. Your serial rapist just hasn't moved to the next step of murder."

"Yeah." Clay glanced at his watch. "The biggest thing the profile noted was the rapist had a really good way of finding victims. Another month gave us another young woman, this time a gal working at a sandwich shop. We thought he was slowing down until we got two missing persons reports."

"Why did you think they were his victims?"

"They fit the type. Both were underemployed, about the same age, and their apartments showed signs of a quick move. So we believe his actual count was three for that month."

I shifted in the chair. "So. Learning and honing his craft."

"And accelerating even more."

"Again, classic behavior of a serial rapist."

"Yeah. And now that clerk's missing. We've usually had more time between his grabbing the gals. Predictable time. We'd worked out that his next victim was going to be taken on Halloween. Now we need to look at that timetable."

"So you're pretty sure Ina Jo is with him?"

He didn't answer. He was staring at my hand. Following his gaze, I discovered I was twirling my pencil like an out-of-control metronome. I stuck the pencil in my pocket.

"He holds 'em someplace remote for up to five days." Clay glanced out the window at the surrounding mountains. "Not hard to do around here."

"He must convince them during that time that their only safety is in fleeing for their lives. Telling them something like

34

he's going to kill her family if she talks." I leaned back in the chair and thought. "From what I remember about this type of rapist, every part of his crime is meticulously planned and methodically executed. And probably recorded somehow for future reference. What about physical evidence? Have you found any DNA?"

"Nope. No body fluids at all. As you said, he's careful. Very careful." He leaned back in his chair and gave me a slight smile. "We've been doing all we can to solve this. Seems like we've reached a dead end, at least for now. Maybe when Ina Jo shows up—"

"Do you have any visual recordings of interviews with the previous victims?"

"Nah. Not really. For the most part, we didn't get a chance to videotape anything. The women bolted before we could set anything up. Why?"

"Sometimes body language or verbal clues will relay a great deal of information."

The sheriff tapped his lips with his finger. "Interesting. We might . . ."

"Yes?"

"We had one woman we interviewed and taped. We weren't all that sure she was a victim of the Hillbilly Rapist."

"Maybe a copycat?"

"Something like that. I can arrange for you to watch the interview."

"Sounds good. And what about surveillance videos? I can develop a sketch should you have something blurry or from a weird angle."

"We might have one," Clay said. "It may not be anything, but the timing was about right and no one could make hide nor hair from the photo."

"Let me look at it and let you know."

Clay punched a button on his desk phone. "Reed here. Have someone set up the conference room and pull the Johnson interview . . . Oh. When will they be done? Okay, set it up for then. Yeah. Okay." He disconnected. "I've set it up for this afternoon. I'll run you back to your hotel." He stood.

"Okay, but—"

"I'll send a car at one thirty to pick you up."

He opened the door to his office and glanced at me.

"One more thing." I rose from the chair. "I was almost hit last night."

Clay frowned at me. "What do you mean?"

"I was walking back to the hotel when someone driving a black pickup tried to run me down."

"Did you get a license plate?"

"No. The truck sped around the corner before I could get a good look at it."

Clay rubbed his chin, then tugged his ear. "Well, Miz Gwen, I suspect that was just a drunk. Why would anyone want to hurt you?"

Except you told the local television station. Which means you're lying. Again.

CHAPTER SIX

CLAY'S RESPONSE PUT ME ON HIGH ALERT FOR black pickups. Unfortunately, black seemed to be the most popular color for trucks in this part of Kentucky.

Driving from one end of town to the other didn't take long. The horseshoe-shaped town of Pikeville had a population of just under seven thousand. Tree-covered mountains rose steeply on all sides.

During the short drive, Clay relaxed enough to update me on the history of the community. "Although folks have lived around here since the mid-seventeen hundreds"—he pointed to a terraced mountain rising above the road—"that's what really helped the town grow. The Pikeville Cut-Through Project. Officially started in 1973, it took fourteen years to move eighteen million cubic yards of earth. That allowed the town to grow to more than four hundred acres."

"Which explains why a lot of buildings look new."

"Yep. We have a university, new library, shopping center—everything a big city has but with a small-town feel."

Including big-city crime. I kept my thoughts to myself as we pulled up in front of the hotel. "Did you grow up here?"

"Nearby."

"You sure seem proud of your town."

"And of Kentucky. We have plans—" He stopped abruptly.

I pretended not to notice a possible slip of the tongue and stepped from the car. "See you later." *Plans? We?*

The stricken look on the clerk's face told me Ina Jo hadn't been found locked up in the laundry room. I didn't much feel like eating, so stopped off at the vending machine on the way to my room. I bought cheese puffs, Oreos, and a chocolate bar. With my daughter safely with her father, I didn't have to be a good example.

The phone was ringing as I entered, but no one was on the line when I answered. I rang the front desk. "Did you just put a call through to my room?"

"No. I mean, it's an automated system. If someone knows your room number, they can dial direct."

I hung up and stared at the phone for a moment.

The maid had cleaned my room, leaving my clutter of art supplies on the table. I opened the cheese puffs and started stuffing my face. Still munching, I strolled to the bedroom, sat on the bed, and kicked off my shoes. My feet constantly hurt. Chemotherapy had permanently damaged the nerves in my soles, making it feel like I was walking on gravel.

The looming vision of returning cancer drove me off the bed. I paced from the bedroom to the living room and back again. What if they gave my interagency job to someone else because I had cancer? How would I pay for treatments? Where would I live? How would I work?

"This is ridiculous." I picked up my cell and dialed Beth.

"Gwen! I thought you'd never call. How are you feeling? How is Pikeville? Have any bodies shown up? Did you catch the rapist? Do you need a partner?" As usual, Beth sounded breathless.

"Fine. Small. Yes. No. No."

Beth was silent for a moment. "You do know I hate it when you do that."

"I'm teaching you—"

"I know. Effective interview techniques." The background musical theme from a forensic show stopped and Winston, my Great Pyrenees, barked.

"How's my dog?" I selected a lead holder from the pencil box and sat at the kitchen table.

"Aha! Something *is* wrong."

"Why do you say that?"

"Because you wouldn't call this early in the morning to ask about Winston and you're tapping a pencil rapidly on some surface."

I stopped tapping and pulled a sketchbook in front of me. "Actually, everything's fine—"

"Ha! Another clue!" Beth sounded jubilant. "You used the word *actually*. That means *actually* there really *is* something wrong."

Doodling Beth's face, I silently vowed I'd never teach Beth another thing about statement analysis. "I need you to research a couple of things for me."

"Sure, but I have houseguests, so unless I can find time, I'll have to email or text you the answers."

"That's fine . . . um, but weren't you just watching one of your forensic shows?"

"It's my cousins from Oconomowoc, Wisconsin, and they're even crazier about crime stuff than I am."

"Is that possible? Don't answer that. Can you look up Sheriff Clayton Reed? *R-e-e-d*. Anything you can find out."

"Will do. Now are you going to tell me what's wrong?"

I drew a halo over her sketched face. Why didn't I tell her? She was my best friend. *Oh, and, Beth, by the way, my cancer's returned. I'm going to die.*

I knew why the words wouldn't come. I didn't want her pity.

"Gwen? Hello?"

"Everything's fine. Just wanted to hear a cheerful voice."

"You dropped the pronoun *I*, so I don't believe you. I'll leave you with this: 'Sufficient unto the day is the evil thereof.' Take things one day at a time, and when you're ready to talk, I'll be here."

My eyes burned. "Thank you, Beth." I managed to disconnect before my throat closed up. Now I was feeling sorry for myself, and that was unacceptable.

I went to the bathroom, got a tissue, and blew my nose. *Stop it!* Returning to the table, I pulled closer the pad of paper I'd been doodling on. At the bottom of the page I wrote *Known* and *Unknown*, then drew a line between them, forming two columns. Under *Known* I wrote: *likes young women, has distinct victim type, has isolated location to hold them, likes torture, gets them to leave town or no report.* I stopped writing. Was that all I had on him? Under *Unknown* I wrote: *smokes? (cigarette burns), convinces them to leave town? knows about forensics? Check photos (if available) to see if similar appearance.*

This wasn't useful. I simply didn't have enough solid information.

Checking my watch, I was startled to see it was almost time to head over to the sheriff's office. I swiftly packed up the items I needed, grabbed a denim jacket, and headed to the lobby. A deputy waited in a patrol car parked by the front door, and I slipped into the front seat next to him.

He greeted me once I had the seat belt fastened, "Ma'am," and drove the short distance to the sheriff's department. We entered through a side door opened with a key card, and I followed him to a well-appointed conference room. Large windows overlooked a colorful autumn hillside, while comfortable tweedy chairs surrounded an oversize walnut table. Clay waited next to the television and video setup. "Have a seat. You'll be happy to know thanks to you we identified the body already. Notified the family."

"Glad I could help. By the way, have you been calling my room?"

"No."

"Did you give out my room number?"

"No. Why do you ask?"

"Never mind." I turned to the set.

"We've been working on the Hillbilly rapes for months," Clay said in an oddly rehearsed way. "This sort of thing reflects badly on our community."

Not to mention the poor victims.

"We welcome your expertise and input to help identify the perpetrator."

There's that elusive "we" again.

"Let's see what you can find on the Teri Johnson interview." He used the remote to turn everything on. A striking blonde in her mid- to late teens appeared on the screen. She sat on one side of a stark metal table while a detective faced her on the other. The detective reminded me of the handsome actor Derek Morgan on the television show *Criminal Minds*. An open file rested in front of him.

Clay handed me the remote. "Push this button to start, this to pause, this to reverse, and this to stop." He hesitated a moment. "Did you want me to tell you why we were suspicious of her?"

"Not yet. Let me watch this, make some notes, and then we'll talk."

"Okay." He moved to the door. "My office is just up the hall. Come and get me when you're ready."

I gave him a half wave.

As soon as he left the room, I started the tape. The young woman was speaking. "You remind me of a TV star or something. Are you, like, famous?"

"No, ma'am," the detective answered. "Are you okay? Can I get you something? Water, a soda . . ."

"I'm fine."

"Thank you for coming down here today. You're not in trouble, and as I said before, I believe you, but I need to be sure we have all the information we need to follow up on this."

"Sure."

He shuffled the papers in front of him. "Now, could you start at the beginning? Just tell me the same thing you said to me in the hospital."

"Sure. My boyfriend drove me home after going to a movie. Some kind of science-fiction flick. I hate science fiction, and this movie was really stupid."

My boyfriend? I jotted a note.

42

"He and I were sitting in the car in front of my house and he started saying stuff like I was flirting with some other boys." She waved her hand as if swatting away the comments.

He and I? Another note.

"Well, I wasn't flirting. They were friends." Her voice rose. "He's so jealous. He saw a delivery guy drop off a box and he was convinced I was dating someone. That night he said some really mean things, like the rapist wouldn't touch someone like me because I was too old and, like, well, he called me a bad name. I told him he was wrong and a pig, you know, stuff like that, and then, you know, sort of got out of the car."

I wrote her story as fast as I could, noting the cluster of "you knows."

She leaned forward. "He drove off, you know, and left me, didn't even see if I was safe or anything—"

"What time was this?"

Bad interview technique, Derek Morgan clone. Never interrupt the witness.

"About ten. It was dark . . ." She took a deep breath. "Do you think this will end up on TV? You know, like a special or maybe in the paper?"

"Your name won't be released, if that's what concerns you." He paused in his writing. "And I don't think he knows where you live."

"Oh." She absently played with her long hair. "That's good. And I know you'll protect me. That's what you do, isn't it? Serve and protect? You know how awful this guy is." She reached for a tissue and dabbed her eyes.

The detective awkwardly patted her arm. "You're safe now."

She smiled slightly at him. "Okay. Like I said, it was dark.

I decided to walk around the block before going in. I was still mad—"

"Were your parents home?"

Interruption number two.

"Yes. I got to the alley at the end of the block, the one next to the Kramer house, and this guy jumped out and grabbed me. I guess he was hiding behind that big maple tree. I was going to scream, but he put his hand over my mouth."

"He grabbed you from the front?"

Leading question. You're flunking the interview, Derek.

"No, from the back. He pulled me tight against his body. He was very strong. He said if I screamed, he'd cut me with a knife. He showed me the knife."

"What kind of knife?"

"A big one. Like this." She held her hands about eight inches apart. "Then he put a blindfold over my eyes. I was so scared."

"I'm sure you were. That had to be terrifying."

"It was. He started to drag me somewhere when I told him I had AIDS. I said I was dying. That's when he let me go. I took off the blindfold when I heard him moving away."

The detective tapped his pen on the paper for a moment. "Did you see him?"

"Mostly just from the back. He was walking away slowly, looking over his shoulder at me. He had dirty black hair and walked with a limp."

"Excellent."

Not really. You just gave direct, qualitative feedback, encouraging her to invent information.

"He disappeared down the alley."

"Did you see him get into a car?"

"Um, no. The alley was dark and he kinda went out of sight."

"What happened to the blindfold?" he asked.

She shifted in her seat and crossed her legs. "Oh. Um. What do you mean?"

"You said he put a blindfold on you and you took it off. Did you drop it at the scene?" His pen hovered over the paper he'd been writing on.

"I'm not sure. Are we going to be much longer? My mom's waiting . . ."

"Nope. I'll just have you read over what I wrote and sign it."

Turning off the video, I tapped my pencil on the table while I thought about what I'd seen. This wasn't a copycat frightened off by the threat of AIDS.

This was a liar.

CHAPTER SEVEN

AFTER ONLY ONE WRONG TURN, I FOUND CLAY in his office. He was once again on the phone.

He finished his call and hung up. "Well?"

"She invented almost the whole thing."

He leaned back in his chair. "We knew there was something wrong about her story. What do you mean, though, when you say she invented *almost* the whole thing?"

I pulled a chair up to the other side of his desk. "She told the truth about the fight with her boyfriend. The rest was an invention."

"How do you know?"

"Forensic artists have about fourteen clues we watch for and two tests we give to determine if someone is being truthful—"

"This wasn't a composite interview."

"I know that. But many of the clues are the same in both a regular police interview and a composite interview."

Clay steepled his hands in front of his mouth as if he were praying. *Great*. Certain body language always caught my attention. Unless Clay always did this action—and in the short time

I'd known him, he hadn't—steepling was a sign of superiority. Steepling in front of the mouth meant he not only felt superior but was holding back telling me. He *knew* Teri Johnson was lying. He was either testing me or wasting my time and keeping me from working on the missing woman.

"Well, anyway, I just thought you should know." I stood to leave.

"No, sit down. I want your thoughts." He leaned forward and folded his hands on the desk.

I hesitated, then sat back down. "Of the clues we look for, the victim or witness needs to display three or more signs to show deception."

"Why?"

"One or even two clues could have actually happened. But as soon as the different indicators start to pile up, we know we have deception in the incident." I pulled out my notes. "She gave nine clues and two verbal indicators." I read them from my notes as I ticked them off on my fingers. "Quasimodo Effect, Betty Boop Display, Scary Movie, Gothic Romance, Indiana Jones Syndrome, Spotlight, Safe Haven, Check-off List, and Revenge Rule." I beamed at him.

"Huh?" Clay frowned.

"Oh, sorry. Those are my nicknames for the different actions and displays she showed."

"Well, that's about as clear as mud."

"Law enforcement likes acronyms. FBI, ATF, DEA, STS. I just use words I can remember and that have a great visual. Don't you know it's all about the visual?"

He twisted his mouth as if smelling something bad but didn't say anything.

"Anyway," I continued, "I wrote it all down." I handed him a sheet of paper with sketches and brief descriptions. "I started with the Revenge Rule. When a witness gives a statement of what happened to them, they'll want someone to know how they came to be in that situation, what happened, and the aftermath, or how this event changed them. Their statement will have three parts."

The phone rang. Clay ignored it. "Go on."

"When the story starts with a fight, say with a boyfriend or spouse, my lie-detector antenna goes up. There's a good chance that the story they're about to tell will be made up to exact revenge on the boyfriend. Kind of a 'Because of you, I was almost killed.'"

"But what if the fight had nothing to do with the event?"

"That's why we need three or more clues." I consulted my notes. "The fight was the truth, as was his jealousy over a delivery-man. Her language reinforced that. She said 'my boyfriend' and 'he and I.'"

"But it *was* her boyfriend. He confirmed he let her off—"

"That's not the point. Calling him 'my boyfriend' without giving his name is what we call an incomplete social introduction. The rule is that in telling a story to a stranger, in this case the detective, the victim wants to make herself understood. She needs to 'introduce' the various people she will be talking about. A complete social introduction would have been 'my boyfriend, John.' *My*, possessive pronoun; *boyfriend*, title; and first name, *John*."

Clay absently pulled out a gold metal cigarette lighter and opened and closed the lid with a small *snap*. The odor of lighter fluid soon filled the room.

"With an incomplete social introduction, plus saying 'he and

I' instead of 'we,' which would indicate togetherness, I concluded they were at odds with each other. Her language confirmed the fight."

Someone knocked softly on the door. "Yes?" Clay barked.

A deputy entered and placed some papers in a file on his desk. "The captain said you wanted this as soon as possible." He nodded at me, then glanced back at Clay. "Got a sec?"

Clay stood and stepped into the hall.

I leaned forward and opened the file. It was a report on Ina Jo.

The two men's voices grew fainter. I jumped up and peeked out the door. They'd moved down the hall and were in a heated discussion.

Leaving the door open a crack so I could hear returning footsteps, I raced around the desk and opened the drawers. They were all locked except the top middle one. Inside was the usual muddle of paper clips, pens, Post-it notes, and scissors, all in a black tray.

Clay's voice rose.

My hand jerked on the drawer handle. The black tray jostled over an inch. Underneath was a sheet of paper.

Footsteps approached.

Heart pounding, I lifted the tray. Underneath was a DNA printout, dated April 17 of this year.

CHAPTER EIGHT

I PLACED THE TRAY IN THE DRAWER, SHUT IT, and stepped over to the bookshelf. I just had time to grab a *Reader's Digest* condensed book when Clay opened the door.

He entered and narrowed his eyes at me.

"I see you like to read . . ." I glanced at the spine. "Ah . . . Nora Roberts?"

"No." He strolled around the desk, sat down, and opened the drawer.

My hand trembled slightly as I shelved the book, then casually returned to my seat.

He was staring at me when I finally looked up.

"Please continue your report."

"Yeah. Sure. Um . . . Teri also had a cluster of 'you knows.' If someone doesn't use that phrase routinely, it marks a sensitive subject. The cluster occurred when she got out of the car, so something happened at that point that she's leaving out of the story. She commented she 'sort of' got out of the car. How do you 'sort of' get out of a car?"

Clay grunted. "Her boyfriend said he shoved her out of the car."

"I figured it was something like that." I checked my notes again.

Clay *snap-snap-snapp*ed the lighter. I glanced at his hand. He stopped and put the lighter away. "I'm trying to quit smoking." He picked up my notes. "Quasimodo Effect?"

"She described him as having dirty hair and walking with a limp. She just needed a hunchback to have a perfect Quasimodo."

"I didn't catch that."

"It's more obvious to a forensic artist. The average person tends to think being a criminal equates to being ugly, so they describe the bad guy as Hollywood's casting of a villain, maybe with pitted skin, large nose, and small, close-set eyes. I call it the Quasimodo Effect. And when you think about it, it makes sense. Victims and witnesses are, shall we say, amateurs. They don't realize that true evil can dress in a clown outfit and entertain at children's parties—"

"John Wayne Gacy, who killed at least thirty-three boys."

I nodded. "Or be a handsome but injured young man in need of help."

"Ted Bundy, with a final body count of over thirty young women and girls."

"My friend Beth would say we shouldn't be surprised. Satan himself can appear as an angel of light." I suddenly missed my friend and sidekick. She lived and breathed forensics and was a whiz at research. She might turn up some interesting information about the sheriff.

"Hello? Gwen?"

I started and dropped the pencil I'd been tapping on Clay's desk. "Sorry. Woolgathering. Back to the clues. Let's see, ah, the victim also said he was strong and walked away . . . slowly . . . looking over his shoulder. As if"—I clutched my hands in front of my chest and spoke in a whispery girlish voice—"he couldn't take his eyes off her. And he was soooo strong." I dropped the voice. "Like a gothic romance novel."

"I can see why your boss, Dave, called and talked you up." He absently rubbed his gold watch for a moment, reached for the phone, hesitated, then looked at me. "This whole thing just dills my pickle." His accent seemed more pronounced. "I'm just a poor country boy and sure do appreciate your help."

I raised my eyebrows.

"Here's what we know about that front desk clerk." He handed me the report he'd just received. "And this here's a copy of the video surveillance image. We got it from a drugstore where one of the gals got grabbed."

I took the material from him. "Do you have transcripts of Teri's interview? And a copy of the profile report?"

Clay's eyebrows pulled together. "I thought you said Teri was lying."

"She was. I just . . . may want to review it again. Something's bothering me."

He unlocked a bottom drawer, rummaged about, then pulled out a file and DVD and handed them to me. "No transcripts, but here's a copy of the interview. I'll get someone to drive you back to your hotel."

"It's not that far. I think I'd like to walk." I was pretty sure no one would run me down in broad daylight with tons of witnesses. I placed the reports into my composite kit.

Clay stood and escorted me to the lobby. "I'll have someone pick you up in the morning."

The afternoon had turned into cool early evening. I paused just outside the door and breathed in the fall air. On my left, a slender, middle-aged man with a lock of dark, unruly hair flopping over his forehead sat next to a plump woman with a long, ginger braid and ankle-length skirt. She was leaning against him, a hankie pressed to her eye, while he read from a tattered Bible.

The man looked vaguely familiar. I tried to picture where I'd seen his face before. His eyes slightly bulged, level eyebrows . . .

The sketch.

The drawing of the unknown remains in the morgue looked like a younger version of the man seated on the bench. A brother? Father?

". . . Naked came I out of my mother's womb, and naked shall I return thither," the man quietly read. "The Lord gave, and the Lord hath taken away; blessed be the name of the Lord."

"Oh, sweet Lord." The woman dabbed at her eye. "I never took a picture of him a'tall this year."

Clay mentioned they'd identified the young man's family. I had no idea why they'd come to the sheriff's department instead of having a deputy deliver the news to them, but with startling clarity, I knew what I needed to do. I reached into my composite kit, pulled out my sketchbook, and approached the man and woman. The couple didn't look up until I stood in front of them. "Excuse me?"

The man looked up. His tortoiseshell glasses slid down his nose and he adjusted them with a quick flick of his hand. "Ma'am?"

"Are you the parents of . . . the young man they found yesterday?"

"Samuel. Samuel Adkins. Yes, he is . . . was . . . our son."

The woman nodded and looked at me with the sweetest face I'd ever seen. "Death has drawn near our family. Again."

"My name is Gwen. I created the drawing that may have helped identify him. I overheard you mention that you didn't have any recent photos, so . . . I thought you'd like to have it." I held out the sketch and my business card.

The man took them with a trembling hand. "Ahhhh." He groped for a blue-and-white handkerchief, then wiped his eyes. "I couldn't—"

"It's okay." I stepped back. "The sheriff has copies, and it's served its purpose."

The man carefully placed the Bible, sketch, and card next to him on the bench, then stood and held out his hand. "Thank you, Miz Gwen. My name is Elijah. This here's my wife, Ruby."

I shook hands with him, feeling the thick calluses across his palms. "I won't intrude any further. Please accept my sincere condolences for your loss."

"We were hoping," Ruby said, "to see him—"

"Ruby, please take my word on this . . ." I touched her arm. "You'll want to remember him the way you last saw him."

Ruby's gaze held mine, then drifted down to the small gold cross on my necklace. She nodded once, then stood. "We'll have the funeral home take care of things."

Elijah picked up the Bible and drawing, then put his arm around his wife. They started to leave, but Elijah paused and turned back to me. "Ma'am, it would be an honor if you would come to Samuel's funeral."

I blinked. "Oh . . . okay. Um . . ."

Elijah held up my card. "I'll call you with the particulars." The two of them walked toward the street.

I took the now-empty bench. Sketching unknown remains and reconstructing skulls are part of my job, but I seldom meet the families of the victims. Unlike television shows where the forensic anthropologists or behavioral scientists run around with guns investigating the cases, the reality is that we each do our part and move on. I rarely even know when my drawings make a difference in the resolution of a crime. Knowing that, in this instance at least, the sketch had brought closure felt satisfying. But sad. Oh, so very sad.

I slowly got up and started back to my hotel. I was starving. Stopping on my way back to the hotel for dinner seemed even more attractive when I spotted the bus parked in front of the lobby. The place would be a madhouse. And the basketball team was probably already warming up in the room above mine.

I found the same restaurant from the night before, this time going inside. The air was rich with the aroma of grilled steak and fresh-baked bread. After ordering dinner from a cheerful waitress who called me "hon," I pulled out the report on Ina Jo.

At 2159, patrol officer Kari Seibel responded to a report on a welfare check on crying baby and possible missing person at the Craftsman's Hotel on Hambley Boulevard, in Pikeville. Gwen Marcey, a guest at the hotel who called in the report, said she'd last seen the mother, Ina Jo Cummings DOB 03/19/1991, and baby when she went out for dinner at 2117 hours. She said she returned at approximately 2150. Shortly after Marcey found the baby, the sitter, Lila Pender (report included), arrived. Officer Seibel called Child Protective Services. Detective Ernest Oropeza arrived at 2221 and found Cummings' purse, jacket, and keys. He contacted her employer, who said she was a trusted employee and had never left during her shift.

Cummings is described as 5'2", 135 pounds, blue eyes, and short black hair with a purple streak on the left side. Her ears have multiple piercings, and her left eyebrow has a vertical silver loop piercing. Her right ankle has a sea turtle tattoo. She was last seen wearing blue slacks, white blouse, navy blazer with the hotel logo over the pocket, and black boots.

My order arrived, something to do with chicken, and I pondered the material in front of me while I ate.

What was most interesting was Junior Reed, Clay's son, was assigned to be the sheriff's liaison on the case. Neither Junior nor the Derek-clone detective I'd just viewed were particularly adept. Why would Clay use those two on the biggest crime wave since the Hatfield and McCoy feud?

I was becoming more convinced that Sheriff Reed didn't want to find the rapist. If that were true, why had he sent for me?

CHAPTER NINE

SURPRISINGLY, THE HOTEL LOBBY WAS EMPTY, the only sound coming from the hidden speakers playing Muzak. The convention—or tour or whatever the noisy group was—must have been out or turned in for the night. I suspected they'd rallied at some other location.

I'd relax with a long, hot bath and read an article in *Forensic News* before turning in.

The scent of dried leaves and asphalt greeted me as I opened the door to my room. I paused, then flipped on the light. The sheer curtains in the living area puffed and swirled as chilly air blew in.

I didn't remember opening the window.

From my position by the door, I could see most of the two rooms. Empty. Swiftly I pulled the pepper spray from my purse. In four quick steps I was in the bedroom. The closet door was open with only my meager wardrobe hanging inside. The bathroom was empty. Nothing looked out of place.

Returning to the living room, I checked the window. The

sash could only be opened a few inches before being blocked. No one could fit through the narrow opening. I was about to turn away when I gave the window a quick tug upward. It opened easily.

Biting my lip, I shoved the window closed and locked it.

Another tour of the room assured me it was empty. I placed the pepper spray back in my purse, took off my jacket, and tossed it on the bed. The white duvet was disturbed from when I sat on it earlier.

The phone rang.

Kicking off my shoes, I picked up the receiver. "Hello?"

A deep male voice said, "You need to leave before you get killed." *Click.*

I gasped and dropped the phone. I spun, trying to remember where I'd placed Clay's phone number.

The chocolate-colored scarf across the foot of the bed shifted.

My mouth dried. I grabbed the duvet and jerked it off.

The coiled snake reared its head and prepared to strike.

I froze.

The snake shook its rattles, starting with a slow *chchch*, then speeding to a continuous *cheeeeeheeeee*. Its head waved side to side, its tongue flickering.

I opened my mouth to scream, but no sound came out. My body refused to move. My heart pounded in my head.

The bedclothes vibrated.

The snake turned its head and looked at the sheet.

I tore my gaze from the coiled beast and glanced down. I was still clutching the covers in a white-knuckled trembling hand. With excruciating slowness, I lowered my hand.

The snake watched, tail vibrating.

I edged backward, one foot, then another. *How far can a snake strike?*

The snake dropped its head.

I fled from the room. Slamming the door shut, I headed to the lobby, clinging to the walls, my legs barely able to keep me upright.

The clerk must have heard me coming. She gawked at my appearance.

Grabbing the counter to keep from collapsing, I stammered, "Ssss . . . snake! There's a ssnake . . . bed. Call-call the police . . . Shut door . . ."

"Now, there . . . is it Miz Marcey?"

I gripped the counter harder and nodded.

"Well, Miz Marcey. Those little ole snakes won't hurt you. They sneak in under the door. I'll get maintenance to catch—"

"Rattlesnake."

The woman paused, phone halfway to her ear. "Are you sure?"

I nodded.

She opened a drawer, pulled out a telephone book, and swiftly flipped pages until she found what she needed. She dialed. After identifying herself, she explained the situation. "I'll meet you outside with a room key. I don't want guests in the lobby or hall to see you or they'll panic. Come and leave through the side door." She hung up. "Jason Morrow, the snake handler with animal control, will be here shortly. This sometimes happens. Can I make you some coffee or tea?"

"No. No. What do you mean this sometimes happens? How many poisonous snakes have turned up in people's beds here?"

The woman wouldn't meet my stare. "Um, well, not when I've been working here. But I've heard—"

"How long have you worked here?"

The woman's eyes narrowed at my tone. "Now, Miz Marcey—"

"Never mind." I rubbed my arms. "Someone opened my window, put that snake in my bed, and called and threatened me. Where were you when I came in earlier? The front desk was unmanned. Anyone could have walked through those doors."

"I only stepped away for a moment."

"Where's your manager?"

Her face flushed red. "We're shorthanded. I'm the manager on duty."

"Listen. Once that snake's gone, you need to get me another room. Someone knows what room I'm in. Last night's attempt to run me down, the snake, the phone calls . . . It's not safe—"

"I can't move you. We're booked solid. Sorry."

She said "Sorry," not "I'm sorry." She left out the pronoun. I moved away from the reception desk, my forensic training in high gear. I understood what people really meant by the words they used. A pronoun shows possession, commitment, and responsibility. By leaving it out, she was saying she wasn't sorry. Was she the one who put the snake in my bed? Or who opened the window to let someone in? Did she know who did? Or was she simply glad I had to sleep in that room, with or without a reptile?

"Would you find me a room at another hotel?" I politely asked.

"Sorry. All the available rooms in town are booked. Have been for months. It's the tournament, you know."

I didn't really know, and I didn't care. As I thought of a suitable comment, a man tapped on the glass outside the lobby. Jason Morrow, the snake wrangler, was a fair-haired, even-featured man in his late twenties, wearing gold, wire-rimmed glasses, and with powerful shoulders and a slim waist. He held what I recognized as snake tongs and a five-gallon plastic bucket with a perforated lid.

The clerk strolled to the door and handed him a key card. "Room 137. Last one."

A hot flash, yet another reminder of my estrogen-positive cancer and the hormone treatment that put me into early meno-pause, left me leaning against the counter. I could see the small television screens displaying the security feeds from the different areas of the hotel. It reminded me of the night before, search-ing for a missing Ina Jo while comforting her wailing daughter. Jason appeared on one, walked directly to my door, looked around, and entered.

The screens flickered, jerked, and two went blank. The clerk stepped over and banged the side. "Stupid thing never works right."

In what seemed like a very short time, Jason appeared on a screen outside my room. The screen flickered for a few moments. When it came back on, the hall was empty.

Jason tapped on the glass doors outside the lobby, held up the bucket, gave a thumbs-up, then nodded at me. The clerk retrieved the key. Walking to the reception desk, the clerk pasted on a smile that didn't reach her eyes. "Well now, Miz Marcey, I can get you clean sheets, but housekeeping doesn't come on until—"

I waved her away, trooped to my room, and locked the door.

Except for the bedcovers lying on the floor, the room looked bland and harmless. Goose pimples broke out on my arms anyway. I found a blanket in the bottom drawer of the bureau in the living room. Wrapping the blanket around me, I curled up on the sofa.

The clock beside my bed in the other room *tick-tick-tick*ed the minutes away. My eyelids grew heavy.

Bam!

I jumped from the sofa, sending the blanket flying.

Bam, bam! "Miz Marcey?" Clay asked through the door. *Bam.*

I raced across the room and let him in. "It's a good thing you're the sheriff. Otherwise you'd be arrested for disturbing the peace."

"I just heard about the snake. Came to see if you were okay." I picked up the blanket and rewrapped it around me. "Snake's gone. I would be, too, if there were another room to rent in town."

"Let me work on that."

"And someone threatened me. By phone."

"Oh? What did he say?"

"'You need to leave before you get killed.' And don't forget the truck that tried to run me down."

Clay's eyes became distant and unfocused. "That's . . ." He reached for the door. "Keep your door locked. I'll have a word with security here."

I trailed behind him to the door. He paused before opening it. "You know, I might have an idea of where you can stay. Let me make some phone calls."

"It's 2:00 a.m."

"I'll wait till a decent hour. Don't worry. Get some sleep. Okay?"

"Okay."

After the sheriff left, the room didn't seem quite so cold and impersonal. I again curled up on the sofa. Like a jerky movie reel in my brain, I pictured the snake coiled in my bed, the baby's sobbing face, the dead man in the morgue, Shelby Lee's bruises.

It wasn't until I woke up and was taking my shower that the thought popped into my head. *I didn't tell the sheriff it was a male voice. Why was he dressed and prowling around town at two in the morning? And who told him about the snake?*

CHAPTER TEN

BY THE TIME I'D DRESSED IN BLACK SLACKS, A beige shell top, and a navy blue jacket and made my way to the lobby, the bus crowd was gone, leaving meager pickings for breakfast. I finally settled on a hard-boiled egg, bowl of canned fruit, slice of whole wheat toast, and coffee. Something wasn't quite right, so I added two Danish and a croissant. Most of the tables hadn't been wiped down, and crumpled napkins, Styrofoam cups, and folded newspapers littered their surfaces. I found a relatively clean table and sat on an upright wooden chair not designed for comfort.

The newspaper was filled with news on the rapes and missing girl. Clay had issued a statement that they would soon begin a door-to-door search in outlying areas, and citizens should remain alert for suspicious activity. I finished reading the latest on the case, discovered the tournament was actually an all-class sports reunion, scanned the local football scores, and moved on to the classifieds. I was well into reading about free kittens, a "spade" dog, and a rabbit hutch complete with rabbits when Clay arrived.

"Ah, good, you're up. Any more death threats?"

I shook my head. "How about you? Did you find Ina Jo?"

He frowned and shook his head.

"I was going to start on the video image you gave me yesterday, unless you have something else you want me to work on."

"We'll get to that." The sheriff wandered over to the coffee urns and poured a cup.

Watching him reminded me of my question. "Clay, who told you about the snake in my room?"

"You did, at least indirectly. The hotel clerk said you told her to call the police. Smart move on your part as well as hers. Insurance, you know. Liability." He sat down next to me and took a sip. "Anyway, I'd left word that if anything came up about you, she was to go straight to me. I got dressed and came over."

"How did you know the phone call was made by a man?"

"That made sense. It was, wasn't it?"

"Yes." I felt like an idiot for asking. "Thanks, in case I didn't say that earlier."

"No problem. You want a new place to stay?"

I nodded.

"So, I have a bit of a confession."

Finally.

He took a sip of coffee. "I've never worked with an artist. I'm not sure if what you do really works, and there's no way our budget would stretch to bring you out. I told your sheriff I wasn't interested in your services. But a . . . friend of mine put up the money to bring you in."

I relaxed. That made so much sense. "Okay. But why?"

"My friend's a politician—"

I rolled my eyes.

"Wait, he's a great guy. Big mucky-muck in helping folks and rich enough to do so. He says crime such as this is a reflection on his leadership."

"In other words, he's running for office, or a higher office, and wants a clean record."

Clay studied his coffee cup for a moment. "I called Arless, the man paying for you to be here, and he said you could stay with him." He saw the look on my face. "And his wife," he added quickly. "You'll be safe there. They're expecting you. Let's get you moved." He finished his coffee, stood, picked up my kit, and strolled down the hall.

I trailed behind. When we reached my door, I pulled out my plastic key card, then hesitated.

The sheriff must have noticed my pause. He took the key from me and opened the door, then swept through the rooms, peering under the bed and sofa, before waving me in.

"Tell me more about the folks I'll be staying with," I said.

"Blanche and Arless Campbell." He glanced at me, eyebrows raised, and smirked.

"Wow. Wonderful!" I pumped my arm.

Clay gave me a thumbs-up.

I pulled out the box I'd shipped the clutter of art supplies, portable drafting table, scanner, and printer in, now thoroughly battered by the airlines. "Who are Blanche and Arless Campbell?"

The sheriff's grin turned into a frown. "You've never heard of them? *The* Blanche and Arless Campbell? Campbell Industries?"

"Oh. You mean *that* Blanche and Arless? Of course." I tried to keep a straight face. "Still never heard of them."

"Arless is one of the richest people in the country." Clay helped me Bubble Wrap the items. "He's a state senator. But he's on his way to the top."

"Top?"

"Sure. He has the good looks, piles of money, trophy wife, and all the connections. Everything he needs to go straight up the food chain to the White House."

"What about his politics?"

Clay snorted. "No one cares about his politics."

"Except he actively cleaned up crime in his hometown?"

He frowned at me, then left to take the box to his car. While he was gone, I tugged out my mismatched suitcases and packed. I'd just finished tucking my toiletries away when he returned.

"Are you sure these folks want a stranger staying with them?" I zipped the second suitcase closed.

Clay lifted it effortlessly. "Sure. Place is always full of folks staying with them. They have a huge home just outside of town, but it's considered their 'mountain retreat.' Their main place is in Lexington." He waited by the door with the larger case while I did a quick, final sweep of the room. I grabbed the smaller carry-on, gave him an encouraging nod, and he maneuvered my suitcase down the hall and into the lobby.

"Your host, Arless Campbell, may be the politician," he said over his shoulder, "but Blanche is the driving force. I wouldn't be surprised if she already has the new china picked out for the White House." A number of people were in the lobby. Clay wove between them, not slowing as we passed the front desk. Apparently the room bill was already taken care of. "Of course, they've had to work hard to get people to take them seriously as presidential material."

"Why's that?"

He stowed my suitcases in the backseat of his sedan next to my box. I slid into the passenger side. Clay got in and started the car. "Well, even though they're from the rich horse country around Lexington, a lot of folks think someone from Kentucky is a backward, uneducated hillbilly. And folks can be snobs. Anyway, they want to meet you. By the way, do you own a dress?" He pulled out into the street.

"What?"

"They're throwing a dinner party in your honor. Tonight."

The Campbell house, make that mountain retreat, was the size of a hotel, sprawling against the hillside, with naturalized flowers, massive boulders, discreet directional lighting, and a waterfall splashing down the front lawn. I was glad I still wore my only suit, albeit secondhand, but my shoes were from a discount shoe rack at Walmart. Clay grabbed my battered luggage from the rear seat of the car. "I'll come back for your box." He headed to the front door. I slunk behind.

The door opened before we could knock, and an attractive woman in black slacks and top ushered us in.

I held out my hand. "Mrs. Campbell, I want to thank—"

The woman looked at me as if I'd kicked her dog. "I'm Mrs. Fields, the housekeeper."

Swiftly stuffing my hand behind my back, I smiled without showing my teeth. "Um . . . how do you do?"

"Well, thank you. Follow me."

I fell in line behind her starched back, and Clay took up the rear with my luggage. We strolled past a massive stone fireplace at one end of a Native American–motif living room to a short hall. Everything smelled of lemon oil and gleamed with polish. My room proved to be an apartment-sized space decorated in neutral beige and off-white colors.

Mrs. Fields pointed to a phone with numerous buttons. "You're in the guest suite. When this button lights up, it's for you."

"Thank you again."

"Lunch is at noon if you're here. We dine at seven." She gave me a short nod and left.

Clay placed my suitcases on the plush carpeting before looking around the room. "Whooee. This is a step or two or eight up from your digs at the hotel."

"Thank you for all this." I waved my arm.

"Glad to help. I'll bring in your box, then I'll have to leave. I've got to get some paperwork done, but I'll see you at dinner." At my expression, his lips twitched. "Arless and Blanche are old friends of mine. I'm almost like another houseguest."

He left, returning shortly with my box of art supplies. After placing it next to the desk, he gave a quick wave and once again left.

Alone, I explored the room. I moaned in pleasure at the bathroom, with a double thick copper bathtub and matching copper-vessel sink. Fragrant rosemary-eucalyptus soap rested in a baroque gold compote dish. The cedar-lined closet had far more hangers, shelves, and space than I had clothes at home. I quickly hung up my meager wardrobe, taking up only a minuscule corner of the huge closet. After stashing my suitcases, I closed the closet door and admired the bedroom. Matching oversize desk, rustic dresser, brown leather accent chair, and end table made up one side of the room with a fieldstone fireplace in the center. The king-sized bed, hosting a dozen throw pillows, invited me to check it out. I pushed, then bounced on its surface like a little kid. I'd be cradled in my sleep. No attempts to run me down, weird phone calls with hang-ups, death threats, or snakes.

The thought wiped the grin off my face. *It's not as if I'm a threat to anyone.* I was just a forensic artist doing her job. I hadn't even identified any bad guys. Yet.

Opening the window, I sucked in the autumn air, then checked the time. I could probably finish the video image sketch in the next few hours if I started now.

My phone buzzed in my pocket. I pulled it out. "Gwen Marcey."

"Miz Marcey, this is Elijah Adkins. We met outside the police department. You gave me and my wife the drawing of our boy."

"Yes, Mr. Adkins."

"We'll have to get Samuel in the ground right quick and all, but we're havin' a celebration of his life on Friday at eleven o'clock. I'd be pleased if you'd join us. Your drawing of Samuel is . . ." A pause, then he blew his nose.

"I'd be honored to come."

He gave me directions, then disconnected.

I shut the window, then slowly placed the phone on the dresser. The directions were not to a church but to their home. I'd need to ask the sheriff what to wear and where I could get a rental car.

Pulling from the box the art supplies I needed, I sat at the desk and removed the video surveillance photo from the file.

A single frame of a video, taken from a camera mounted above the street, showed the image of a man wearing a cobalt-blue sweatshirt and dark pants. The blurry series of pixels suggested light-colored hair, and the individual facial features were nothing more than impressions. Although many video images led to identifications, the equipment used by businesses varied in quality, and it wasn't unusual that someone like me would be used to help clarify the images.

Propping the photo up against the desk lamp, I stood and walked halfway across the room. With my back still to the image, I tugged out a facial identification catalog and block of Post-it notes from my composite kit. Counting to five, I turned and looked at the photo from a distance, then squinted. The pixels blended together and I could see the suggestion of a face. Before that image disappeared, I flipped through the pages of the catalog and applied Post-it notes to the closest photo matching the surveillance appearance. I returned to the desk and looked closely at the picture. A hint of something white, just a couple of pixels in size, showed by the man's temple. I knew what that was. I'd seen it before. Gold-rimmed glasses, with sunlight glinting off the frames.

I moved the photo to the dresser across the room, then set up my drawing area on the desk. The slanted drawing board, ruler, circle template, erasing shield, electric eraser, kneaded rubber eraser, and Bristol board soon littered the surface.

Drawing a six-inch line down the center of the paper, I bisected it with a four-inch line halfway down. Within the four-by-six-inch box would be the proportioned face of a typical Caucasian male. The width of the eye would fit five times across the middle of the average face. I'd marked my ruler to that measurement. The nose would be about one and one-eighth inches from the eye line, and the opening of the mouth would be one-third the distance between nose and chin. Once I'd scaled the proportions, I opened the book and sketched in the features I'd selected. With glasses, I wouldn't have to be overly accurate on the eyes. I thinned the face a bit and added ears.

I stood to get some distance on the sketch, but before I could move away, my cell phone buzzed.

"Hi, Mom. Dad wants to talk to you."

Before I could say a word, my ex-husband, Robert, was on the line. "Gwen, I've got a problem. Caroline's father had a heart attack." Robert had married Caroline four months earlier. I attended the ceremony and had since become tentative friends with her.

"Oh, I'm so sorry—"

"I'm flying with her to Seattle, then I have to be in Los Angeles for a meeting. I need Aynslee to come stay with you."

I felt a slight tug on my heart that Robert showed such care for his new wife's father. He'd divorced me the first chance he got after I'd been diagnosed with breast cancer. "I'd love to see Aynslee, but I'm not in my hotel room anymore. Can Beth—"

"Believe me, Gwen, I would far rather have her go anywhere than with you."

I opened my mouth to protest but he went on.

"I tried Beth first. She has houseguests. And before you ask,

I did try Dave as well. He's off on some Torch Run. I really need for you to take her. It's only for a week."

I picked up a pencil and tapped it on the desk. "Robert, I told you—"

"If you're about to say you're in danger again, then I'll figure out something else."

"Well—"

"But hear me clearly on this. If your stupid job has again threatened your life, the second I'm back in town, I'm petitioning for sole custody. You are an unfit mother."

"Robert!"

"So? Are you in any danger? Or more importantly, would Aynslee be at risk with you?"

"You know I'd never put her in jeopardy."

"Well then, Aynslee told me you flew into Lexington, so I've put her on the 4:15 p.m. flight tomorrow." He disconnected before I could say anything.

"Robert, you skunk!" I redialed, but he'd obviously turned off the phone.

I paced from the desk to the window and back. *If I tell him about the two attempts on my life, he'll go after sole custody in a heartbeat. But by saying nothing, am I placing my daughter in the sights of . . . who? I don't even know who wants me off this case.*

I'd just have to keep her safe.

I sat on the chair, rubbed my toes, and looked around the room. The bed was big enough, and the room spacious, but how much was I stretching my hosts to announce my fifteen-year-old daughter would be joining me? I hadn't even met them yet.

Then there was the small problem of my reoccurrence of

cancer. "Buck up, Gwen," I whispered. "You don't know how long you have. Enjoy your time with your daughter."

And lest you forget, the local rapist is keeping busy. And someone threatened me.

Robert called me an unfit mother. If anyone got near my daughter, they'd see just how fit I could be.

A divorced, menopausal mother with nothing to lose.

CHAPTER ELEVEN

THE PHONE RANG, LIGHTING UP THE GUEST SUITE button. I picked it up.

"Miz Marcey, lunch is served," Mrs. Fields said.

Glancing at my watch, I stood and moved to the bathroom to check my appearance before exiting the room. I made a wrong turn and ended up in a short hallway with three doors. The first door proved to be a half bath, the second another guest room, and the third door was locked.

I reversed and found the wide staircase going downstairs. I went down and followed a murmur of voices across the living room to French doors leading to a natural stone patio. To my right was a seating area around an outdoor fireplace. Straight ahead, a tall, angular man with broad shoulders and a woman with long, dark hair sat on ocean-gray wicker chairs pulled up to a glass-covered, wicker table. Matching hand-painted dishes on papaya-colored place mats graced five settings. The sun was warm, but a large umbrella offered shade. A hint of blooming roses perfumed the air.

The man had been watching something on a laptop. He shut the computer and stood as I approached. "Ah, so there you are. The renowned forensic artist. I'm Professor Thomas Wellington." In his midthirties, he wore a blue oxford shirt under an earth-toned tweed jacket. He reminded me of Paul McCartney.

"Professor Wellington." I shook his hand.

He turned to the slender woman who looked to be in her late twenties. "And this earnest young lady is my research assistant, Trish Garlock."

Trish had an infectious grin and a smattering of freckles. She wiggled her fingers at me. "Hey."

"Hey, Trish." I took the unoccupied seat next to her.

Mrs. Fields rolled a cart stocked with food from another door, apparently leading to the kitchen. "Mr. and Mrs. Campbell will be slightly detained. They have asked that you not wait for them." She placed lunch on the table—an array of salads, sliced meats and cheeses, an overloaded bread basket, condiments, and fresh fruits. Trish and the professor dove in, filling their plates.

I sighed, feeling slightly guilty for enjoying the glorious day, beautiful setting, and abundance of delicious food served by trained staff.

But only *slightly*. I dug into the chow.

Halfway through my strawberry spinach salad, the French doors opened and a man crossed to the table. "I'm so sorry I'm late." He smiled when he saw me, displaying perfect teeth.

I made a concerted effort not to gape at him. *Please don't let there be spinach between my teeth.*

Arless Campbell was easily the most gorgeous man I'd ever seen. In his mid- to late thirties, he had thick black hair framing

a square forehead, with a hint of gray dusting his short side-
burns. His face was chiseled with a strong jaw and full lips. He
wore a charcoal suit with a cranberry silk tie and a blindingly
white shirt.

I felt like I should stand, or curtsy, or bow, as if in the presence of royalty. I couldn't figure out what to do with my hands, so
I stuck one out for a handshake. That might be an Appalachian-
royalty faux pas, but Arless didn't blink. He took my hand in
both of his. "So we finally meet. Welcome to our home."

My mouth didn't seem to work, my brain locked up, and
heat rushed to my face. *Since when did you become such a bumbling
refugee from a turnip truck?*

I'd been so busy staring at Arless Campbell I hadn't even
seen his wife. If he was gorgeous, she was breathtaking. She'd
swept up her blonde hair into an elegant bun. No, make that a
chignon. Women who looked like her would never simply have
a bun. The hairstyle emphasized her graceful Audrey Hepburn
neck. She had huge dark eyes that dominated her delicate face.
Her dress was a simple black sheath that clung to her slender
body. She carried a Coach purse the color of butterscotch.

"Mrs. Marcey, welcome." Her voice was without accent and
finishing-school modulated.

"Please call me Gwen." I resisted offering Blanche a hearty
handshake.

"And you must call us Arless and Blanche."

Arless pulled out a chair for his wife, then sat in the remaining unoccupied seat and placed the cloth napkin in his lap.

Trish leaned close. "I saw your face as you met Arless," she
whispered. "I had the same reaction. He's beautiful."

"I feel like an idiot. I hope *he* didn't notice," I whispered back.

"I think he's used to it. Their nicknames are Ken and Barbie."

Mrs. Fields appeared, placed a frosty glass of iced tea in front of each of them, and just as quickly disappeared. "I'm sorry to be so tardy." His voice was rich and deep. "I was tied up in a meeting, and my dear wife waited for me." He looked at her with such an expression of love that it took my breath away.

Robert, no man for that matter, had ever looked at me that way. I shoved down the self-pity and concentrated on my surroundings. If I stared at his face, I'd start looking for pores, maybe a wart, some indication he was human and not a perfect robotic creation. "Your . . . uh . . . home is beautiful."

"Thank you." Blanche picked up a spoon and added some sugar to her tea. "I'm glad we could provide you with someplace to stay while you're here. It's not fancy, but I hope you're comfortable."

Not fancy? I'm in a different reality. "I understand you provided the funds to bring me out from Montana. Thank you."

Blanche stirred her drink. "Darling, you didn't tell me you'd arranged for Gwen to come out and work on the recent cases."

Arless waved his hand. "It was nothing. Clay told us about you and we insisted on getting your help. He was pretty stubborn about 'bringing in an outsider,' as he put it."

I gave a noncommittal grunt.

Blanche placed her spoon on the table and looked at me. "But it seems this has put you at considerable risk. Clay told me someone tried to run you down, and you found a snake in your bed at the hotel."

"A rattlesnake."

Wellington and Trish exchanged glances. "How'd they get the snake out of your bed?" Trish asked.

"The hotel called animal control."

"Jason Morrow?" Arless asked.

"I think that was his name. Why?"

"Small town. Everything tends to be connected." Arless glanced over my shoulder.

"Jason is my son." Mrs. Fields refilled my glass.

"Oh!" I hadn't noticed her approach.

Arless said, "If you're concerned about your safety—"

"I'm here to do a job. Please don't worry about me." I didn't mean for that to sound so abrupt. I smiled through stiff lips.

"We shall see to it that you're not harmed while here in Pikeville," Blanche said.

"Really, I'm fine, and grateful for your hospitality."

An uneasy silence fell on the gathering.

"What does Clay have you working on?" Trish finally asked.

"Pretty much what I do back home in Montana." I took a sip of water. "Unknown remains, composites, signs of deception—"

"Deception?" Trish sat up straighter.

"Sure. Being able to tell when people lie." I took a bite of spinach salad.

Blanche looked surprised, Arless amused, and Trish excited. "You mean," she asked, "like body language?"

"Mmmm." I quickly swallowed the mouthful. "That, plus written and verbal clues."

"Fascinating." Blanche touched her lips with her napkin. "Are you always checking to see if people are lying?"

I laughed. "That's what everyone thinks when they find out I've studied deception, but no, it's too much work to do all the time. Unless, of course, something sets off my warning bells."

Arless leaned forward. "And you studied this because of your work?"

"When I interview, I have to know if my victim or witness is being truthful."

"That would be useful knowledge during a campaign to assess the other candidates," Arless said thoughtfully.

Wellington laughed. "Most people feel that you can tell a politician is lying because his lips are moving."

Blanche shot him an annoyed look. "I'm sure, Gwen, that most parents would find your lie detection handy if they have teenagers."

"You bet," I said. "Though studies show that even young children lie at about the same rate as teens and adults. But speaking of teens, you folks have been so gracious in taking me in that I hesitate to even ask you this."

Blanche and Arless gave me encouraging smiles.

"My fifteen-year-old daughter needs a place to stay for a week or so. I hate to impose on your hospitality—"

"Think nothing of it, Gwen," Blanche said. "Of course she's welcome. We have a big house."

Arless nodded in agreement, then turned to Blanche. "See? If Gwen were worried about her safety, she'd never bring her daughter out." He patted her on the knee.

"Er, right. And thank you so much. She won't be a bother. She's a really good kid . . . most of the time."

"Is she flying in?" Blanche asked.

"Yes. She arrives tomorrow in Lexington. I'll rent a car—"

"You don't have to do that." Blanche took a scoop of fresh fruit. "I'd be happy to drive you."

"But—" I began.

"A splendid idea, my dear." Arless stroked her hand. "Maybe once your daughter is here, she'd enjoy taking in some local culture. Does your daughter like live performances? We're patrons of the local small theater."

Trish laughed. "You're patrons of all the cultural activities."

"Hmm, well, Aynslee likes live musical groups." *Like Neutral Stench, but undoubtedly not on their list of favorites.* "She'd probably like the theater. I'm usually too busy to take her," I finally offered lamely. *And too broke to buy the tickets.*

"This play's great. And spooky," Trish said.

"It's the story of Octavia Hatcher," Arless said. "A local woman, married to one of the richest men in town. Have you heard of her?"

I shook my head.

"The story goes," Blanche said, "young Octavia had a child, a son, Jacob, born in January of 1891, who died shortly after birth. Octavia became severely depressed, then fell into a coma. On the second of May that year, the doctors pronounced her dead."

"And she was buried right away," Trish said. "'Cause they didn't have a way to embalm her body."

"A number of other people in town developed the same symptoms," Professor Wellington said. "But after slipping into a coma, after a couple of days, all of them woke up."

A cool draft from somewhere brushed against my neck. "But Octavia . . ."

"Woke up also," Professor Wellington said. "In her coffin. She was buried alive."

CHAPTER TWELVE

MRS. FIELDS APPEARED AGAIN AND BROKE THE silence following the professor's statement. "Would anyone care for coffee?"

"I . . . I would." I caught the professor's attention. "How did they find out she'd been buried alive?"

"Once her husband realized others were waking up, he had her exhumed. Her fingernails were ripped to the quick, and frozen on her face was a look of horror."

I shook my head, trying to get the image out of my brain. "Did anyone ever figure out what happened? What the disease was?"

"No. It's been quite the mystery." Blanche nodded at her husband. "We need to get you and your daughter tickets to the local theater production. And if Clay will give you any time off, you and your daughter can visit the statue her grieving husband placed over her grave. She looks down on the town from the cemetery."

"Aynslee would relish the idea of visiting a cemetery with

a ghoulish story attached," I said. "Especially with Halloween approaching." I hesitated a moment. "But I'll probably keep her out of sight."

"I understand," Blanche said.

"You'll both be safe here," Arless said. "Traditionally we host a Halloween costume party. We'd be delighted if you and your daughter joined us."

"I can get you costumes," Blanche added. "I just need to know what size your daughter is."

"That sounds like fun," I said.

Blanche gave Arless a small nod. "We may be making a big announcement—"

"Now, Blanche . . ." He wagged his finger at her. "No hints." He took a proffered cup of coffee and changed the subject. "If you'd rather stay out of sight, maybe you both could spend a few nights at our cabin."

"Darling, no one's been there for a long time. It's probably a mess."

"I'll have Mrs. Fields get someone up there to clean it. Even if Gwen doesn't want to stay there, no sense in having it fall down." He nodded at the hovering woman and she nodded back.

Professor Wellington glanced at his watch, then jumped to his feet. "Excuse me. I'm afraid I must eat and run. I have an appointment over in Grundy, Virginia. I found a church practicing shape-note singing."

"Will you be here for dinner?" Mrs. Fields poured a cup of coffee and handed it to Trish.

"I'm not sure. It depends on how long everything takes. I'll call." The professor left.

Arless wiped his lips with his napkin, then placed it on the table. "I'm afraid I must rush off as well."

I glanced at Trish. "Okay, I gotta ask. What's shape-note singing?"

"It dates back to the early eighteen hundreds in America. It's a way of quickly learning music by placing a shape on the note heads. It's mostly done for religious music, hence the professor's interest. Anyway, you should ask Professor Wellington about it."

"Okay." Clay would be calling soon about the sketch, so I excused myself and headed to my room. The propped-up drawing on my desk was almost finished.

Stopping at the door, I stared at the sketch. I'd seen that man before, with a slightly fuller face.

Jason Morrow, the snake wrangler. And Mrs. Fields's son.

Swiftly I shut the door behind me. What if Mrs. Fields saw this?

It's not a positive ID. It's a sketch. There could be a number of people who look like that.

I resisted the urge to widen the face and increase the resemblance.

Using the house phone, I dialed Clay's number. He answered on the second ring. "Hi. I'm just finishing up the video surveillance drawing."

"I'm tied up right now, but I'll send someone." Clay's voice was clipped.

I wanted to tell him that I thought I'd recognized the man, but I didn't want to influence his own possible recognition. And I could be wrong. "Okay. Do you have anything else for me?"

"Not right now. See you tonight." He disconnected.

I put the finishing touches on the drawing, scanned it, and printed several copies. After backing it up on a flash drive, I placed the printouts in a folder. Taping some tracing paper over the top of the original sketch to keep it from smudging, I placed it in a separate folder. Before I could take it to the front door for pickup, Mrs. Fields tapped on my door. "An officer is here for you."

Following her, I spotted Junior in the foyer shifting his weight from foot to foot. His restless fingers danced around the hat he held.

"Here you go, Junior." I handed him the folder. He glanced at it, then left without a word. Mrs. Fields shut the door behind him. I wanted to ask about her son's whereabouts, but instead said, "Odd fellow."

"Always has been." She sniffed, then headed for another part of the vast house.

My cell phone was ringing as I entered my room. "Gwen Marcey."

"How's the case going?" Beth asked. "I picked up your mail and phone messages. You have someone who has a case for you in Folly Shoals, Maine. How much longer are you going to be? I finished the research you asked me to do."

"Challenging. Thank you. Where's that? I don't know. Tell me."

Beth was silent for a moment. "Okay. Point made. Let me try again. Folly Sholes is an island off Summer Harbor, Maine."

"At least I'll have some work waiting for me."

"How's the case going?"

"Interesting. Someone tried to run me down, I've gotten a death threat, and someone put a rattlesnake in my bed."

"Oh! Really? Doesn't that enervate you?"

"I have no idea what you just asked. Is that your word of the day?"

"It is. I didn't think I'd be able to use it. What does Robert think about all that? Isn't he sending Aynslee to be with you? He called me, but I didn't have room."

I rubbed my forehead. "Aaah, Beth, I'd appreciate it if you didn't mention anything I just said to anyone."

"So he's threatened you. Talk about being between a rock and a hard place."

"Yeah, well."

"Meeting someone new, a decent guy for a change, would—"

"Don't go there, Beth. I'm still not ready for the dating scene. Just tell me how the research went."

"Hold on." Paper crackled in the background. "Your Clayton Reed is divorced with one son and has a BA in criminal justice from the University of Pikeville. He ran for state representative four years ago. Lost. Ran for city council the year before that and lost that as well."

"So. He's ambitious, but not very successful at it. Could be one of the reasons he hangs around Blanche and Arless. The allure of power."

"Who are Blanche and Arless?"

"The folks who paid for me to come here. Check them out next. Last name of Campbell. Also look into a Jason Morrow and Mrs. Fields."

"Do you have a first name on Fields?"

"No, but she's Jason Morrow's mother. Works for the Campbells."

"Okay. One last thing on Clayton Reed. He has several

luxury cars registered in his name and pays some pretty hefty taxes on his house."

I thought about his gold watch. "Thanks, Beth. I think, as the saying goes around these here parts, I'm fixin' to look into that ole boy."

CHAPTER THIRTEEN

I FOUND MYSELF PACING THE ROOM LIKE A caged cat. How would I find out how Clay could afford all the luxury items in his life? *Hey, Clay, who's bribing you? Or are you brewing and selling your own moonshine?*

I'd just have to keep my eyes and ears open tonight. Preparing for it physically wouldn't take long. I had one dress. My hair was still growing back after chemo and formed a layered, feathery cap on my head. Naturally wavy, it didn't need anything more than a quick comb to be presentable. Makeup would take another two minutes. Entire preparation for the dinner party: ten minutes.

I had several hours to kill, and pacing this room, although it was beautiful, was driving me crazy. I *could* read a book. Watch TV. Think about cancer. Or snakes. Or death threats.

The Indian-summer afternoon suggested a walk. I grabbed my camera and a jacket, then left my room. This end of the house was a rabbit warren of closed doors and short hallways. Eventually I found my way to the patio doors leading off the living room. All the lunch dishes and food had been cleaned up, chairs returned to order, and throw pillows fluffed. On the left of the outdoor fireplace, a landscaped hot tub burbled, and a meandering, stone-paved path began on my right. I took the path.

The Campbells had poured a lot of money into making their grounds appear natural. The stone path wove through densely planted trees and shrubs, occasionally opening up to a log bench or meandering past a man-made stream. I passed by the window to my room, then worked my way to the side of the house, pausing to snap a photo of an interesting leaf or light pattern. The house was tucked into the hillside, and the trail now ambled downward. The mossy soil perfumed the air, and a squirrel briefly checked me out. I found a bench next to the tiny brook and sat. Whoever designed this site was an artist. Dappled sunlight painted the trunks of the aspens in shades of peach and cameo rose. The leaves were every shade of golden yellow, from amber to azo. I longed for a paintbrush and my watercolors. I could stay here forever, cocooned by the forest. Leaning against the trunk of the nearest tree, I closed my eyes and listened to the birds sing to each other.

The soothing sounds did nothing to slow my clicking mind, replaying what I'd seen and heard so far. When I'd mentioned the type of snake appearing in my bed, Wellington and Trish had exchanged glances. That tidbit of information held some special meaning to them. The snake theme emerged again with the possible identity of Jason Morrow from the video surveillance drawing I'd completed. And a connection to this house. Then there was the dead body, compliments of an untreated snakebite.

I really hated snakes.

A cool draft slipped uncomfortably up the back of my jacket, raising goose pimples. I opened my eyes. The breeze stopped, but the uncomfortable feeling didn't. Someone was watching me.

I stood and stretched, rolling my head and rubbing my neck, casually checking the landscape around me. The foliage was simply too dense to see through. Looking toward the house, I searched for prying eyes. I didn't see anyone, but they could have moved away from the window.

Clouds covered the sun, and the thick plantings cast dark shadows around me. Standing, I hurried down the path toward the front of the house. I arrived at a small, stone-lined patio outside open French doors on the lower level. *A shortcut to my room?* I sped toward it.

"Ah, there you are." Arless's voice carried clearly through the opening.

I was about to answer when he spoke again.

"No. The problem will be resolved no later than the thirty-first. Don't worry." He passed by the open door, phone pressed to his ear. I stopped, sure he'd seen me.

He hadn't. He was in an office, with a partner desk and wall of bookshelves behind him. Strolling to the shelves, he pushed on one side. The shelving unit opened, revealing another room beyond.

I melted into the background foliage, not wanting him to think I was eavesdropping or spying on him. The trail continued to a gazebo, then opened to a short slope to the street.

The gazebo was a white octagon with a triple roof, Victorian braces, and gray roofing. The entire structure was screened in.

A silver sedan, looking very expensive, pulled up to the house and parked. The driver stepped out and opened the rear door, then helped an older woman from the backseat. An older gentleman exited from the other side. They looked vaguely familiar.

Dashing into the gazebo, I hid behind a window column. I didn't need folks to know I was here. Not yet.

The driver was about my age, with sun-bleached hair tumbling over drawn brows. He wore a sports jacket over a black T-shirt and jeans. Gold-rimmed sunglasses glinted in the sunlight. From a distance, he was easily in the Arless category of gorgeous men. My eyes lingered on his broad shoulders.

"What time should I pick you up?" he asked the older man.

"We'll call. Thank you."

The driver, or chauffeur, gave a two-fingered salute, then glanced around. His gaze stopped on the gazebo.

I felt like he was staring right at me.

Heat rose to my face. *He can't see me. The screen is blocking his view.*

He waited until the couple was almost to the door before returning to the car. I could see the car's symbol, a letter *B* with two wings, as he turned around and drove off. A Bentley. I suddenly recognized the older man: he was a fantastically wealthy Oscar-winning director known for his charitable organization. Arless's visitors, or more probably campaign contributors, were top rung.

The driver, however, made my fingers itch for a pencil to sketch him.

It's high time you started noticing men. I heard Beth's voice in my head. Until now, I hadn't had any desire to meet new people. The scars from my divorce were too fresh, and Robert kept picking at the scabs. But here I was, staring at a chauffeur as if he were a shop window full of chocolate.

Well, admiring a nice-looking man wasn't a crime. It was like . . . studying the menu, not ordering out.

I could hear Beth's sniff.

Okay then, like appreciating the handcrafted lines of the Bentley. It wasn't as if I was racing out to buy one tomorrow.

A chauffeur is hardly a Bentley . . .

"Let it go, Beth." I stood and left the gazebo, allowing the screen door to slam behind me with a satisfying *whack.*

A large boulder marked the end of the path, and I dropped down the small incline to the pavement. The house now perched to my right and loomed above me. Walking up the street past the house, I found the driveway leading to a three-car garage.

Mrs. Fields stepped from a hidden doorway. "I saw you walking around the house."

Although the words were innocent enough, she stated it like an accusation. Had she seen my sketch? Did she think I was setting up her son?

"I needed some fresh air." I approached the house and tried to breeze past her.

She put out her arm. "Understand one thing. I'm watching out for Mr. and Mrs. Campbell."

And your son? "I'm not here to cause anyone any grief."

She dropped her arm.

A luxury, American-made car took up one of the three bays of the oversize garage. On the side opposite of the garage doors, a raised concrete area held sporting equipment: bicycles, two kayaks on a rack, shelves with neatly labeled plastic bins, and a large laundry sink. Keeping my head up and back straight, I marched through the garage, up the three steps to the raised area, then to the interior door. The kitchen beyond was immense, with professional stoves, pots, pans, and mixing bowls. The aroma of baking bread filled the air. Extensive counter space provided enough room to prepare a dinner for the entire White House staff.

Considering the Campbells' ambition, that was probably the goal.

A rounded man in a white chef's jacket paused in his chopping of something green, frowned at me, and pointed with a rather large carving knife to the exit.

Given his rather hostile attitude toward my intrusion into his lair, I decided not to share my recipe for tuna noodle casserole with potato chip topping.

I could hear Beth's voice. *Ah, Gwen, not sharing that noxious concoction with the chef is returning good for evil. I'm proud of you.*

Sometimes I wondered why she was my best friend.

Checking my watch, I figured I'd have enough time for a bubble bath before dinner. I returned to my room. The phone was ringing.

I picked it up.

The same deep male voice was on the line. "I told you to leave. You need to learn to take me seriously." *Click.*

My skin prickled between my shoulder blades. I ran to the living room. "Mrs. Fields? Mrs. Fields!"

The woman appeared. "Yes?"

"My phone . . . I mean, the phone in my room. Who has that number?"

"The guest suite? I suppose someone could look it up. It's not unlisted, if that's what you're asking."

"Mrs. Fields, did you tell anyone I was staying here?"

She folded her arms. "Of course not." She pivoted and stalked off.

I stared after her. Should I call Clay and mention Jason? Was he the one threatening me? Slowly walking to the suite, I replayed the day. Clay mentioned Arless's name in the lobby, and a number of people could have heard him as we carried the luggage outside. Clay could have told someone he moved me. Technically, Clay could have even made the phone call. The voice was disguised.

Terrific. I had someone I suspected, actually several people, but who could I turn to if Clay were involved? And what did the caller mean by, "You need to learn to take me seriously"?

I found a small sketchbook in my kit and wrote Clay's name at the top of a blank page. Underneath I wrote: *said caller was male, doesn't want me working on the case, smokes (cigarette burns on Shelby Lee), knows forensics, not around when calls come in, knows my location, living beyond his means? DNA results in desk.* I thought about Shelby Lee's reaction to the sheriff's presence. She'd stared at his hand and watch. If he wore a disguise, maybe she recognized his watch. A useful piece of information would be if he owned a cabin in the mountains or if his house were remote. He was divorced, according to Beth. Lady friend? Or did he live alone?

I turned to a fresh page and wrote *Junior Reed.* Underneath his name I wrote: *knows forensics, likes snakes, not around when calls arrive, knows my location, weird.* Just being weird wasn't a crime, but torturing women wasn't the most socially acceptable behavior.

I knew even less about Junior. Another call to Beth was in order. She could find out if Clay, Junior, or Jason drove a black pickup truck.

On a third page I wrote *Jason Morrow.* Underneath I jotted:

could easily find out I was here, likes/handles snakes, resembles sketch from surveillance still.

One thing was for sure. I needed to keep my eyes and ears open tonight at the dinner party.

CHAPTER FOURTEEN

BY THE TIME I NEEDED TO PREPARE FOR THE dinner, I'd decided not to mention the second phone call. Whoever made the calls might slip up and give himself away. I also needed to be more mobile. Depending on Clay or one of his officers to cart me from place to place limited me too much.

The burgundy velvet sheath dress was a great find at the secondhand store, and I loved the way it fit. I just hoped we wouldn't be required to dress every night for dinner, and if we were, they'd better like the color burgundy.

I followed my nose and the sound of voices to the living room. The conversation ceased when I appeared. Clay, looking quite dapper in a black sports coat, designer jeans, and loafers, stepped beside me and quickly took my elbow.

"You look lovely." He led me to Arless Campbell, who was busy pouring drinks from a wet bar.

Blanche waved at my outfit. "What a lovely dress. An Oscar de la Renta?"

"I believe so."

She smiled slightly. "May I get you a drink?"

I didn't need alcohol to cloud my thinking. "Club soda, please."

Blanche nodded to Arless, who proceeded to pour my drink. Before I could say anything to either of them, Mrs. Fields appeared. "Dinner is served."

We moved toward the dining room, an alcove surrounded on three sides with glass and two intricately detailed bronze sculptures.

Arless seated me to his right, with Trish across the table and Clay next to me. The array of silverware was impressive, as was the Waterford bone china and crystal. I tried not to think of my own chipped dinnerware, now wrapped in newspaper and sitting in storage.

"Clay told us about all the stuff you've already done with the surveillance drawing and watching the video and looking for lies," Trish said to me as a uniformed maid served our first course of tomato aspic on a bed of lettuce. She gave an impish grin to the sheriff. "He's most impressed."

Clay shifted in his chair and a slight flush spread up his neck.

"But I got to wondering," she continued, "don't computers do it all now? I mean, I don't want to offend you by saying you're obsolete, but . . ."

"That's a common question, and I'm not offended," I said. "That's like saying now that computers have spelling and grammar check, any writer can become a novelist and crank out a bestseller."

"Good point."

I tried the aspic. Spicy and interesting. "Even with a computer, you still need artistic knowledge about the face, shading, and facial features. Computers become obsolete before you can take them out of the box, and the learning curve on programs is steep. Most of the forensic artwork is still done with a pencil, especially in smaller cities and rural areas."

"So you don't use computers at all?" Trish asked.

"Well . . ." I took a sip of water. "*I* don't, but there is a newer program out, horribly expensive, that takes hand-drawn composites, puts a grid over them, assigns facial feature priorities, then runs the results against a huge database of mug shots and driver's license photos. It then narrows down the likely suspects with a series of possible photo matches. The victim or witness looks at the results for a match. The better the witness and drawing, the more the suspect range is narrowed down. I understand the match rate is very high."

"You've never used it?" Trish asked.

"No, well, not in its present format. I sorta helped develop it."

"Really." Wellington scooped some aspic into his mouth.

"For a time," I said. "I taught at the police academy. Forensic art, cognitive interviewing, that kind of thing. A computer company approached me about developing a program. One that used composites. I told them what they needed to do. They left and I didn't hear from them again. Things got a bit complicated at home . . ." *Now's not the time to talk about divorce, cancer, and rebellious teens, not to mention massacres and bombs . . .* "Well, anyway, I read about the program in a law enforcement magazine," I finished lamely.

"So what's this program called?" Arless asked.

"Um, Compositfit? Comp-Fit? Something like that."

Clay took a small notebook from his pocket and jotted a note.

"You mentioned the surveillance photo you worked on," Arless said. "Has there been a change since a lot of businesses are using surveillance cameras?"

"Yes, to a point, but many of the photos are at weird angles or blurry. Someone needs to be trained in what to look for in the human face." I took another bite of the aspic.

"What do you look for?" Blanche asked.

"If I can see the ears, I'll start there."

"Really?" Blanche asked, blinking rapidly.

"Sure. Ears are probably as distinctive as fingerprints. And you can tell a bit about the family tree. For example, earlobes are either attached or unattached, though there are variations within that, and the shape is inherited."

Professor Wellington inspected Trish's ear, while Clay gazed at mine. "I see what you mean," Clay said. "You have a bump on your ear."

"Darwinian tubercle." I touched it. "A congenital thickening of the helix. I noticed your ear on one side is smaller than the other, Blanche." I glanced at Clay, then blinked. "And Junior isn't your son," I blurted out.

Everyone's gaze shot to me. Heat rose in my face. "I'm sorry. I just noticed your lobe's attached and Junior's isn't. I should have asked to see a photo of his mother."

Clay shifted in his seat. "No. You're right. He's adopted. You're very observant."

"Ah, well, it's things like that I look for," I said.

"Now I'm going to look at everybody's ears," Trish said.

"Occupational hazard," I said.

The first course was whisked away to be replaced by an attractively presented main course. "Traditional Southern food to welcome you," Blanche said. "Fried catfish, cheese grits, okra, and cornbread."

"Yum." *I hope.* Everything *smelled* heavenly, but the cornbread was the only thing I'd ever tasted.

"Did you get hold of that church in Grundy?" Wellington asked Trish.

"Darling," Blanche said to Arless. "Are we having music this time?"

While the conversation swirled around me, I forked some of the catfish, then leaned over to Clay. "I'm wondering if you know somewhere I could rent a car? I don't need to tie up your officers carting me around the countryside."

"Where did you need to go?" Clay asked.

"I've been invited to the funeral of Samuel Adkins, that young man I sketched."

Conversation ceased. Everyone stared at me.

"Elijah and Ruby Adkins invited you to their place? For a service?" Trish asked.

"A funeral. I think they were grateful when I gave them the sketch of their son. Why?"

I took the last bite of the catfish. It was delicious.

Blanche carefully placed her wineglass on the table. No one spoke for a few moments.

"Well, well, well," Arless finally said, looking at each person sitting at the table. "Shall we retire to the study?"

After carefully folding my linen napkin and placing it on the table, I followed everyone into the room with floor-to-ceiling bookshelves on three walls. Table lamps cast pools of golden light on the mahogany leather furniture, and handmade rugs covered the oak floors. Arless lit the logs in the fireplace, filling the room with a flickering amber glow and the scent of burning applewood.

I could feel eyes on me, but when I looked around, no one seemed to be paying me any attention. They'd settled in a semicircle around the fireplace, cupping the lead crystal glasses Blanche had filled from a bar in the corner of the room. She'd held up a bottle of Kentucky bourbon and raised one eyebrow, but I shook my head.

"It's your call," Arless said to Clay. "It didn't work with Trish."

Clay swirled his bourbon, then took a sip. "Of course, we can't predict how this will go either."

"It is a matter of trust."

"We know what *doesn't* work. But with that program . . ." Blanche leaned forward. "I think it's a fabulous idea. When could we start?"

"We could put the plan together as early as tomorrow."

"Excuse me." They obviously needed to discuss something without me. "I have a long day coming up. Thank you for the lovely dinner. I'll leave you alone—"

"Please have a seat, Gwen." Arless nodded at a chair near the fire. "I'm sorry we were being so cryptic. We"—his gaze rested on each individual in the room—"have a proposal for you."

Everyone's gaze focused on me. I wiped a damp hand on my dress.

Sheriff Clay cleared his throat. "I'm afraid I haven't been completely up front with you."

I frowned at him and waited.

The sheriff shifted in his chair and took a sip of bourbon. "I told your boss, Dave, about the serial rapist. I didn't think about the other . . . problem."

"Problem?" I asked.

"We've had a lot of bodies showing up. Quite frankly, it never occurred to me that a forensic artist would be useful for sketching someone for identification. Most of these bodies, including the one you sketched, belong to a particular group of people."

Professor Wellington cleared his throat. "What do you know about the people who call themselves Signs Following Believers?"

"Never heard of them."

"The full name of their church is the Church of the Lord Jesus Christ with Signs Following. They're snake handlers," Blanche said through stiff lips. "Pentecostal snake handlers."

CHAPTER FIFTEEN

SNAKES AGAIN. THE ROOM WAS WARM, BUT I felt a chill.

Only the crackle of the fire and the tinkle and clink of melting ice cubes in the old-fashioned glasses broke the silence. Arless finally spoke. "We should start at the beginning."

I nodded.

"Kentucky is the only state"—Arless smoothed his perfect hair with a well-manicured hand—"that passed laws specifically prohibiting snake handling in religious services. But it wasn't enough. People continued to die from snakebites. I was able to introduce a bill to substantially increase the fines and jail time."

"Arless thought that would be the end of it," Blanche said, "that the churches would simply go to West Virginia where it's legal. Instead, they went underground and stayed in Kentucky."

"And the bodies started to pile up," Clay continued. "Not just snakebites. They also drink poison—strychnine and lye—and burn themselves with fire."

I swallowed hard, wishing I'd taken that glass of bourbon. "I don't understand. Why?"

"Partly because these are uneducated, backwoods people. And they take their Bible literally," Arless said.

Professor Wellington stood, walked to the bookshelves, and pulled down a gold-labeled Bible. "It comes from Mark 16:17–18. 'And these signs shall follow them that believe; in my name shall they cast out devils; they shall speak with new tongues; they shall take up serpents; and if they drink any deadly thing, it shall not hurt them; they shall lay hands on the sick, and they shall recover.'"

"I confess I'm not all that familiar with that passage," I said.

"Snake, or serpent handling, as they call it," Professor Wellington said, "was practiced in Virginia and West Virginia as far back as the late eighteen hundreds. You'd basically find it at coal-mine revivals." He looked toward the ceiling and slightly nodded his head. I could almost see him mentally composing his thesis.

Wellington continued. "But it was a charismatic traveling preacher, George Went Hensley, who linked serpent handling with tongues and the other signs and seemed to make it more . . . popular. They believe this biblical passage is a commandment of Jesus."

I shook my head. "But it seems to me that there's a First Amendment issue about passing a law prohibiting—"

"The free exercise of religion." Professor Wellington snapped the Bible shut. "And the Fourteenth Amendment says state legislators can't pass laws either. But the Kentucky Supreme Court ruled that the state could regulate snake handling to protect citizens. And believe me, they need protection."

"Children—" Blanche glanced at her husband. "Some of the . . . victims of this cult have been children. Forced to drink poison and handle deadly snakes."

I wiped my damp hands on my dress. "That's terrible. Did you identify the children? Do you need me to draw—"

"Yes, we identified them." Clay's face tightened and a vein pounded in his temple.

"Then I don't see how this has anything to do with me."

"We know Elijah and Ruby are members of this so-called church," Clay said. "But we need to identify everyone involved, especially the leaders."

I was beginning to see where this conversation was going, and I didn't like it at all. I waited until the mild hot flash passed before speaking. "Tomorrow I'm picking up my daughter. I won't—can't—put her in any danger."

"She won't be in danger." Professor Wellington carefully placed the Bible back on the shelf. "It's only the members who are . . . shall we say 'allowed,' or forced, to follow the bizarre beliefs."

"And you know this because . . . ?"

Trish spoke for the first time. "Six months ago we came down here and started working on Tom—er, Professor Wellington's thesis on Appalachian church music and beliefs. That's when the first body, a twelve-year-old girl, turned up."

"So I asked Trish if she'd help us," Clay said. "All we thought we needed was the right clothes. She already had the long hair and, since she was from West Virginia originally, the right accent."

"I went undercover," Trish said, "and tried to infiltrate the church, but they quickly figured out that I wasn't much of a Christian, let alone a Pentecostal holiness believer."

"You said 'holiness believer,'" I said. "That means . . . ?"

"That's one of the names they call themselves," Trish said. "For them, uncut women's hair, modest clothes, stuff like that were some of the outward signs."

"Okay, but why me, and why now?" I asked.

"*Why you* is that you have a foot in the door with the invitation to the funeral," Clay said. "And can draw the faces of the members."

"Can't you just take their pictures?"

"Believe me, we tried," Trish said. "I had a camera with me, but they found it."

Professor Wellington rubbed his hands together. "As to the *why now* part of your question, we know a big revival, a brush-arbor homecoming, is coming up soon. We also have heard that this time all of the children will be forced to participate. Burned, poisoned, and bitten by snakes."

A log in the fire popped.

I jerked, then licked my dry lips. "But what about the rape cases?"

Clay swirled his glass. "I think you've done all you can on them for now. We'll keep looking for the missing woman, and this time we'll put her in protective custody until we can get that drawing and the information we need. And given the threats and all to you, it wouldn't hurt for you to lay low for a bit." He glanced at Arless, then back at his glass.

"I don't know—"

"I'll tell you what. When I drive you to the airport tomorrow, I'll fill you in on our plan and the background of this group," Blanche said.

"And I'll pull the police reports on the bodies we've found," Clay offered.

"We'll get you a car," Arless added.

"And the right clothes to wear for that funeral," Blanche said.

My head ached and I rubbed my forehead. "But Elijah already knows I'm connected to the police—"

"Don't worry," Clay said. "We'll arrange everything."

I stood to leave.

The men also stood. "There's a substantial reward should you be able to expose this cult," Arless said.

"Reward?" As soon as the word left my mouth, I regretted it.

"I put the money up, personally, when I got the laws passed," Arless said. "Any person who identifies members of this snake-handling group will receive a reward. I'm dangling a carrot, the monetary reward, with the intent of then getting new laws on the books." He mentioned an amount that left me breathless.

I studied my clasped hands. "I'd like to think it over. I'll give you my answer in the morning." Quickly leaving the room, I headed to my suite, my brain buzzing. I held my thoughts in check until I'd firmly shut the door. *Reward*. The kind of money Arless mentioned would pay my expenses for the upcoming battle with cancer. A losing battle.

I tugged off my dress and hung it in the closet. I could choose to not fight the disease and use the money for Aynslee's college. Robert had put some funds aside, but this would get her into a first-rate school.

But I would have to either leave her in town with a serial rapist loose or take her into the mountains to a snake-handling cult.

CHAPTER SIXTEEN

I SPENT A RESTLESS NIGHT RUNNING FROM snakes and spiders, waking up in a cold sweat. Failing to inquire the night before about breakfast, I showered and dressed, then went looking for coffee. If need be, I'd call a cab and scour the town for some morning brew. Fortunately Mrs. Fields spotted me crossing the living room and pointed to an alcove off the kitchen where coffee, orange juice, fruit, and pastries waited on the sideboard.

Professor Wellington sat next to the window, deeply engrossed in a newspaper. He wore a worn, umber-brown corduroy jacket over an open-necked plaid shirt. Trish, seated on his right, was just finishing up a muffin. She looked fetching in an oatmeal sweater with an oversize taupe scarf around her neck. "Morning." She popped another bite into her mouth. "Try the pumpkin spice," she managed around a mouthful. "It's heavenly."

I joined them. "You're up early."

"Not really. We're fellow houseguests." She stood and retrieved a second muffin. "Blanche and Arless insisted when

Professor Wellington asked about a place in Pikeville while working on his second PhD."

"That was nice of them."

"They're the most generous people I've ever met. They work in a food kitchen, helped fund a shelter. They're even building an orphanage in Haiti."

"Impressive." I turned to Professor Wellington. "What are you getting your PhD in?"

He lowered the paper enough to see me. "Religion."

I took a sip of coffee. "And your thesis is on . . . ?"

"Music played and sung in the Appalachian churches."

"Like the Scottish-Irish roots to gospel—"

"Hardly." Professor Wellington put down the newspaper. "I was following up on K. Y. Young's 1926 analysis that revealed the infantile desire found in the church lyrics was nothing more than a repressed desire for an absent father's protection and comfort."

"Oh." I took another sip of coffee. "Or maybe the music is meant to lift you up and get your mind on worship." I wanted to kick myself as soon as I said that. Wellington was a longtime friend of my host and hardly someone I wanted to antagonize.

Wellington stared at me for a moment, then returned to his paper.

Before I could think of anything suitably neutral to resume the conversation, Blanche breezed into the room wearing a sharply tailored, black-and-white-striped jacket and gray boot-cut trousers. Her hair was held back with a pair of sunglasses. "Arless sends his regrets that he won't be joining us this morning. He's expecting visitors." She glanced at her diamond-encrusted watch. "What time does your daughter arrive in Lexington?"

"Four fifteen."

"We should leave after lunch then." She filled a coffee cup and took a seat next to me. "Have you made up your mind about helping us?"

"I have. I'll help."

"Outstanding!"

"Just to be clear, you want me to draw a composite of the people directly handling the snakes?"

"And anyone bringing snakes in a snake box. Yes."

"What are you going to do with the composites? Release them to the press or—"

Blanche smiled. "You'll help, but Clay already made inquiries into that computer program you spoke about last night—Composit-Fit ID, by the way, is the name. Now that you're on board, Arless will purchase it. As soon as you get us the composites, we'll be able to identify the suspects and put a stop to all this here in Kentucky. According to Clay, it interfaces with the DMV as well as other facial databases."

"Are you going to arrest the identified handlers?"

"Clay said they pretty much have to catch them with the snakes, but if he knows who they are, he can keep an eye on them and wait until they make a move." She paused. "I'm assuming that because you are both the witness and the artist, the drawings will be extremely accurate."

"They should be. I may not remember a name, but I'll never forget a face. But there's still the problem of me getting accepted by the group."

She patted my hand. "Don't worry about that. I'm sure you'll be able to do it. I'm thrilled with your answer. Now, you'll have to excuse me. I have some phone calls to make." She turned and strolled off, leaving behind a whiff of Joy perfume.

Trish raised her eyebrows at me. "So. You're going in."

"Looks like."

"I see you wear a cross. Are you by any chance Pentecostal?" Trish asked.

"No."

Professor Wellington folded his paper onto the table. "So what do you know about the holiness Pentecostal traditions?"

"Um . . . well, Trish talked about long hair and clothing and . . . maybe they talk in tongues?"

"That's what I thought." Wellington tilted his head back and his eyes became unfocused as if he were addressing a classroom of college freshmen. "The practice of glossolalia, or speaking in tongues, is not limited to Pentecostals. In America, that phenomenon occurred in such groups as the Mormons and the Shakers of the nineteenth century." His gaze sharpened on me. "You'll need to brush up on what they believe."

"And I would need to know this because . . . ?"

"You'll be hard-pressed to join them at their homecoming if you can't show some familiarity and acceptance of their faith."

"What's a homecoming?" I asked.

Wellington stood. "It's similar to a church revival. Different churches get together to support a single church. In this case, they'd not only be helping the local congregation but showing contempt for the law. I'll be right back."

Trish watched him leave, then sighed. She caught me watching her and her face flushed red.

"He seems like a nice enough fellow," I said.

"He's . . . wonderful. But doesn't seem to know I'm female."

"Umn," I grunted noncommittally.

Trish shrugged, then lifted her chin. "Well, back to earth.

Big day today. Lots of churches to scope out for the professor."

"How do you find or choose the churches for his music research?"

"Professor Wellington finds them. I think he grew up around here." She stood. "Oh, I have a magazine article written about the snake handlers. It's old, but I think it's still accurate. Let me find it and get it to you. Okay?"

"That'd be great. Anything you have will help."

She stood and left the room.

After placing my cup on the sideboard, I started to leave, but Wellington appeared in the door. "Blanche will fill you in on the background of the locals, but you might want to read this." He shoved a thick paperback into my hands. The title was *The Traditions of Holiness Pentecostals.* "This will catch you up on some of the origins and beliefs. There's a chapter in here about the serpent handlers, which came out of this movement."

"Thanks." I rather expected him to assign me a research paper as well.

Mrs. Fields appeared at the door. "You have a phone call." She held up a receiver.

The book dropped from my suddenly numb hand. "Who . . . Who is it?"

Mrs. Fields's knuckles whitened on the receiver. "It sounds like Sheriff Reed." She thrust the phone into my hand.

"Hi, Gwen. Clay here. Tried to call you on your cell. We found Ina Jo."

"Fantastic—"

"Not really. She's dead."

CHAPTER SEVENTEEN

TWENTY MINUTES LATER CLAY PICKED ME UP.

"Is this the work of the Hillbilly Rapist?" I asked.

"We'll know soon enough. Her body was found in the Levisa Fork of the Big Sandy River." He drummed his fingers on the steering wheel. "We were pretty sure she was one of his victims because of her background. I suppose she could be a suicide—"

"Not with a baby."

He shook his head. "The state crime lab will process the scene, but they've held off until we get there. They may even wait until their forensic anthropologist arrives from Frankfort."

The location was less than ten minutes from the center of Pikeville, but it took us almost twenty to drive up Highway 23, exit, weave around a sporting goods store and Walmart, then cruise through the parking lot of a Hobby Lobby to a short paved road. The road proved to be a boat launch for the river, with a parking area, before it dropped to the river and crime scene. Police, sheriff, and a variety of other emergency vehicles crisscrossed the parking lot. Across the river was a major highway, and cars were backed up for miles while passersby tried to see what all the excitement was about. A waiting deputy wordlessly escorted us through the parked vehicles, past a female deputy interviewing a couple of pale-faced teens, to the river. The stink of dead fish floated on the air.

A solid row of uniformed officers parted as we approached, revealing a sprawled body, her lower half still submerged in the murky, khaki-green water.

I slowed, as always reluctant to confront death, and waited until my analytical brain took over.

Ina Jo was still wearing the outfit I'd last seen her in and lying facedown with her arms under her body. Her legs moved gently with the current. The defiant purple streak in her hair now merely looked sad.

"Thank you fellows for waiting." Clay's face had turned pale. He took a deep breath and nodded at a gloved crime scene technician.

The technician rolled her over.

Some color returned to Clay's face.

Mud caked her face, masking her features. Only a glint of silver showed where the silver loop pierced her eyebrow. The slim, blue-and-white braided rope still wrapped around her neck left no doubt as to her fate. Her wrists showed purple-red abrasions.

"Well—" Clay rubbed his nose. "That rules out her jumping in the river as a suicide. That's a pretty distinctive rope, though. Even a blind hog finds an acorn now and then. Maybe that will give us a lead."

I frowned at him. When we were at Blanche and Arless's

house, Clay's accent was far less pronounced and he dropped the quaint country sayings. Trying to fit in? That matched my speculation that he was obsessed with the allure of power.

Clay turned to one of his officers standing nearby. "Billy, you fish here. How far do you think she traveled down the river?"

The young man half shrugged. "Could be she was thrown in as far away as the Pauley Bridge."

"Yeah. Makes sense." Clay strolled over to where I was standing. "The Pauley Bridge is around that big bend." He nodded upstream. "It's a pedestrian crossing over the river. There are a few other places the killer could have used, but the water's low right now. If he dumped her on the riverbank and pushed her in, she'd washed up pretty fast."

"You'll know a lot more after the autopsy."

"Yeah. Told ya he was smart, though. Throwing her in the river like that. Water washes off forensic clues."

I pulled out a small pad of paper and a pencil, then drew a line down the center. On the top of one column I wrote *Known*, on the other *Unknown*.

"Are you sketching?" Clay asked.

I turned the pad so he could read what I'd written. "This is how I organize my thoughts. I can figure out the questions I need to ask from this." Under "Known" I wrote: *used rope, woman dressed, strong—*

"Why did you write that he was strong?" Clay asked.

"Whether he threw her off the pedestrian bridge or transported her to the bank, he'd have to be able to pick her up and carry her, and she's not a tiny woman."

"Sure."

We strolled up the bank to the car. "Clay, I couldn't help but notice your reaction before they turned the girl over. You were very pale."

"Yeah. A lot of years ago my buddies and I were fishing in this river. We found a body. It was facedown and we turned it over. I'll never forget that face, or what was left of it. The police never identified the body. I . . ." He grinned sheepishly and shrugged. "I hope you won't mention it. Not good for a cop to be weirded out by dead bodies."

"It's understandable."

He grunted in response.

We'd arrived at the car. Clay got in and started the engine.

I slipped in beside him and looked at my notes. "You know, I was thinking . . . One possibility is the Hillbilly Rapist got spooked when you announced a door-to-door search. Instead of the leisurely several days, he discovered you'd soon be pounding on his door. He needed to get rid of the evidence. Did you announce where you were starting your search?"

Clay didn't answer, but sat up straighter.

While he concentrated on driving, I added to my *Known* column: *water washes off forensic clues.*

I jotted: *Is this what the caller meant by "You need to learn to take me seriously"?*

"Now what did you think of?" Before I could stop him, Clay grabbed my notebook and read what I'd written. "What's this? You got another call?" He looked at me, a vein throbbing in his forehead. "And you didn't think it was important enough to tell me?"

My face burned. "I . . . I—"

He threw the notebook into my lap. "What else did he say?"

"Um. Not much. 'I told you to leave.'"

"You came in to help us with this investigation. I knew bringing in an outsider would be a mistake."

We were soon at the Campbell house. Clay turned to me. "I'd send you home right now if you hadn't agreed to help Arless and Blanche."

Still blushing, I got out of the car and Clay drove away. What could I say to Clay? "I'm suspicious of you"?

Glancing at the house, I spotted a curtain moving on the second floor. Good ole Mrs. Fields was at it again.

In response to my ringing the doorbell, Mrs. Fields opened the door and stepped aside to let me enter.

Blanche breezed in from the living room, phone to her ear. "Hold on." She put her hand over the receiver. "Ready to go pick up your daughter?"

"Be right there." Strolling to my bedroom, I threw my sketchbook across the room. I hated being thought of as an outsider and not doing my best work on a case.

Robert's voice intruded on my thoughts. *You're a failure yet again, getting dumped off the Hillbilly case.*

"Go away, Robert," I whispered.

This isn't the first time you've been thrown off a case either.

"Pouring salt on the wound? I'm perfectly capable of beating myself up without your help." The whipped-cream topping to this whole goat rodeo would be if Clay were somehow involved and my carelessness led to another woman being hurt. Or killed.

I punched a pillow on the bed for good measure, then picked up the paperback book on Pentecostals that Wellington gave me.

Blanche was waiting in the kitchen, now minus the grumpy chef, and I trailed her to the garage beyond. The raised concrete storage area gave me a clear view of all three bays now occupied with expensive vehicles. A second luxury car had joined the one I'd seen earlier. Blanche walked down the steps and climbed behind the wheel of a carmine-red Porsche Cayenne Turbo. The seats were two-toned natural leather.

I stroked the leather. Even the air smelled rich.

"Are you okay?" Blanche asked, touching my arm with a perfectly manicured finger.

No. Clay wants me off the rape case, I'm broke, and I have cancer again. Robert's planning on getting full custody of my daughter, I don't have a home, and to top it all off, I'm green-eyed with envy over this stupid car. I'm probably ugly, fat, and if I had a mother, she'd be dressing me funny. "I'm fine, thank you."

She handed me a fabric bag imprinted with the name of the Pikeville library. Inside was a small stack of file folders. "That should get you started."

I added the paperback to the folders. After opening the garage door, we backed out and turned toward Lexington. The earlier sunshine had surrendered to a chill, and wisps of low-hanging, blue-gray clouds clung to the mountains surrounding the town. The leaves on the trees sported Indian yellow, olive green, and a hint of rust. My black mood lifted slightly. I waved my hand toward the mountains. "This is a painting waiting to happen."

"It *is* beautiful, isn't it? I want everyone to see this country the way I do, to love this state the way I love it." The corners of her mouth turned up slightly and her eyes softened with a wistful look. We drove in appreciative silence for a few miles, watching the autumn landscape unfold.

"I should take up painting," Blanche finally said. "You can paint almost anywhere, right?"

"Yes, it's a wonderful hobby, and watercolors are quite portable." *And expensive.*

"Mmm." She nodded.

"Does Arless have a hobby?"

"Sailing. We keep a sailboat at Kentucky Lake."

Blanche's cell rang. She answered. "Yes. Okay." She looked at her watch. "We'll turn it on. Bye." She disconnected and dropped her phone into her purse. "Clay said to turn the radio on in about ten minutes. The lead news at the top of the hour."

"Are they announcing something about the homicide?"

"He didn't say." She turned on the radio, found the right station, and lowered the sound so the gentle words of an old-time gospel song formed background music. I thought of Wellington and his research.

"Welcome to the sound of Pikeville, station WXWD. This afternoon we have a special guest here with us in the studio. Sheriff Clayton Reed joins us for some exciting news. Welcome, Sheriff."

"Thank you." Clay's voice sounded tense. "We finally have a lead on the serial rapist, the so-called Hillbilly Rapist, preying on women here in Pikeville. A composite sketch, made from a video surveillance image, led us to Jason Morrow, an employee of the county's animal control. We've put out a warrant for his arrest."

"Jason Morrow!" I exclaimed. "Poor Mrs. Fields." I *really* hoped she wouldn't blame me.

"So your sketch artist was able—"

"It was good police work. The artist was threatened several times and someone put a rattlesnake in her bed. Only the Hillbilly Rapist would care if a forensic artist worked on this case, and when I viewed the security tapes, I saw Morrow bringing the snake to the hotel."

"Have you linked Morrow directly to the rapes?"

"Ah . . . I'm not at liberty to say. As for the sketch artist, as a matter of fact, she's no longer connected with the sheriff's department."

CHAPTER EIGHTEEN

I WASN'T SURPRISED. CLAY SEEMED FURIOUS AT my not telling him about the phone call. But something he said bothered me a lot. I just couldn't put my finger on it.

Blanche turned off the radio. "What's that all about?"

Blanche and Clay were friends. I had to be very careful what I said. "It's a . . . misunderstanding."

"Not to worry. Sounds like Clay caught the rapist, so your work there is done. You can now concentrate on our project of sketching and identifying the snake handlers." She took her eyes off the road for a moment and glanced at me. "Breathe, Gwen."

I gripped the stack of file folders in my lap.

"This all might work out." She nodded to herself. "Yes. This might be the break we need."

"I'm not sure I follow."

"You need to find a way to be invited to the snake-handling revival. Ruby and Elijah know, because of the sketch you gave them, that you work with the sheriff's department. They're going to be super cautious of you. Clay distancing himself from you helps. What if . . ." She thought for a moment. "What if you tell them at the funeral that you're in trouble for giving them the sketch? Ask for it back, then offer to do a portrait of their son. We'll pay you extra for the drawing, of course. Set it up so the only time you can meet with them to do the sketch is during the revival."

I pulled a pencil out of my purse and twirled it in my fingers. "I'm not sure . . ."

"Because it's well known that Arless introduced the legislation to increase the fines and jail time for snake handlers, obviously you won't be able to stay with us."

"But all the rooms in town are taken."

"We have something better. Remember that cabin we mentioned the other night? Back when Arless and I were first married, and before we built our home, we bought a cabin here in Pikeville. Well, actually not in town, but nearby. It's simple, but does have electricity and running water."

"Won't folks know you own it?"

"No. The paperwork just lists an LLC and we've never actually lived there. We also have an old pickup you can drive. Mrs. Fields will pack your clothes and send them with Trish and Tom. The two of them offered to straighten up the cabin and stock it with groceries. You'll be able to move in when we get back from the airport."

I clenched my teeth thinking about Mrs. Fields touching my things. "Thank you, but—"

"I'll call Arless just before we get to Coal Run Village and he'll meet us or get someone to drive over with the truck."

I wanted to point out that I wasn't convinced Clay had

arrested the right man. If not, whoever had been threatening me was still out there. And I was picking up my daughter. "I'll do this on one condition."

"What's that?"

"You can tell no one where I am. That includes Clay."

"Some people already know, but I'll make sure everyone who's aware of your whereabouts keeps it a secret from Clay and anyone else, if that's what it takes."

A hot flash shot up my neck and onto my face. I ducked my head, then opened the top file for something to do while it passed. A black-and-white photograph of a rawboned man, mouth open, holding a large snake, was clipped to the inside. A missing person's report, a single sheet of paper, was enclosed.

MISSING PERSON REPORT
TYPE OF MISSING PERSON:

___ Disability

___ Juvenile

_X_ Involuntary

_X_ Endangered

___ Other

Name: Maynard, Grady Earl **Sex:** M **Race:** W **DOB:** May 20, 1958 **Height:** 6'1" **Weight:** 185 **Hair:** Brown **Eyes:** Blue

Scars/tattoos: Left index finger missing tip, scar on right arm

Employment: CAS Coal Corporation (dozer operator), Church of the Lord Jesus with Signs Following (pastor)

Home address: 54637 Pine Ridge Holler, Pikeville, KY

Last seen: Disappeared around October 31, 1996

I checked the back of the form. Blank. "This is it? Nothing on the type of vehicle he owned, who filled this out, anything?"

"I didn't think you were investigating Grady."

"Sorry. Sometimes I get carried away. What does this mean—disappeared?"

"He worked for a coal mine. Most folks believe he went in a slurry pond."

"What's a slurry pond?"

"It's an area where the coal waste products are impounded. It's a bit like quicksand. If you happened to fall in, your body would never be found."

I licked my lips. "So. Yet another Pikeville resident buried alive."

Blanche jerked on the steering wheel and the car swerved. "Sorry. I'd never heard it expressed like that before. Grady Maynard started the snake-handling church in Pikeville. When he disappeared, everyone thought the church would simply dissolve."

"But that didn't happen."

"Right. Then when Arless got the law changed, we again expected the group to go away, but it went underground. And the members became even more prone to drink poison, burn themselves, and handle serpents. Indirectly, Grady also was the reason Arless and I became so involved in stomping out the practice." She tapped the paper on my lap. "We didn't know it at the time, but the cabin we bought, the one you'll be staying in, was Grady's home."

Several hours later Blanche dropped me off in front of Arrivals, then headed over to the parking lot set up for cell phone calls.

The arrival/departure screen informed me Aynslee's flight was on time. I strolled toward security. The crowds were thick with families holding Welcome Home signs, boyfriends with wrapped bouquets, and distraught mothers with crying babies.

I spotted my daughter almost immediately. Her long ginger hair hung in spiral curls halfway down her back, and her cheeks were flushed with excitement. Her face appeared, then disappeared in the milling passengers coming out of security. I raised my arm so she could find me in the crowd. She saw me and waved with a new smartphone with a pink bling cover.

She finally cleared the throng and I could see her clearly. Her jeans were ripped and shredded all the way up the front, exposing a large amount of leg and thigh. Her black T-shirt stopped a good two inches from her hip-high jeans, revealing her belly button and an expanse of tanned stomach. Open-toed sandals and a large backpack completed the look.

What was Robert *thinking*? I'd seen bathing suits less revealing.

I hugged her. My vision blurred and I swallowed down the lump in my throat. She may have been half naked, but she was *my* beautiful, half-naked daughter.

"Mom! Let go. I can't breathe."

I released her.

"Gosh, Mom, it's only been a couple of days."

"Well, I'm happy you're here. Where did you get the . . . new clothes?"

"Caroline bought them for me. And the phone."

I clenched my fist, then made an effort to relax my hand. My ex-husband's new wife would get a phone call when I got back. "She saw you wearing this? And let you go out in public—"

"Whatever. I'm hungry."

Glancing around the airport, I could see only one restaurant. "How about we get your bags, then see if Blanche will take us somewhere to eat."

"Who's Blanche?" She fell into step beside me as we ambled to baggage claim.

"Long story." Something chirped. Then another chirp.

"What's that sound?"

"I got some texts." She continued to walk with me, eyes now glued to the phone, thumb giving a flipping motion on the screen. She stopped flipping, read for a moment, then started texting.

We stopped away from the baggage claim carousel so I could catch her up on the events of the past few days without anyone overhearing. She kept her head down, cradling the phone, thumbs flying.

A loud horn sounded and the carousel started. The passengers surged forward. We remained stationary, like rocks in a human stream, with Aynslee's gaze riveted on her cell.

"And in three days," I finally said to her bent head, "I'm turning into a rutabaga, going to Paris, and will be performing opera onstage. *La bohème*."

"That's ridiculous." She didn't look up.

"I was just seeing if you were listening to me."

"Whatever."

"So what did I just tell you?"

She finally looked up and rolled her eyes. "You said we're going to hang out with a bunch of people who worship snakes. I was texting Mattie about it."

Mattie was the young girl we'd rescued from the streets, drugs, and prostitution. She now lived with her aunt.

126

"They don't worship snakes," I said. "They handle them."

"Sounds creepy." Aynslee looked at her phone, apparently now part of her hand, and started to text again.

"And I'm not sure if I'm taking you with me," I said. "It may not be safe."

She ignored me.

"Who are you texting now?"

"Mattie answered. She loves the snake thing."

"Aynslee, I need you to watch for your suitcase."

"It's black."

I looked at the parade of black bags slowly drifting by. "Can you be a bit more specific?"

She didn't look up. "Look for the one with crime scene tape."

I checked the suitcases again, this time spotting the one with yellow and black plastic tape on the handle. Several people stared at me as I retrieved it.

I dialed Blanche. "The eagle has landed."

"Be right there."

By the time we made it outside, Blanche had pulled up to the curb. Aynslee stared at the gleaming Porsche. "You didn't tell me they're rich," she whispered.

"They're rich," I whispered back. "But I'll be living in a cabin in the mountains."

"Oh."

After introductions and before I could suggest it, Blanche said, "Let's have an early dinner, then drive around a bit so you can see some of the stables around here. Lexington is called the horse capital of the world." She drove us to a charming bistro where she suggested we try the regional dish "hot brown," which proved to be an open-faced turkey sandwich covered with some kind of delicious gravy. Aynslee placed her phone near her hand. It chirped and whistled with annoying regularity.

"Please turn that thing off," I told her.

She rolled her eyes again and put the cell into her lap. The chirps and whistles ceased, but she now stared downward.

Blanche politely ignored Aynslee's antics.

I wondered if I could smash the phone on the floor or if I'd have to stomp it into cell purgatory.

"Did you grow up around here?" I asked Blanche.

"No." She touched her lips with the linen napkin. "My family perished in an accident long before I left for college. I'd liked the arts program at the University of Kentucky, got accepted, and moved here. I fell in love with the area."

"I'm sorry about your family," I said.

She nodded. "I held down two jobs putting myself through college. Then I met Arless, and the rest, as they say, is history."

We ordered derby pie for dessert. Aynslee giggled.

"What's so funny?" I asked.

"Nothing. Just a boy I met." Both thumbs flew as she tapped a message on her phone.

"How did you meet him?"

She didn't look up. "At the mall. Not a big deal."

Teenagers were part of Job's trials and the unwritten plague of Egypt.

I gave up on communication with her and, with Blanche's blessing, dove into the files I'd brought in with me. Trish had scrawled notes in the second file. "What does she mean, 'Check out baptism'?" I asked.

Blanche cleared her throat. "Well, I have to ask you a personal question."

I slowly placed the forkful of pie back on my plate. "Ookay. Shoot."

She shifted in her seat. "What are your feelings about baptism?"

Aynslee giggled, still without looking up, and in spite of myself, I joined in.

"What's so funny?" Blanche asked.

"Oh, I'm sorry. I didn't mean to laugh. When you said personal question, I was expecting you to ask how much I weighed, or whether I flossed daily." I wiped my eyes. "Baptism is supposed to be a public proclamation of your faith. Why did you ask?"

She sniffed. "At my church, we baptize babies. This . . . group will want to baptize you."

"But I've already been baptized."

"According to Trish"—Blanche tapped the file—"they encourage everyone to rededicate themselves during the homecoming revival."

I read Trish's notes.

We were in a small clearing somewhere in the mountains. I was totally lost, and they'd blindfolded me for a part of the trip.

They asked me if I'd been baptized in the name of the Father, Son, and Holy Ghost. I said to the best of my knowledge, I hadn't been baptized. They asked me if I wanted to be and I agreed.

They'd hung blankets from the trees to create an area to change clothes. The women pointed to the blankets and told me to undress and put on a plain white robe. After I did, the women led me to a creek with a waist-deep pond. About ten people, both men and women, were present, standing around in the water. I didn't recognize any of them. I waded out to where a man and woman were waiting. They asked me about my "testimony" or favorite Bible verse. I had no idea what a testimony was, and the only verse I could remember was "Jesus wept." They led me back out of the water and said I wasn't ready. When I got dressed, I was sure someone had gone through my things. I had a small camera to record the snake handlers, and it was missing.

It's clear to me that they are extremely cautious about anyone joining them who isn't part of the group already.

I closed the file. "So they essentially stripped Trish down, went through her things, got rid of the camera, then sent her packing."

"Yes. She remembered a few first names, but I don't believe they were useful."

"Why did they ask her if she'd been baptized in the name of the Father, Son, and Holy Ghost? That's the usual wording."

"It has something to do with 'Jesus only' versus 'the Trinity.' You'll have to ask Professor Wellington or Trish when we reach the cabin." She counted out a hefty tip. "Trish was lucky they let her go. You'll need to be very prepared if they invite you to their revival. Who knows what they'll do if they find out why you're really there." She smiled at me, but the smile didn't reach her eyes.

CHAPTER NINETEEN

BLANCHE ACTED AS A TOUR GUIDE, GIVING regional history. When Aynslee heard about Octavia, the woman who'd been buried alive, she wanted to visit her grave. By the time we'd toured some of the horse country and headed back toward Pikeville, the sun had set.

Blanche made a phone call and a rusty, Hooker's-green Ford pickup with a gray primer–painted fender waited for us alongside the road in Coal Run Village.

My stomach clenched when Junior stepped from the truck. Instead of his uniform, he wore dusty jeans, a faded red T-shirt, and a blue flannel jacket. His hands were at his sides, fingers convulsively wiggling.

"I thought we agreed my location would remain a secret," I said.

"Don't worry about Junior." Blanche nodded approvingly. "He's good at not talking to people, as I'm sure you've discovered. In your files you'll find a map, but for today, Junior will drive you to the cabin and ride back with Trish and Professor Wellington. Aynslee, you'll—"

"Aynslee will be going with me." Even though Clay had supposedly captured the Pikeville rapist, I had serious doubts. And I didn't want my daughter out of my sight.

Blanche raised her eyebrows. "Well then, we'll see if we can find suitable clothing for both of you for the funeral."

"What's wrong with my clothes?" Aynslee asked.

"You'll want to dress respectfully and put everyone at ease as much as possible," Blanche said. "Trish noted that holiness women wear ankle-length skirts, don't cut their hair . . ." She eyed my short locks.

I self-consciously touched my hair. After months of chemo, my bald head finally had enough hair for a trim, although my hairdresser tut-tutted about the texture. "I should have brought one of my wigs."

"Don't worry." She looked at Aynslee. "You'll need to remove what they call your ear baubles—"

"What?" Aynslee asked.

"Earrings. And your . . . um . . . nose ring."

The tiny nose ring was the remaining sign from Aynslee's rebellious period, a time I hoped was far behind us. The cell phone, boys, and choice of clothing told me a new chapter had opened. Oh joy.

We got out of the car, retrieved Aynslee's suitcase and backpack, and waved good-bye to Blanche. Junior returned to the truck, leaving Aynslee and me to lug her bags into the back. Before I could say anything, Aynslee slid in next to Junior. I followed.

The cab smelled faintly of mildew, old cigarettes, and pine air freshener from the disposable stylized evergreen dangling from the rearview mirror. Junior rested his hand on the stick shift, nearer than I liked to my daughter's leg. I clenched my teeth and pulled her close to me.

She stiffened with my hug, glanced at me, and rolled her eyes.

We turned off the highway and started climbing. The forest pressed inward on both sides, reminding me a bit of Montana, but with hardwoods rather than pines. Junior soon switched on the headlights. The pavement gave way to dirt and gravel, and he slowed so we wouldn't bounce off. Gouged out of a steep hillside, the road was barely two cars wide.

Junior's fingers tapped a calypso beat on the steering wheel. Something about his actions tickled a memory. "Junior, do you like snakes?"

"Yes."

"What is the name of the snake with the hood?"

"Cobra. Over two hundred and fifty types. Family of *Elapidae.*"

"Do you . . . handle them?"

"Sure. I have two boa constrictors as pets."

After rubbing down the goose pimples on my arm, I opened the fabric bag and found the map Blanche had drawn up, then pulled a tiny key-ring flashlight out of my purse. After clicking it on, I held up the map. "Where are we now?"

Junior glanced over, then slowed down and stopped. "This is the big turn we took about a mile back. And here's the first bridge." He traced out the route with a dirty fingernail. "We'll be coming up on this spot really soon. It's hard to see, but that's the turnoff to the cabin."

I nodded and clicked off the light. Junior shifted gears and started forward.

"Wait." I pointed. "Up ahead."

Junior nudged the truck forward. "Yeah."

A car's reflectors glinted. As we grew closer, the truck's headlights illuminated the rear of a late-model sedan. "That looks like one of Blanche's cars," I said.

Junior grunted an answer, parked, and got out. "Stay here." He slammed the door shut.

I slipped from the seat and followed with my key-ring penlight. "Aynslee, stay in the truck," I called over my shoulder.

Junior was staring at a flat on the right rear wheel. When I reached him, he frowned at me and moved toward the front.

I squatted next to the car and peered closer. The valve stem of the tire was broken off. Standing, I held the light higher. The gravel was rough on the side of the road, and I didn't see any footprints. After peeking into the backseat, which was spotless, I slowly turned, scanning the surroundings. The trees sighed in the cool breeze, and a few golden leaves drifted past. An owl hooted on the hillside to my left, and the trees clung to the abrupt drop on my right.

Someone touched me on the arm.

I jumped and fumbled the penlight, catching it before it fell.

"Sorry, Mom. What's going on?"

I couldn't answer. My flying light had briefly illuminated something on the steep slope below. Holding the light steady, I peered over.

Crumpled against a sturdy tree trunk was a woman's body.

CHAPTER TWENTY

AYNSLEE LET OUT A SQUEAK, THEN ASKED, "Who . . . who's that?"

"It looks like Trish. She was wearing that sweater and scarf this morning." A gust of cold air sent the leaves flying around us. I tugged my jacket closer. "Aynslee, please go back to the truck."

My daughter slowly backed away, then jogged to the pickup.

Before I could warn him, Junior shot past me and plunged down the hillside, creating a small avalanche of dirt and rocks. He grabbed a tree to keep from hurtling to the bottom of the ravine. He touched her body, then snatched his hand back. "She's dead."

A lump formed in my throat, and I swallowed hard in order to speak. "That was clear from up here. Necks don't usually bend like that."

Junior scrambled back up to the road, sending another batch of gravel and dirt cascading down the hill and over Trish's body. "She must have slipped when she got out to fix the tire."

"Slipped . . . or was pushed." I folded my arms. "And if she was pushed, this is a homicide scene, and you've just destroyed any evidence by thundering down there like a rhino."

Junior stared at me, fingers wiggling away.

I tugged out my phone. No service. "Do you have your radio with you?"

"No." His fingers twiddled faster, his gaze riveted on the body below.

"How far to the cabin?"

"Maybe a mile."

"Junior?" He didn't seem to hear me.

"Junior!"

This time he looked at my feet.

"You need to drive me to the cabin and call for help, then get back here and wait for the sheriff to show up. Do you hear me?"

Still staring at my feet, Junior nodded and walked back to the truck.

I joined him in the cab.

Aynslee pressed against me and I put my arm around her. "He's creepy," she whispered. After taking an almost hidden turn, we drove another mile to the cabin, buried deep into the hillside. A gray Honda Civic with New York plates was parked on the side.

The cabin was a simple log structure with a porch spanning the front. A path, outlined with round river stones, led to the front. Leaves formed a thick padding on the ground. The porch light, swirling with bugs, illuminated matching rustic rockers. Light glowed from the multipaned windows on either side of the door. Wellington appeared as we got out of the pickup. "Leave it to Trish to not show up. I've had to do all the cleanup as well as—"

"She's dead," Junior blurted out before I could stop him.

"What do you mean she's dead?" Wellington let the screen door slam behind him.

I'd reached the bottom of the steps and grabbed the rail.

Wellington looked at my face, then the white-knuckled grip I had on the railing. He took a step backward, then another, then fumbled his way into the cabin. I followed, with Aynslee behind me.

The single room had a kitchen area on my right, river-stone fireplace with a crackling fire straight ahead, and large brass bed with a navy-and-red quilt on the left. A door in the corner appeared to be for the bathroom, and next to it was a free standing, full-length mirror. A ladder on the opposite corner led to the attic door in the ceiling. A coffee table, a small, cranberry plaid sofa, and two chairs embraced the fireplace. A simple maple table with two chairs sat under the window next to me. A box of groceries rested on the table beside some files. The cupboards were two rustic crates with a few neatly stacked dishes on one side and some canned goods on the other. The room reeked of a liberal application of lemon-scented air fresheners.

Wellington had his back to me, holding on to the white farm sink. "I kept thinking, then hoping, she was simply late," he said without turning around. "But she's never late." He pulled out a handkerchief and blew his nose.

Junior joined us, his fingers doing their dance.

Wellington turned around, eyes bloodshot and skin pale. "What happened?"

"Got a flat tire," Junior said in his blunt way. "Went to fix it. Foot slipped off the edge of the road and she hit a tree. I gotta call the sheriff." He strolled to a rotary phone hanging on the wall.

I wasn't sure I agreed with his accident reconstruction. Hopefully Clay had good technicians who could decipher crime scenes, even ones that had been totally messed up by his fumbling son.

"Yeah, this is Junior. I need to speak to the sheriff."

A short pause.

"Huh? Yeah. I'm at the cabin. With . . . Wellington. Yeah. Trish is dead." Junior stuffed his twiddling fingers into his pocket.

Wellington moaned and groped for a chair. I placed my purse and library bag on the floor, then nodded to Aynslee to sit on the sofa. I moved to Wellington and patted his arm. "Can I get you something?"

He shook his head.

Junior was on a roll, giving his dad the blow-by-blow. Wellington put his hands over his ears. I wanted to yank the phone from Junior and tell him to sit in the truck.

After a series of "Yeah . . . okay . . . yeah . . . yeah . . . ," Junior hung up. "The sheriff wants Professor Wellington and me to go to the site of the accident and wait for him and the ambulance."

Wellington stood and stiffly walked to the front door. Junior placed the truck keys on the table, then followed the other man outside. A moment later Wellington's car started and they drove off.

Even though I wasn't working with Clay anymore, I felt useless stashed in this cabin while the department investigated poor Trish's death. Back home, I'd be sketching the scene, taking photos, and assisting in the case.

Aynslee stood, strolled to the door, and twisted the lock. She rattled the door, checked the lock again, then moved to the windows and tested to see if they would open. Pulling the curtains closed, she moved to the window over the kitchen sink and did the same.

When she glanced at me, I raised my eyebrows.

"Do you believe in ghosts?" she asked.

"I believe in angels, both good and fallen." I thought for a moment. "I'm sorry you had to see Trish's body."

"I've never seen a dead person before. At least not one, like, that wasn't a skull you were working on. And skulls don't seem all that real. More like a Halloween decoration, you know?"

"Mm," I grunted.

"And that lady, you know? The one buried alive?"

"Octavia Hatcher."

"Yeah. What if she's still mad? What if she meets that other lady, Trish, and they decide to, like, get even? That dead lady was just a little ways away." She backed away from the door, her eyes searching the room.

"I promise you no ghosts will get in here. You're safe."

She bit her lip.

"Tell you what. Why don't I make us some hot chocolate? There's some of the powder stuff on the counter."

"Hot chocolate makes you fat."

I stared at her size zero jeans and skimpy top. "Okay, why don't we add marshmallows and whipped cream to it?"

Aynslee rolled her eyes. "Whatever." She moved to the fireplace and added a log, sending up a flurry of sparks.

Pouring bottled water into a pan on the stove, I turned on the burner. I could hear Aynslee restlessly moving around the room behind me.

"I can't stay here. I can't *stay* here."

"Why not?" I asked, turning.

She held up her phone. "No cell service." She paced across the small room.

"Think of it as roughing it. Pioneers. Back to nature."

"There's no one to talk to."

"What am I, chopped liver?"

"You don't count. You're not a person. You're Mom."

I *knew* I was missing something in this whole mother-daughter connection.

"And I'm hungry."

Turning off the burner under the now-boiling water, I dumped some powered chocolate mix into two mugs and poured the hot water into the cups. "I lied about the whipped cream and marshmallows, but here's your hot chocolate. That should hold you until I make dinner."

She picked up a mug and moved to the sofa.

"Give me a minute to see if my clothes made it here." Strolling to the door in the corner, I winced as each step sent a protest from the pine floor. Sure enough, a small bathroom lay beyond, with a closet holding my suitcases to the right. The box, getting quite worn with all the packing and unpacking, held all my drawing supplies and materials. I pulled it out. A hot flash dampened my forehead. I ran some cold water and splashed it on my face, then brought the box into the main room, emptied it onto the coffee table, and replaced it in the bathroom closet.

Returning to the main room, I found Aynslee had unpacked the box of groceries onto the table. I picked up the small stack of files and opened one. Inside were some police reports on the bodies they'd found. Blanche must have gotten these from Clay before he got so angry with me. I added the files to the other research materials in my library bag. Returning to the kitchen area, I surveyed the array of items sent over: several gallons of bottled water, baking soda, flour, cornmeal, various spices, rice, grits, and numerous canned goods. Having neither the faintest idea how to cook nor any talent in the kitchen, I realized this could prove to be a bleak stay in the mountains. "From the bottled water, it looks like we need to stay away from drinking tap water."

"Whatever."

"I hate that word."

"Whatever."

I opened a gallon of water and poured a glass before shifting the grocery box to the floor. Underneath was a duplicate of the map Blanche gave me, a key to the front door, and several more files. Adding the map and files to the library bag, I set the bag alongside my art supplies on the coffee table. I stuck the key on my key-ring flashlight and dropped it into my purse.

"What is this stuff?" She held up a jar of locally made succotash and a can of black-eyed peas and beans.

"Welcome to the South." I helped her transfer the canned goods to the crate cupboard. Just as I placed the last can on the shelf, the whole thing gave way and crashed to the floor.

I leaped back, then stared at the mess. Picking up a dented can, I fought the overwhelming desire to throw it out the window.

"Mom?"

"I know, it's not your fault. It's mine." I started picking up cans.

"Mom!"

I looked up. Silently she pointed. The back of the crate was still attached to the wall with two hinges on the left side.

After placing the cans on the counter, I carefully felt along the edge of the wood opposite the hinges. My fingers encountered a tiny latch. I shoved downward. *Click.*

A small door swung open.

CHAPTER TWENTY-ONE

A GAUZY WEB COVERED THE OPENING. A SPIDER the size of a Chihuahua glared at me.

Shudders rippled over my body. I couldn't get air in my lungs. My vision narrowed.

Mist enveloped the spider and web. The pungent odor of Black Flag bug spray filled the room. The spider writhed, clung for a moment, then dropped to the kitchen counter. A can of green beans crushed the insect into a memory.

I wrenched my gaze from the arachnid remains to my daughter, still holding the insect spray and can of green beans. "I think you just saved my life."

"Mom, you really need counseling for your spider phobia."

"It's not a phobia. It's an intense dislike."

"Whatever. What's in here?" She reached for the opening.

"No! Don't put your hand in there. That spider could have relatives." I couldn't stop the small, tippy-toe spider dance. "Let me get a light." For a few moments, we checked the drawers for a flashlight. I was about to pull out my penlight when Aynslee spotted one by the door. It was a hand-crank, powerful LED emergency flashlight.

"Maybe there's a treasure hidden in the wall. We could be rich!" She handed me the light.

"Whatever we find belongs to the owner of the house." I cranked the handle to power up the flashlight, then carefully checked the small enclosure for more multi-legged critters. Nothing moved or crawled, so I pulled out the contents: a leather-bound Bible and a Mason jar holding coins and bills. I placed them on the kitchen table.

Aynslee emptied the jar of money and began counting.

I opened the Bible and a photo of a beautiful woman dropped out, her eyes closed as if in a trance, and wearing a scarf around her head. I set the photo aside and examined the Bible. The fly-leaf, in bold ink, stated:

PRESENTED TO PASTOR GRADY MAYNARD, IN
GRATEFUL APPRECIATION, FROM THE MEMBERS
OF THE CHURCH OF THE LORD JESUS WITH SIGNS
FOLLOWING, HOMECOMING, OCTOBER 1995

"Fifty-seven dollars and forty-four cents," Aynslee said with disgust.

"So much for buying the mansion and Jaguar this week." I flipped through the worn pages. In the center of the Bible was a page for recording births and deaths. A different hand had written:

GRADY MAYNARD, B 5/20/58
MIRIAM MCCOY MAYNARD, B 2/15/62, D 9/8/83
MARRIED 6/2/78

I worked out the math in my head. *His wife married young and died young.*

Under the date of marriage was simply: *Devin Maynard.*

"They had a son." I looked at my daughter. "But no birth date. I wonder if he lived long. Maybe he died in childbirth."

"This is sincerely creepy." Aynslee had been staring at the photograph. She handed it to me.

In the same handwriting as the center of the Bible, someone had written *Miriam.* I turned the photo back over and looked at it closely. What I'd originally thought was a scarf wrapped around the woman's face was the body of a large snake.

I dropped the photo and wiped my hand on my pants. "So his wife was a snake handler also. That could be why she died young. We'll turn the photo, Bible, and massive cash treasure over to Blanche and Arless. I suspect there's not much rush, though, with Trish's death and all." Once again a lump rose in my throat.

"Why would anyone hide a Bible?" Aynslee picked up the book.

"I suspect Grady wasn't hiding *a* Bible—he hid *that* Bible."

"Because it was from his snake-handling church?"

"Yep. Tangible proof of his connection that could have landed him in prison."

Aynslee shrugged, jumped up from the table, and checked the freezer. "Thank You, Lord. We shall not starve. Pizza!"

"Why don't you preheat the oven while I unload the pickup. And we'll have a vegetable with that, just to ward off scurvy. Just not"—I couldn't help the involuntary shiver, thinking about how she'd smashed the spider—"green beans."

After dinner, Aynslee wandered around the cabin. "What if there's another hiding place?" she asked.

"I don't think they had much to hide. Most of the time in this region it'd be moonshine, but I doubt a pastor would be brewing illegal hooch."

Aynslee climbed the ladder in the corner of the room. "We didn't look up here."

"That's because there's probably spiders." My shoulder muscles twitched.

She reached the top of the ladder and pushed on the attic door. Nothing moved. She inspected it closely. "It's nailed shut."

"Well then, that's that."

She climbed down the ladder. "I'll look again in the morning."

"You do that." I finished washing and stacking the dishes, then wiped down the table and straightened up. A quick sweep with a broom I found leaning against the wall by the refrigerator and I'd tidied up the small space. I was too sleepy to start my research on Grady's church. Aynslee'd already sacked out on the sofa in front of the fireplace. I pulled the covers back on the bed and checked for more spiders or snakes, then got on my knees and did the same under the bed. No sign of critters or toe monsters, but the mattress had a dark stain and the floor was scratched. I stood and moved around the bed. The scratches matched each iron leg. It looked as if the bed was originally closer to the fireplace.

I retired to the bathroom and put on my pajamas, then woke Aynslee with a touch on her shoulder. "Okay, sleepyhead, time for bed." She padded into the bathroom while I turned off the overhead lights and partially closed the damper. With only the embers from the dying flames in the fireplace and a pinpoint red light from the smoke alarm in the ceiling, I left on the bedside lamp so Aynslee wouldn't trip in the dark.

The bed let out a squeal when I crawled under the covers, and I immediately rolled to the center. Aynslee got in on her side and crashed into me. "What's with the bed?" she asked.

"It appears"—I grabbed the side and tried to move over— "that we have a thin old mattress over a metal spring foundation. We'll just have to make do tonight and let me see if I can locate a piece of plywood in the morning."

"Won't that be too hard then?"

"Plywood and an extra pad," I amended.

"I feel like the hamburger in a taco."

"Then I'm the lettuce, so lettuce get to sleep. Get it?" I nudged her. "Let us?"

"Mom, there's something seriously wrong with you."

I fell asleep with a smile on my face.

I woke to the coral light of morning.

Aynslee was up and trying to light a fire. A smoky haze was all she had to show for her efforts.

The floor was icy and the room freezing. Shivering, I swiftly opened the front door and all the windows to keep the fire alarm from going off, then grabbed a pair of socks and a sweater before joining her in front of the fireplace. "You need to open the damper more. I closed it down for the night. And you'll need some kindling and paper."

"Whatever." She stood. "I was never in Camp Fire." She grabbed a bowl of cereal and sat at the table.

The room quickly cleared of smoke and I soon had a fire blazing. A quick check of the alarm told me why it didn't sound: the red light was off. After shutting the windows and the door, I turned to the next critical item. Coffee. A blue enamel percolator coffeepot sat on the small stove and a bag of Duncan coffee rested on the counter.

While I assembled my morning brew using the bottled water, Aynslee headed to the bathroom and soon emerged fully dressed. "There's still no Internet. Or cell service. How can people live like this? What am I going to do today?"

"You're going to a funeral and working on your homework." I'd started homeschooling my daughter the previous year when she'd become such a rebellious handful.

"I can't do homework without the Internet."

"Yes, you can. You still have to write a story or poem for Creative Writing."

She looked at me as if I'd sprouted horns. "How'd you know my homework?"

"I'm a trained investigator."

She rolled her eyes.

"And I'm checking up online."

"Mom!" She managed to draw the word out to three syllables.

"Okay. Finish searching for buried treasure, then do your homework."

She immediately cheered up, grabbed the flashlight, and started knocking on the walls.

I retrieved a box of pencils, sketchbook, and small voice recorder from the stack of art supplies in the living area and moved them to the kitchen table. The file folders Blanche gave me along with the book from Professor Wellington joined the supplies. With a fresh cup of coffee, I settled at the table.

"I found something." Aynslee held up a tiny object.

"Bring it here."

She placed half a clear capsule on the file in front of me. I picked it up and sniffed. No odor.

"What was in it?" she asked.

"I have no idea."

"I wish I could text Mattie. She's an expert on drugs."

"Yes, well." I placed it on the side of the table. "Watch out for the other half. Maybe it has something left in it."

My daughter moved to the bathroom where she continued banging on floors and walls.

Even though I wasn't on the serial rapist case anymore, something still bothered me about the arrest of Jason. I decided to update my thoughts before moving on to the snake handlers. Opening the sketchbook, I found my notes on Clay: *said caller was male, doesn't want me working on the case, smokes (cigarette burns on Shelby Lee), knows forensics, not around when calls come in, knows my location, living beyond his means? DNA results in desk.* I added: *knows water washes off forensic clues* and *strong enough to throw murder victim off bridge.* But Clay was furious when he found out I'd received another phone call. I put a negative mark next to the words *"You need to learn to take me seriously."*

I still needed to find out if Clay owned a cabin in the mountains or if his house was remote to facilitate his holding a woman captive for any length of time.

Junior Reed's name was on the next page. Underneath his

name I'd written: *knows forensics, likes snakes, not around when calls arrive, knows my location, weird.* I added: *still knows my location,* then added: *not strong enough to throw murder victim off bridge.* Of course, he could have dragged her to the river. I added a question mark.

On page three was Jason Morrow's name with: *likes/handles snakes, resembles sketch from surveillance still.* I thought about Clay's remarks on the radio: *"When I viewed the security tapes, I saw Morrow bringing the snake to the hotel."* The security tapes were at best spotty, going off and on at different times. I pictured Jason as I'd seen him on camera. He'd walked into and out of the hotel room carrying a five-gallon plastic bucket with a perforated lid and snake hook. There was something . . . something . . . yes! The recordings didn't have a time or date stamp. Clay could have seen Jason retrieving the snake, not placing it in my room.

I leaned back in my chair. If Jason was indeed the Hillbilly Rapist, my work with Clay was done anyway. But the rapist had crossed the line into murder with his last victim. If another woman was taken, then Clay arrested the wrong man. And now he'd moved on to killing his victim.

"It's not your problem anymore." I stood to get another cup of coffee.

"What?" Aynslee asked from the bathroom.

"Nothing." *Or at least nothing I can do about it.*

Sitting down, I closed the sketchbook and pulled the stack of file folders in front of me. The first folder had a list of deaths and homicides over the past six months, with a summary paper clipped to the cover. I could see why Arless and Blanche were concerned over the snake handling church.

AGE	SEX	CAUSE OF DEATH	DATE	IDENTIFIED?
12	female	poison	4/15	yes
32	female	hit-and-run	5/11	yes
8	male	undetermined; body burned	6/7 approximate	yes
37	male	poison	6/29	yes
62	female	snakebite	8/1	yes
64	male	snakebite	8/1	yes
29	male	car accident	8/2	yes
27	female	car accident	8/2	yes
5	male	car accident	8/2	yes
3	female	car accident	8/2	yes
6 mo	female	car accident	8/2	yes
21	male	snakebite	10/?	yes

Samuel, the young man I'd sketched, was handwritten under the last entry. Counting him, that made three snake fatalities, and the poison probably all related to church members. The burned body could be yet another death from their practices.

Opening the sketchbook again, I turned to a clean page and wrote at the top *Known* and *Unknown*, then drew a line between them. I picked up the recorder and turned it on. "Today is October 29th. I'm in Pike County, Kentucky."

Aynslee now crawled on hands and knees, looking under the furniture and tapping the floor. The sound was giving me a headache. I turned off the recorder. "Aynslee—"

"I think I found something else." Aynslee's voice was an octave higher.

I stood and moved to where she was kneeling. She'd pulled the small area rug away from the pine flooring near the front door. "Listen." She tapped the floorboards.

They did sound hollow. And they moved slightly with her tapping. The boards lined up, forming a seam. I found a sharp knife and used it to pry along the seam.

A trapdoor lifted slightly. With Aynslee's help, we pulled it open. Musty stale air arose from the onyx-black opening.

CHAPTER TWENTY-TWO

A HANDMADE ROPE LADDER DANGLED INTO THE inky darkness. "Well, what do you know?"

"Let's go down there."

I took the flashlight from her and shone it into the opening. The powerful beam revealed a hard-packed dirt floor about nine feet below. The ladder ended slightly above the ground. Around the stone walls were empty aquariums and wire cages, with several bales of wood chips, one of which was open, in the corner. A dirty fan leaned against the wood chips, and a stack of plastic containers spilled across the floor. Spiderwebs drifted in the slight air like lacy curtains. I clenched my teeth to keep from making any wimpy squeals.

"What do you see?" Aynslee asked impatiently.

"Spiders."

Something ran up my back.

I jumped to my feet, slapped at my shirt, and made wimpy squeals.

"It was just me, Mom." Aynslee smirked. "I tickled you."

"There are times that I think you are the devil's spawn." I tugged gently on one of her spiral curls but remained standing. "Looks like you discovered Grady's snake room."

"Why would you use a ladder to get the snakes up and down?"

"I suspect there's another entrance. This is probably a way to check on the snakes without going outside."

"Let's go find it." Aynslee was up and out the door before I could say anything. I shut the trapdoor, pulled on a pair of clogs, and followed.

The cabin was built on a hillside, with the rear tucked into the slope. We crossed the porch and went down the steps to the front. In daylight, the river-stone foundation was easy to see. We crouched and peered under the steps. Dried grass, more pine needles, and a few rocks filled the space. Using the flashlight, I illuminated the foundation to check for doors or windows. Everything appeared solid.

A complete search around the perimeter of the house proved unsuccessful in finding an access to the basement. I did find a neatly curled garden hose attached to an outside faucet, a small stack of firewood, and an ax. I brought several pieces of wood, along with the ax, to the steps. I could split some kindling later today for tomorrow morning.

"Why aren't there any outside doors or windows, even?" Aynslee stared at the front of the cabin.

"I'm not sure. The roof is new, and the logs have been recently refinished. I'd say they went ahead and just put a stone facing on the foundation, covering over any openings."

"I could climb down that ladder and see if there's another way in."

"No. You're not going into that snake room."

154

She rolled her eyes. "But all the snakes are gone."

"The spiders still live there. No."

"What if I found a way in through a tunnel somewhere in the woods?" Her eyes sparkled.

"You still couldn't go down there, but you might have the start of a good story for your Creative Writing paper."

"Turn around slowly," a male voice said from behind me.

A bolt of adrenaline raced through my veins. I raised my hands and did as he said.

The snake handler, Jason Morrow, stood behind me, a rifle leveled at my waist. Dirt was smeared across his pale face and his jacket was ripped.

I stepped sideways, blocking Aynslee with my body. "What do you want, Jason?"

"So you know my name."

"Everyone does now. There's a warrant out for your arrest as the Hillbilly Rapist."

Jason spit on the ground. "Yeah, well, don't believe everything you hear. Face the cabin and sit down."

I really didn't want to sit on the ground with my back to him, but he raised the gun slightly. I sat. Aynslee thumped to the ground in front of me and I put my arms around her. "Did your mom, Mrs. Fields, tell you—"

"Leave my mom out of it!"

Please don't hurt my daughter. Please don't hurt my daughter. The words hammered in my brain with the pounding of my heart.

"I've done a lot of things wrong—" His voice wavered and he cleared his throat.

"Just turn yourself in—"

"Shut up and listen!"

Aynslee grabbed my arm. She was quivering like an aspen leaf. A hawk shrieked overhead and a puff of cold air raised goose pimples up my arm.

"They paid me, okay?" Jason's voice was stronger. "So I took the money. It was supposed to be a joke. That's what they told me. So I turned the snakes loose. And the next day I put one in the car. No one was supposed to get hurt. When they called again for me to do something else, I said no way, I wasn't going to be up for murder." Jason was babbling now, the words tumbling over each other.

"Jason. Jason!"

He stopped.

The cold from the earth under me seemed to run up my body. "I'm sure you never meant for anything to go wrong—"

"That's right! But it did, and now this."

"Why are you here?" I asked.

"I wanted to talk to you. To tell you."

"You're trying to convince me you're not a killer? Or the rapist? With a gun in my back?"

He was silent for a moment. "Gun's not loaded. It had to be you. You're an outsider. And they're afraid of you."

"Who is, Jason?"

"And I didn't put that rattler in your bed. I swear."

"Jason, give me a name. Who paid you?" I held my breath.

"Don't trust anyone." His voice grew fainter. "Anyone. Do you understand? The snake—" The hawk screamed again, drowning out his final words.

Taking a chance, I looked behind me, then jumped to my feet. Jason was gone. Aynslee leaped up and together we raced into the cabin, slammed the door, and leaned against it. "We gotta call the police!" Aynslee said.

I pulled the curtains, checking first that Jason hadn't returned. "We will. But we need to be sure the police aren't involved."

"He was going to kill us!"

"No. Not with an empty rifle. I think he was warning us."

"What was he talking about?" Aynslee's eyes were wild and her lower lip trembled.

"He mentioned 'next day' and 'murder.'" Strolling to the table, I rummaged around until I found the chart Clay had given me on the deaths of the past few months.

AGE	SEX	CAUSE OF DEATH	DATE	IDENTIFIED?
12	female	poison	4/15	yes
32	female	hit-and-run	5/11	yes
8	male	undetermined; body burned	6/7 approximate	yes
37	male	poison	6/29	yes
62	female	snakebite	8/1	yes
64	male	snakebite	8/1	yes
29	male	car accident	8/2	yes
27	female	car accident	8/2	yes
5	male	car accident	8/2	yes
3	female	car accident	8/2	yes
6 mo	female	car accident	8/2	yes
21	male	snakebite	10/?	yes

Sure enough, an older male and female had died of snake-bite, and the next day there was a car accident in which a number of people perished. Had a snake loose in the car caused them to crash? No wonder he'd wanted to confess. He could be responsible for the deaths of seven people. But Jason hadn't said who'd paid him.

That still left two people poisoned. And the others.

Clay told me the bodies and the Hillbilly Rapist were not linked, but Jason formed a connection—assuming he was the rapist, which he denied.

"What are you going to do now?" Aynslee slouched on the couch and wrapped her arms around her legs.

I picked up a pencil and tapped it on the table. "Did you hear the last things he said?"

"Something about snakes."

"That's all I heard." I stopped tapping and picked up the phone.

No dial tone.

Aynslee watched me.

"I'm going to check something. Lock the door after me, okay?"

"Don't go."

"I'll be right back." I peeked through the curtains, then waited until my daughter got off the sofa. "Ready?"

She nodded.

Unlocking the door, I stepped through and waited until I heard the *click* of the lock. Still no sign of Jason. I trotted down the steps and around the cabin, looking for the phone line. I quickly found it. The phone cable appeared to be untouched, but when I gave it a slight tug, half of it pulled out. Someone, probably Jason, had cut the line.

I hurried to the front of the cabin just as one of the Campbell luxury cars drove up and parked. Both Blanche and Arless stepped out. They didn't notice me at first. Arless grabbed a paper sack from the backseat. He wore an open-collared golf shirt with an embroidered logo proclaiming its designer origins. Khaki slacks and loafers completed the GQ look. She wore a cap-sleeve, black sheath dress with a simple silver embellishment at the shoulder. Her hair was again swept up into a carefully tousled series of loops.

I was still wearing plaid flannel bottoms, oversize white socks, clogs, and a snaggy gray sweater.

Blanche paused when she spotted me beside the cabin. "Um, good morning."

"Good morning." I strolled over to her. Up close, I could see her eyes were red and face pale. Continuing up the stairs, I tapped at the door. Aynslee opened it. She opened her mouth to speak, but closed it when she saw Blanche and Arless. I gave her a tiny shake of the head and she retreated to the chair in the corner.

"I tried calling, but the phone is out of order," Blanche said.

"Yes . . . so I just discovered." Jason's voice rang in my brain. *Don't trust anyone. Anyone. Do you understand?*

"You wouldn't have heard." Arless placed the sack he held on the kitchen counter, then leaned against it.

"Heard what?"

"Jason Morrow's been caught. Less than a mile from here." Blanche glanced at the pulled curtains. "Did he come here? Did you talk to him?"

Don't trust anyone. "Why would he come here?" I didn't look at Aynslee.

"He *was* the person who put the rattler in your bed," Arless said. "Maybe he was trying to get to you again."

"Well, I'm glad he was arrested." This time I did look at my daughter. She raised her eyebrows at me but remained silent.

Blanche picked up the sack. "I brought some clothes for Aynslee and you to wear to the funeral. What time does it start?"

I checked the clock. "Eleven. You brought the clothes just in time. I'm sorry, I'm being rude. Would you like some coffee?"

"Please, if it's already made." She noticed the partially emptied jug of water. "I'm sorry. I meant to mention the tap water wasn't great, but I see you figured that out." She placed the sack and her small purse on the table, then sat on the sofa in front of the fireplace. Arless took the chair on the right. I brought each of them a cup, clearing a small area on the coffee table for their cups. "Do you have any news about Trish?"

Blanche cradled her mug in both hands. "Poor Trish. I feel responsible. If I hadn't sent her up here to straighten—"

"It's not your fault." I sat next to her. "She . . . slipped?"

"That's what Clay said." Arless leaned forward. "He thinks her head hit a rock on the way down, then got twisted . . ." He paused when he glanced at Blanche's face. "Uh . . . we're waiting on the autopsy."

She sipped her coffee, swallowing audibly.

I wanted to ask more questions about what Clay discovered at the accident site, but Blanche was clearly in no mood to talk about it.

"How's the cabin working out?" Arless asked.

"Well, since you're here, in addition to the phone being out, I don't think the fire alarm is working either. And I need to confess that we've done a bit of damage to the cabin."

Blanche looked at me, raised an eyebrow, then glanced around the small room. She quickly spotted the missing "cupboard," the attached door still slightly open.

"I'm afraid we overloaded the shelf and brought it down."

Arless stood and examined the wall. "Not to worry. We'll get someone up here to see to the phone, fire alarm, and cabinet." He looked at his wife. "In fact, we should just go ahead and order the matching upper cabinets we talked about. The wooden boxes seemed rustic at the time, but we need to keep this place in good repair for when we go to sell it."

"You're putting this place up for sale?" I asked.

"We're hoping for a big move." Arless gave me a hundred-watt smile.

"Now, darling . . ." Blanche shook her head slightly.

"Well . . . anyway, when the wooden crate fell off the wall, there was a space behind it with some items you should have." I rose and brought them the Bible, money, and photograph, shoving more art supplies aside and placing them on the pine coffee table in front of them. "The Bible belonged to the original owner of the cabin, Grady Maynard. The photo is of his wife, Miriam. They apparently had a son, Devin."

Arless returned to his seat and picked up the Bible.

Standing, Blanche strolled to the sink and placed the half-empty cup on the counter. "We could locate no family when we bought this place. It was sold for back taxes."

"Oh, I didn't mean to imply that someone else may have a claim to this place—"

"No, no, I know you weren't saying that."

"Speaking of the prior owner," I said. "Aynslee discovered the snake room in the basement—"

"Yes." Arless wrinkled his nose in distaste. "When we renovated the cabin—what was it, five years ago? Anyway, we just left everything down there and sealed it up."

"I see," I said. "Um, about Trish . . ."

Blanche took a deep breath. "I'm sorry. I'm still pretty shaken up over her death. She lived with us for several months. She was almost like a sister to me." She reached into her purse and took out a lace hankie, then dabbed her eyes.

Aynslee stood and approached the woman. "I'm really sorry, too, Mrs. Campbell."

Blanche turned away and blew her nose, a quiet, ladylike toot.

I'd really like to learn the art of crying neatly, instead of my big, red-faced, sobbing boo-hoos.

Blanche kept her back to us for a few moments before turning around. "We need to get going. Do you have a sack or bag for those things?" She waved her hand at the Bible still in Arless's hands.

I found the small box that had originally held some of the groceries, then loaded it with the items on the coffee table. Arless handed me the Bible. "About Trish's funeral?" I asked.

"We're trying to locate next of kin." Arless stood and took the box. "We'll let you know." He strolled to his wife and gently rubbed her back. "Ready to go?"

Blanche nodded, grabbed her purse, and started for the door, then paused. "Oh, and when you have the drawings done of the snake-handling church members, bring them to our house and we can cut you a check for the reward right away. Or you can call and we can arrange to meet you someplace—"

"Can it be Octavia's grave? At midnight? On Halloween?" Aynslee grinned at me.

"I thought you were afraid of ghosts," I said.

"Whatever."

Blanche smiled for the first time. "A bit theatrical, don't you think?"

"I love this cloak-and-dagger stuff," Aynslee said. "Except for . . . um."

"Yes?" Blanche said.

"Nothing." Aynslee glanced at me, then down.

"Well," Arless said, "if you finish on Halloween and want to deliver the drawings, best come in costume. That's the night we have our big party."

"We actually start with a gathering at the shelter for the less fortunate in our community." Blanche lightly stroked Arless's face. "Some small gifts, bobbing for apples, that sort of thing. We do that every chance we get. We love being around the children . . ." She touched the hankie to her eyes.

"After an hour or so, we'll head to our place for our big political fund-raiser." Arless caught Blanche's hand in his and gently kissed her fingertips.

I looked down, feeling like an intruder to their intimate moment. "So . . . ah, when does the computer program arrive?"

"The marvels of modern technology," Arless said. "I've already downloaded and installed Composit-Fit ID at the department. The instructions say they've developed it to the point that rough sketches will still spit out possibilities. Amazing." He took his wife's elbow and escorted her to the car, opening the door and making sure she was comfortable before closing it. He gave us a casual wave, then drove off.

I sighed. *What would it feel like to have a husband like that?*

"Now what?" Aynslee said.

"Now we get ready to go to a funeral."

CHAPTER TWENTY-THREE

I SAT AT THE KITCHEN TABLE AND BENT OVER the file on the snake-handling group. The answer to the accidents, murders, and rapes somehow was tied up with snakes. I shifted in my chair and glanced around the room.

Clay was unable, or unwilling, to do the necessary police work to stop the crime spree. That left me. I couldn't wait for another person to die, or another woman to be tortured and raped. But sitting around a mountain cabin without any way to communicate and waiting for something to happen was stupid. I shouldn't have let myself get talked into this isolation.

But all the official channels were closed. I couldn't interview Jason, work the crime scenes, view tapes, or use any of my skills.

I did have one avenue open. The invitation to the funeral with the snake handlers.

Aynslee got up and wandered to the window, opened the curtain, and leaned against the glass.

How can I keep Aynslee safe? I trusted no one. No way would I leave her here at this cabin.

But if the snake handlers were involved . . .

I needed to talk to them, to get invited to the revival, not just to draw them, but to see if I could find answers. I didn't want to botch the invitation to join them by saying or doing the wrong thing. Beth usually relished doing my research for me, and I missed my friend's purple highlighter and notes. Fortunately someone had condensed the materials for me.

Aynslee screamed.

I shot to my feet.

She stepped out of the bathroom. "Just *look* at me! I can't go anywhere dressed like this." She turned to the freestanding mirror and screamed again. She'd put on the outfit Blanche had dropped off: a black, ankle-length, gathered skirt; white, long-sleeved blouse; black socks; and clunky black shoes.

I bit the inside of my cheeks to keep from smiling. "Perfect."

"Perfect? Are you kidding me? I look like-like a nun or something."

"Wrong denomination. You look modest. Be sure you wash off all your makeup and take off your ear baubles."

Aynslee left to wash her face. I finished reading the file, then closed it and tapped the outside with a pencil. This wasn't going to be easy.

Don't trust anyone.

"Guess what?" Aynslee held up a skirt and blouse for me. "If possible, your stuff is uglier than mine."

She was right. The blouse was a strange, vaguely unhealthy shade of green, and the full skirt was a dark sepia brown.

She wrinkled her nose. "Your shirt looks like puke."

"Um. Put that on the sofa. I'm going to make a casserole for the funeral and don't want to get anything on it. Not that food items wouldn't improve the appearance."

"Oh, Mom, you're not going to take those poor people your tuna noodle casserole, are you?"

"Of course. You always bring food for the family."

"But that's not food. It's . . . it's not edible."

"You eat it all the time."

"I'm immune. Pleeease?"

"It's the thought that counts." I ignored her lack of support and located a white Pyrex dish, box of pasta, can of tuna, and can of cream of mushroom soup. After cooking the pasta, I mixed the other ingredients together, adding water to make it all smooth, and placed it in the dish. The presentation looked rather . . . monochromatic. I located a can of peas and added them to the mix. I'd hoped the peas would add a cheerful note of sap green. Instead, they were closer to the gray-green of terre verte. I couldn't find any potato chips to crush for the topping, so I settled for sprinkling different colored spices on top, forming leaf shapes. "Ta-da!"

Aynslee wandered over. "That's kinda pretty. What are the sprinkles made of?"

"Um, the green one is basil. The yellow one is curry, and the red one is . . ." I picked up the jar. "Something called mace." I put the lid on the dish. "Give me a minute to get dressed."

After scrubbing my face and running a comb through my hair, I tugged on the skirt and blouse. The waist of the full skirt was too big, so I safety pinned the extra fabric. It flowed to my ankles, covering the black socks. The blouse was new, with sharp creases where it had been folded. I didn't spot an iron anywhere, so I smoothed it out the best I could. I left the blouse untucked to cover the safety pin and wad of extra fabric.

Aynslee made no effort to hide her mirth. With the green

top and brown skirt, I looked like a tree stricken with some exotic disease. Without makeup and with my light-colored hair, I looked pale and drawn. *Maybe the cancer is spreading.* I shoved down the thought and concentrated on keeping Aynslee cheerful.

Grabbing the library bag, I emptied out the files I'd placed there earlier, stacking them on the coffee table. I stuffed a pencil, eraser, and sketchbook in it along with the contents of my purse. Aynslee reluctantly picked up the casserole and her cell.

"No." I pointed at the cell.

"Why not? They'll probably have cell reception."

"You are not going to be texting or calling someone during a memorial service."

"But you have your phone."

"I'm not turning it on." *Not until I know who to call and who I can trust.*

She let out a snort worthy of a startled deer, put the cell down, and stomped to the truck. We'd driven several miles before she spoke to me again. "What happens during a snake-handling funeral?"

"I'm not sure. The material I read stated that the practices and beliefs of a particular group came down through the families, and if someone disagreed, they would likely go down the road or across the street and just start a new church."

"What would they disagree about?"

"Hmm. Well, a 'Jesus Name' group, or Oneness, believes that there is only one person in the Godhead, Jesus Christ. To be baptized in the name of the Father, Son, and Holy Ghost doesn't count as baptism."

Aynslee turned to watch me.

"There are some who believe you have more than one baptism: a first by water and a second by fire."

"That sounds painful."

"A metaphor. Baptized by the Holy Ghost."

"Like in the Bible," Aynslee said. "On the day of Pentecost."

"Finish the example."

"Oh, Mom, do you ever stop?"

"Don't you have a term paper coming up in Bible Studies?"

"Yeah."

"I'm giving you a potential topic. And firsthand research." She didn't look convinced. "Think of all the things you'll have to share with Mattie."

Aynslee brightened, leaned back in her seat, and recited to the ceiling. "The Jewish Feast of Weeks, which was . . . forty?"

"Fifty."

"Fifty days after Easter—"

"Passover."

"Yeah. That's when everyone got together from all over. In Jerusalem. The apostles were there as well. Suddenly a bunch of fire—"

"Technically, a sound like wind."

"Whatever. A wind came in and dropped fire stuff on them and they were able to talk to each other in their own language."

"Something like that. And speaking of tongues, some believe that if you don't—or can't—speak in tongues, you won't go to heaven."

Aynslee scratched her chin for a moment. "But I read somewhere that people believe if you do speak in a language you couldn't have known, it's a sign of possession by the devil."

"Not within the Pentecostal group."

"What about snakes?" She rubbed her arms.

"Some of the groups feel if you don't follow all five signs given in Mark 16: drinking poison, handling serpents, healing, speaking in tongues, and . . ." I tapped the steering wheel. "Yeah, casting out devils, that you were picking which part of the Bible you wanted to follow."

"What if you got bit by the snake?"

"Again, some disagreement. Some say that person wasn't anointed by God."

"How would they know when they're actually anointed?"

"From what I've read, it's a special feeling."

Aynslee raised her eyebrows. "What else?"

"You might get bit, according to some, because you were doing something wrong in your life, or you were a lesson to an unbeliever that the snakes were somehow not dangerous."

"But the doctor treating—"

"They usually don't seek any medical attention after a bite, relying on prayer."

"But what if you die?" Aynslee's voice was barely a whisper.

"It was your appointed time to die. Or your death is a lesson to others."

She nodded. "Okay, but it all sounds confusing."

"It makes sense to them. Just remember, sweetheart, we're there to pay our respects and hopefully get invited to their homecoming, okay?"

"What if they bring out snakes?"

"Stay behind me. I'll keep you safe."

CHAPTER TWENTY-FOUR

WE ONLY GOT LOST TWICE. THE ROADS TWISTED through the mountains and were seldom marked with a name, but Elijah's directions came with descriptions of landmarks. We finally pulled in front of a modest white house surrounded by a large array of older cars and trucks. A cow pasture on the right held a couple of Holsteins casually chewing their cud, while a freestanding garage squatted on the left.

People had spilled out onto the porch, and everyone stopped speaking, turned, and stared at us as we got out. I tugged my skirt straight, took the casserole from Aynslee, and marched bravely forward.

A smiling Elijah stepped out of the house wearing a white shirt and black dress pants. "Praise the Lord. You came."

"I hope you don't mind, but I brought my daughter, Aynslee. Aynslee, this is Mr. Adkins."

He nodded at her, and his gaze went from head to toe on our outfits. He nodded and turned to the fellow mourners. "Folks, this here's Miz Gwen and her daughter. Miz Gwen's the one that drew Samuel's picture."

I wiggled my fingers at the assembled crowd. *Trust no one.*

He gave a small jerk of his head, and Aynslee and I followed. The guests made a path for us like Moses parting the Red Sea.

The living room was equally crowded, and I was relieved to note that my attire was in keeping with the women's clothing. Mine wasn't even the ugliest outfit. Taped on the wall in front of me was my drawing of Samuel. Under it on a small table was a Mason jar with store-bought flowers—still in the plastic wrapper—lit candles, a Bible, and a very old teddy bear.

I swallowed past the lump forming in my throat.

An unlit, woodburning stove rested on a slightly raised hearth on my left, with a door next to it. The kitchen opened directly into the living room ahead and right of the table. I guessed that the opening on my right led to the bedrooms.

"Elijah." I cleared my throat. I hated to lie. "I . . . I shouldn't have given you the drawing. It was evidence. If you'll let me return it to . . . the, uh, sheriff's department, I can do another. A portrait. I'm sorry—"

"That's a mighty nice offer, Miz Gwen. That would be a blessing to us." He approached the table, stared at the drawing for a few moments, then took it off the wall and handed it to me. "Render to Caesar the things that are Caesar's."

I felt like a lying sneak, but part one of Blanche's plan seemed to be working. I handed the sketch to Aynslee. "Take this to the truck and put it in my sketchbook." She nodded and left.

Ruby moved into the room, gliding through the mourners, and came to my side. "Thank you, Miz Gwen, for coming."

I smiled at her and handed her my casserole. She took it, then did a brief double take at the leaf pattern on top. "How . . . thoughtful."

Another woman took the casserole and hustled it away to the kitchen. Ruby took my elbow. "Come, meet the others." She moved around the room. "This is Beulah, Carol Ann, Lee, Earl, Ida, Jeremiah, Ivy, Tyrell . . ." Each person smiled warmly, often through tears, and greeted us. The women offered a hand or touched me; the men kept a distance.

Aynslee returned. Several of the younger men stared at her and nudged each other.

A young girl, probably about six, sidled next to Ruby. "This is my daughter, Sarah."

"Hello, Sarah." I pulled Aynslee from where she was lurking behind me. "This is my daughter, Aynslee."

"Nice to meet you, Aynslee." Ruby's gaze slid to my ringless left hand.

Sarah grabbed Ruby's skirt and peeked at us from behind her mother. Aynslee smiled at her and wiggled her fingers. Sarah grinned back.

At some unseen signal, everyone moved into the living room. It took me a moment to realize the men had gravitated to one side of the room and the women to the other. I caught Aynslee's blouse and tugged her into place on the women's side.

"Let us pray," Elijah said. All heads bowed and Elijah launched into a long prayer. I peeked at the people around me. Were some, or all, of the group part of the snake-handling church?

What if they start pulling out snakes?

I sucked in a quick breath. Aynslee glanced at me and raised her eyebrows. I shook my head slightly. In the tightly packed bodies, an irritated rattler could take a chomp on almost everyone in the room.

I kept my eyes open, watching for any indication that the prayer would move into more sweeping gestures of faithfulness. Elijah finished, but someone else—Jeremiah? Tyrell?—spoke. The prayer went on, with different members speaking after a slight pause, apparently to make sure the previous person had finished. All of them gave thanks for our presence and thanked Jesus for my drawing skills.

I was humbled.

A woman started singing, and they all joined in. I'd never heard the song before, and my western Montana brain couldn't understand the deeply accented words. As soon as they finished, Ruby began another song. Her voice was untrained, but beautiful.

When the last note ended, Elijah spoke. "I want to thank all of you, my family, friends, and neighbors, for joining us." He continued talking about the life of his son, at times barely restraining tears. When he stopped speaking, a second, then a third mourner took over.

When the cancer kills me, will everyone speak as kindly?

I shoved the sooty black thought down and concentrated on memorizing the people around me. Although at times I can barely remember what day of the week it is, I have a photographic memory of faces. Even if I didn't get invited to the homecoming, I could draw those present.

A prayer followed the final speaker. "Lord, bless all the folks attending here today, and bring comfort to the family of Jason Morrow."

I jerked my head up.

After a chorus of "amens," the memorial service was over.

Everyone shuffled toward the kitchen. I touched the arm of the nearest woman and she paused.

"Do you folks know Jason?" I asked.

"Some might. I didn't know him personally. It was all over the news."

"His arrest—"

"Then he tried to escape. Police shot him dead." She turned and followed the others.

My feet seemed rooted to the floor. *Dead?*

How deep did this cover-up go? I swayed slightly. I needed to use the restroom. Making a guess that the layout of this house was similar to the cabin, I reached for the doorknob nearby. A large, calloused hand grabbed my wrist.

I jumped.

"What are you doing here?" a rough male voice whispered in my ear.

"You're hurting me." I turned to the man towering over me. I recognized him immediately. He was the handsome chauffeur I'd seen driving the older couple in the Bentley. He wore a white dress shirt without a tie and black pants over heavy work shoes.

He let go, but continued to invade my personal space. He smelled faintly of freshly cut wood and aftershave.

"I was looking for the powder room," I said.

He continued to stare at me, but the corners of his lips pulled down in confusion.

"Ah . . . restroom? Bathroom?"

The glower returned to his face, but he stepped aside and jerked his head to the opposite wall. A door opened beyond that, and one of the women emerged from a tiny bathroom.

I pushed past the man and headed to the restroom. After rinsing my face in cold water, I turned to check my appearance in the mirror over the sink.

A frame outlined where a mirror once hung, but only the plywood backing remained. I returned to the living room. Aynslee was the only person left.

"That's where you were." She shoved a hunk of hair off her face. "I'm starving, and everyone's already filled their plates and gone to the backyard. Come on!"

Obviously Aynslee hadn't heard the fate of Jason.

We moved into the kitchen. It was like a step back in time. A white-painted kitchen table with red trim strained against the quantity of food: ham, turkey, biscuits, sweet potatoes, and something that looked like tater tots. An older woman was stirring something on the 1950s stove, which also held large pots of green beans, some other type of dark green vegetable, and two pots of different-colored beans. All the cabinets were painted white, with vintage mint-green-and-red wallpaper. The farm sink under the window had matching fabric hanging below instead of cabinet doors.

I took a deep breath, sucking in the aroma. I didn't think I was hungry, but my stomach let out an angry growl.

"Best you eat up now," the woman said.

"This room is amazing." I picked up a paper plate. "Perfectly preserved, what, 1950s?"

The woman stopped stirring and smiled. "The 1940s, but not preserved. Designed. Ruby is an interior decorator specializing in vintage kitchens." Her smile widened at my expression. "And Elijah is a contractor. You equate simple folk like Ruby and Elijah with illiterate and uneducated."

My cheeks burned.

She tapped the wooden spoon on the pan and placed it on a spoon rest. "Get to know them. They're good folks." She left.

"Well," I said to Aynslee, keeping my face down so she couldn't see my blush. "That was awkward." I busied myself filling my plate, then nudged my daughter and nodded toward my empty casserole dish. "At least they loved my cooking."

"Check the garbage."

I gave her a withering look, which she ignored. I couldn't help it. I peeked into the trash.

A number of used paper plates filled the space. All had remnants of tuna noodle casserole. When I looked up, Aynslee was grinning at me.

"Don't say a word, young lady."

We took our overloaded plates to the yard where tables and folding chairs were scattered under the trees. Elijah raised his hand and patted the space across from him. Several people moved closer together to make room for us.

After sitting, I grabbed Aynslee's hand and said a quick, quiet prayer, then picked up my fork. God already knew I'd pray, but Elijah needed to know I had a passing conversation with Him.

Both Ruby and Elijah were staring at me when I looked up. He glanced at his wife. She smiled slightly and he nodded once. He turned to me. "Miz Gwen, I told my dear wife about your offer to redraw Samuel." Everyone stopped talking. The birds chirped around us and a light ham-scented breeze lifted my hair. "We . . . that is, Ruby and I . . . would like for you to join us. We're having a revival starting tonight and running through this weekend."

Yes! I refrained from pumping my arm.

Before I could answer, the man who'd confronted me in the living room placed his hand on Elijah's shoulder. "A word with you, Elijah?"

Elijah stood and the two men moved a distance away.

"Um . . . ," I said to Ruby. "I'm afraid I've forgotten his name." I jerked my head in the direction of the two men.

"That's Blake, Elijah's cousin." Ruby watched the two men for a moment. "Wonder what has him so riled?"

Blake was bent forward in intense conversation with Elijah. Elijah shook his head, then placed an arm across Blake's shoulder. Blake shrugged it off and glanced at me. His jaw tightened and he pointed at the house, then me.

Did he see me in the gazebo the other day? Is he now telling Elijah about my connection to Arless?

Elijah again placed his hand on Blake's arm and spoke to him for a few moments. Blake listened. The two men ended the conversation with a handshake. Elijah returned to the table and sat. "Miz Gwen, as I was saying, we'd love for you and your daughter to join us at our revival."

"Aynslee and I would be honored to come."

Aynslee poked me in the leg. I ignored her. "We just need to return to the cabin and—"

"Oh, that's not necessary." Elijah caught Ruby's gaze, then looked at me. "We have everything you'll need. We're leaving shortly."

"Oh, but—"

"It's quite a distance, you know, and there wouldn't be time for you to go home and return. We all go up as a group, so there's just this one opportunity." Elijah rubbed his forehead, tugged his ear, then placed a gnarled finger in front of his lips.

He was lying.

I wasn't going to be able to tell anyone I was going to the revival. That was probably the concession he made to Blake. *She can come, but no one can know where she is.*

I'd be on my own, with my daughter, with a snake-handling cult.

CHAPTER TWENTY-FIVE

AYNSLEE AND I FINISHED OUR MEALS IN SILENCE
while conversations swirled around us. I listened for any mention
of snakes or serpent handling, but all I heard was mind-numbing,
convoluted stories about car troubles, relative problems, and local
politics. Throw in the regional accent and I was hard-pressed to
follow anyone's discussion.

Little Sarah, Ruby's daughter, brought over a hand-stitched
teddy bear made of sturdy burlap for Aynslee to admire. "Hello
there, Mr. Teddy." Aynslee handed the bear back.

Sarah took Aynslee's hand.

Aynslee glanced at me.

"Go ahead."

The two of them scampered off.

"Sarah don't usually take to strangers," Ruby said, watching
them. "She doesn't talk."

I wanted to ask why, but considering I just attended her son's
memorial service, probing into her daughter's problems might be
a bit intrusive.

But I was supposed to find out more about these people. "Was she born like that?"

"No. No." She sighed. "Her sister, she was just twelve. Well, she died. April 15. Sarah stopped speaking when that happened."

I thought about the list of deaths. Was her daughter the first? Mentally I kicked myself for not bringing the folder with me. I finally said, "Aynslee has a big heart. Maybe Sarah can sense that."

"She's probably a lot like her mother that way."

I looked down. She wouldn't be nearly so kind if she knew I was infiltrating her church to have the congregation arrested.

The women started collecting empty plates and cups, and I stood to help. Ruby caught my arm. "Let them clean up."

Nodding, I sat down. "That was a beautiful memorial service. I noticed you . . . um . . . prayed for someone named Jason Morrow. Did you know him?"

"I didn't. It was just so sad."

"Hmm." I wanted to press the issue, but this didn't seem like the right time.

"I'd like to get to know a bit more about you, seeing you're joining us for the homecoming."

"Ahh . . ." I scratched my nose and glanced away. "What do you want to know?" *Brilliant, Gwen. If Ruby's an expert on deception, you just gave her three clues that you're going to lie.*

"Your husband?"

Robert was a relatively safe topic, and I relaxed slightly. "Ex-husband. He divorced me when I was diagnosed with cancer. Then wrote a book, a novel, loosely based on me. It made me seem like a flaky idiot."

She made a *tut-tut* sound.

A fly discovered my empty plate and I swatted at it before looking at her kind face. "I forgave him. Finally."

"That must have been hard. If I can ask . . . Why did you marry him in the first place?"

"Oh, he was handsome . . . and brilliant. And I was young, just nineteen—"

"Around these parts, you were practically an old maid."

I smiled. "Well, maybe the word I should have used was naive. He loved my starry-eyed adoration."

"Is he—?"

"Remarried. And happy." I nodded toward Aynslee. "And he gave me my daughter."

"Behold, children are a heritage from the Lord, the fruit of the womb is a reward."

"Uh . . . yeah, that's what I always say."

Blake approached. Now that he wasn't towering over me and growling, I could see he was even better looking than I'd originally thought. Most decidedly eye candy in that store window.

Heat crept across my cheeks and I ducked my head so no one could see my blush.

"We're full up," Blake said. "Can you ride?"

"Ride?" I glanced up.

Blake's jaw twitched and he folded his arms.

"What he means," Ruby said, "is all the four-wheelers are taken up with people and supplies, and the only other way to get to the homecoming is by horseback. Can you and your daughter ride horses?"

"Oh. Sure. I mean, I'm rusty, but—"

"Then let's get going." He turned and stomped off.

He might be the best-looking man in four counties, but his manners placed him squarely with the Neanderthals.

"You'd best follow him," Ruby said. "Horses take longer and you'll want to be settled by nightfall."

Standing, I caught Aynslee's attention and waved her over. "We're leaving now, and guess what? We're going horseback riding."

"No way," Aynslee said.

"Way." We threaded our way through the yard and into the house.

The kitchen bustled with women transferring the food into a host of coolers. Blake waited impatiently in the living room. "You'll be blindfolded for a portion of the trip." He held out two strips of fabric.

"You're kidding me. I can't ride a horse blindfolded—"

"Not that part."

"Not any part." I put my hands behind my back.

"Fine with me. Don't go." He turned to leave.

"Wait." *They blindfolded Trish. She made it safely home from the revival.* I slowly held out my hand.

He dropped the blindfolds into my hand. "I have the black Jeep Cherokee parked out in front. Get in the backseat and put on the blindfolds. I'll be there shortly."

I snatched the fabric from his hand, stuck my head in the air, and marched from the room. The hot flash caught me halfway to my truck, leaving me breathless. I paused.

Aynslee turned, saw my face, and waited.

"I'm fine," I finally said.

"Do you think they know why we're really here?" she asked.

"No." *But Blake may suspect.* "They're just cautious and we're

182

strangers." I handed her the blindfolds. "Wait in the car. I need to grab my art supplies from my truck, then I'll join you."

Aynslee already had her blindfold on by the time I joined her. I pulled out my cell, but the slam of a door made me throw it back into my bag.

The back of the Jeep held a pack saddle and a pair of canvas panniers, containers of supplies for a pack animal. The rich odor of horses filled the small space. I slid next to my daughter and covered my eyes. I felt helpless and exposed.

"He's cute," Aynslee said.

"He's a Neanderthal."

The Jeep rocked as Blake climbed into the driver's seat. After a moment, we began to move.

Aynslee slipped her hand into mine. I squeezed it with a reassurance I didn't feel. "Ruby told me you're Elijah's cousin," I said to Blake. "Is that why you go to his church?"

"No."

"You go because you're . . . anointed to handle serpents?"

"I don't handle serpents."

"But—"

"How much are you charging Elijah and Ruby to draw their son?"

"I'm not. It's a gift—"

"Yeah, right. Look, get something straight. I'm taking you to the homecoming, but I don't trust you. I'm keeping my family safe from people like you."

I was glad my face was mostly covered by the blindfold.

The car turned off the pavement, slowed, and began bumping and turning. We drove for what seemed to be hours in silence. Finally we stopped. "You can take off your blindfolds," he said.

We were in a small clearing covered with freshly fallen leaves and smelling of hay and horse manure. High rolling mountains surrounded us, and a steep, muddy trail shot up the hill on our right. A makeshift corral held four horses munching hay from corner feeders. Parked nearby was a two-horse trailer and black pickup.

Black pickup?

Blake stepped from the Jeep and opened the tailgate. He must have changed clothes back at Elijah's place and now wore jeans and a plaid shirt. The outfit highlighted his broad shoulders. I tried not to stare as he unloaded the pack saddle and panniers. He'd also put on the same sunglasses I'd seen him wearing the first time I saw him. Up close, I could see they were prescription transition lenses.

Transitional lenses mean they're clear part of the time. Gold, wire-framed glasses just like my drawing from the surveillance photo.

Jason said he wasn't the rapist.

No one knows where I am.

The last victim, Ina Jo, was murdered.

"You'll ride the bay gelding," Blake said. "The kid can ride the sorrel mare."

"Her name is Aynslee."

"She can still ride the mare." He strolled to the trailer, opened the door at the front, and pulled out two saddles. After laying them on the ground, he grabbed a third saddle, blankets, and bridles, adding them to the tack. "The bay takes the snaffle bit. The sorrel gets the curb."

"Mom," Aynslee whispered. "What did he just say?"

I pointed. "Grab that bridle and follow me. You're riding

that brown horse over there. I'm riding the brown one with the black mane and tail."

The horses glanced up as we entered the corral, then went back to eating. "Wait here," I said to Aynslee. I approached the bay, easily close to eighteen hands, his withers above my head. That was a long way to fall should my rusty riding skills abandon me.

Bridling both horses, I led them to the pile of saddles. Blake had already put a halter on the third horse and tied him to the fence.

Aynslee and I led our rides outside the enclosure to the pile of tack. "Any particular saddle you want us to use?" I called to Blake.

"No."

I selected the one with the padded seat for Aynslee. Fortunately saddling a horse was like riding a bicycle, and it didn't take me long to get them ready.

I handed both sets of reins to Aynslee. "Hold on. I need to get my stuff." Strolling to the Jeep, I opened the rear door, grabbed my bag, and turned around. I bumped into Blake.

He snatched the bag from my hand. "Oh no you don't." He moved to the open tailgate of the Jeep and dumped the bag into the cargo area. My art supplies, wallet, cell phone, several pens and tubes of lip gloss, and key-ring flashlight scattered. He picked up my cell and, with a swift toss, threw it into the woods.

"Hey!" I grabbed his arm.

He looked down at me.

I let go and punched his arm. It was like punching a brick. "That was *my* phone. How dare you!"

"I'll buy you a new one when we get back. What did that cost you? Ten bucks?"

"Thirty-nine."

"You won't need it where we're going. Mount up. We've a long way to ride."

I stuffed the contents into the bag, slung it over my shoulder, and slammed the tailgate shut as hard as I could, secretly hoping the window would shatter. It didn't. Stomping over to Aynslee, I took the reins of my horse and tied him to the fence. I helped her mount, arranged her long skirt, then handed her the reins.

"What do I do now?" Her eyes were huge and shiny.

"Hold on to the saddle horn if you need to. Lean forward when we go uphill and lean back when we go down." I gave her a few more riding tips.

"Can we buy a horse when we get home?"

"We'll see." I left her turning her mount in circles and returned to the bay. The stirrups were so high I'd need a ladder to reach them.

"Give me your leg."

I spun. Blake was standing close. Very close. I had to tip my head back to see his face. Turning around so he wouldn't see my blush, I grabbed the pommel and saddle strings, then bent my left leg. He swiftly boosted me up. My wretchedly long skirt hiked past my knees, exposing the equally ugly black socks, ending at midcalf, and clunky shoes. I was ridiculously grateful I'd shaved my legs.

Blake stared at my leg for a moment, a smile twitching his lips, and let go of the reins.

My bay snorted, tucked his head, and crow-hopped. I tugged on one rein trying to get his head turned to my leg. The crow-hopping turned into full-fledged bucking. Grabbing the saddle horn to keep from flying off, I hauled back on the reins and clutched him with my legs. The ground blurred under his flying hooves. The horse gave one last spine-cracking kick before settling down.

I scrunched the reins on my mount's neck and glared at Blake.

Blake gave me a half smile and two-fingered salute, then mounted his handsome chestnut.

Aynslee's eyes were wide open. "What if my horse does that?"

I worked at unclenching my teeth. "You seem to have a calm mount. Don't worry."

Trailing the packhorse, Blake turned his chestnut toward the steep trail. I let Aynslee fall in behind him and I brought up the rear. We climbed single file through a thick grove of trees before the narrow trail leveled and swung to the left. The ground was firm under a thick blanket of leaves, and the thud of hooves, squeak of saddles, and chirping of birds were the only sounds. The grass-scented air mixed with the aroma of leather and horses, taking me back to when Dave and I would go riding in Montana.

I thought about Blake putting me on a horse he knew would buck. A broken arm or leg would be one way to keep me from going to the revival.

The trail disappeared at times and we'd ride single file, following Blake's lead. At last it widened, and my long-legged mount pushed ahead, drawing level with Blake's chestnut. The chestnut pranced sideways, swishing his tail.

"Why are you going to the homecoming?" he asked while controlling his horse.

"Elijah and Ruby invited me. And I offered to draw Samuel."

"Have you ever been to a revival?"

"No. I've never even been to a Pentecostal church. Why are you going?"

He didn't answer for a few moments. "Ruby and Elijah have strong beliefs, but a lot of people disagree. They've been shunned by their family. The people in their town are ashamed of them. The law is after them, documentary films exploit them, and other religions mock them." He glanced at me. "I'm protective."

My stomach twisted. He'd already tried to get me injured. He could have been the one who tried to run me down. What would he do when he found out the real reason I was here?

CHAPTER TWENTY-SIX

I PULLED BACK ON THE REINS AND ALLOWED Blake to lead again. Aynslee gave me a questioning look as she passed, and I smiled slightly. She continued ahead until she rode alongside Blake.

"What's my horse's name?" she asked.

"Cinnamon. I call her Cindy."

"Cindy." Aynslee stroked the horse's neck. "Hi, Cindy. You're so beautiful." She looked up. "What's your horse's name?"

I expected him to brush off "the kid's" questions, but he continued to answer her. Once on a roll, Aynslee peppered him with equine questions, offered fifteen-year-old insight into social media, and shared her miserable time at the boarding school I'd had to send her to last year. Barely pausing for breath, she launched into her friendship with Mattie, then her crush on a boy named Carson.

He listened and commented when she paused.

I upgraded his status to saint, albeit one on the lowest rung of the saint hierarchy.

Trying to keep my mind off Blake, I focused on the trail, but my thoughts kept returning to him. While being married to Robert, I'd never thought of another man in any way but neutral. If I met someone handsome, like Blake or Arless, my fingers would itch for a pencil and paper. I had certainly never blushed or become a bumbling fool until after my divorce.

My identity had been Robert's wife. *Mrs.* Robert Marcey.

Robert was a gifted writer, hailed as the next Hemingway or Steinbeck. I'd been over-the-moon happy when he proposed to me. Early in our marriage, Robert and I would talk about growing old together, sitting in rocking chairs on a summer's afternoon. Then life interfered with our fairy tale. The words dried up for Robert, and he blamed me. My cancer diagnosis was the excuse he needed both to be free and to write again.

I'd been surprised and horrified at Beth's hint that I think about dating. Now here I was thinking about Blake as more than an artist's model.

Forget it, Gwen. He's just a chauffeur.

Beth's voice intruded on my daydream. *You're a woman worth loving. You're a catch.*

Catch and release. Like a fish. Ha-ha.

He could be married, Dave's voice cautioned.

True. With ten kids. But he somehow didn't act married. *Or like a crazed rapist and killer.*

You're kidding yourself, Gwen. Robert's voice now joined in my mental discussion. *No man, even a driver making minimum wage, wants damaged goods. You used to be a looker. Now you're—*

"Shut up, Robert."

I didn't realize I'd spoken out loud until both Blake and Aynslee looked at me. I coughed to cover my embarrassment.

190

So what was my new identity? A woman worth loving . . . or damaged goods?

The trail took a sharp right. At the bottom of a steep slope, the road leveled and opened into a field ringed by a hodgepodge of tents surrounding a series of campfires. On the far side of the field sat a variety of off-road vehicles. The rich aroma of food cooking made my mouth water. The sun had drifted behind the mountains, casting Prussian-blue shadows and causing the temperature to plummet. Aynslee hunched forward and rubbed her arms. The thin blouses we'd put on that morning were hardly sufficient for a late-October evening.

Several men paused in their various activities to come forward and take our bridles. Blake dismounted and helped Aynslee get down. By the time he turned to help me, I'd dismounted. Tugging my blouse straight, I did my best to hide the pain in my backside and thighs from the saddle. It *had* been a long time since I'd ridden.

Shivering from the cold, I pulled off the bag of art supplies and started unsaddling my horse when an oversize coat settled over my shoulders. It felt so good I pulled it close before turning to see the source.

Blake draped a man's sweater over Aynslee. "Thanks. Mom says you're a Neanderthal, but I think you're nice." She grinned at him.

I could see why some animals eat their young.

I concentrated on loosening the cinch and pretended I didn't know my daughter.

Before I could unsaddle, Blake was beside me. He lifted it off the horse effortlessly. "Neanderthal?" he whispered, his lips so close to my ear that my hair fluttered.

A flood of heat rushed to my face. I turned to watch him. He easily hefted the saddle, then sauntered to the area where he'd stacked the other tack.

At least he didn't ask for his coat back.

An attractive but simply dressed woman sidled up to my horse and stroked his cheek. "So. Blake put you up on Rowdy."

"Rowdy?"

She patted the bay's shoulder. "This is Rowdy. Blake's favorite horse. He never lets anyone ride him." She raised one eyebrow at me.

"Well, I guess he figured anyone from Montana who can saddle and bridle a horse should be able to ride a mount with an attitude. Do you know Blake pretty well?"

She glanced at Blake, patted my horse again, shot me a swift look, and walked away.

A middle-aged woman wearing a denim skirt and a sweater bustled over. She'd been at the memorial service.

"Hi. Is it Ida?" I asked.

"No names here, child. We have a lot of enemies. I bet you're starving." She took my elbow and aimed me toward the campfires. I nodded for my errant child to follow.

Thirty to forty people sat in folding lawn chairs or on blankets, eating, talking, and laughing. Many stopped when they spotted us, but soon continued. Blake's back was to me, and several women peeked in his direction between bites of dinner.

The woman led us to a log with a flattened top where plastic plates, silverware, and a roll of paper towels lay.

Little Sarah Adkins spotted Aynslee and pulled her into a tour of the campsite.

"Grab a plate and silverware," the older woman told me.

"Then help yourself to whatever looks good." She pointed at the different campfires, each with a suspended pot or fry pan on a grill. "The drinking water is over there. You're the one that came to the service today and brought that . . ."

"Tuna noodle casserole," I offered.

"Well bless your heart. Enjoy. When you're finished, the garbage is over there in that plastic bag."

I nodded.

Everything smelled heavenly. I chose a pot of what looked like stew and looked around for a place to sit. Ruby caught my gaze and patted the scarlet blanket next to her. I joined her.

"Good choice," Ruby said. "Squirrel stew."

"Oh yum." I eyed the hunk of meat I was about to bite into. I ate most of it anyway. It was much better than my tuna noodle casserole. Casually I glanced over at Blake. Before I could look away, he looked over at me and winked. I ducked my head and stared at my plate. When I finally looked up, Ruby was staring at me.

"My, my," she said. "Well, he's a good-looking man. All the women have their caps set for him, as you can see. Has a good job selling cars."

"I thought he was a chauffeur. He's a used car salesman?"

She chuckled. "Something like that. He owns the largest car dealership in Kentucky. Also a bank, a stable, and a number of other businesses."

I shut my mouth. "He's-he's rich?"

"Has the Midas touch."

"But I saw him driving a couple of people around in a Bentley. I thought he was a chauffeur."

"He helps out folks who have trouble driving. That's his

personal car." She touched her lips with a napkin. "He can be very generous to his friends. And dangerous to those he thinks are enemies."

I tried to keep from flinching.

She nodded in his direction. "He seems to fancy you. About time he showed more than polite interest. His fiancée ended things with him this past year."

"Really."

"Foolish woman. But I heard he put you up on his bay gelding. And you stayed on."

I shrugged. "Luck."

"You've caught his attention. If you want to keep it, well, you know what they say. The fastest way to a man's heart is through his stomach."

"The only way I'll ever get close to a heart is by becoming an open-heart surgeon. The only thing I've successfully made in the kitchen was a mess."

"That's a start." Ruby smiled.

Feeling the blush starting up again, I asked, "How do the restroom facilities work around here?"

She pointed. "Men in that direction. Women over there. If you see a roll of toilet paper on the branch, the facilities are empty. Take the TP with you, return it when you're finished."

"There's no TP in the outhouse?"

"Outhouse? Oh my. You'll find a shovel at the correct spot." She giggled at my expression. "It's simple but effective."

My face was under control by the time I returned. I was beginning to feel relaxed and comfortable here, letting my guard down.

Don't trust anybody.

Sitting next to Ruby, I asked, "How do you let people outside your congregation know if there's to be a revival?"

"We have a most efficient phone tree. We call it the buzz. Works for this and is crazy good at spreading gossip, unfortunately."

I pushed the remaining squirrel stew around in my bowl. "Tell me, Ruby. Did you know Grady Maynard?"

"Why do you ask?"

Answering a question with a question. Was she going to lie to me? "Just wondering. I'm staying in his cabin."

"We moved here after Grady . . . disappeared. We're originally from Tennessee. I never met him."

"I accidentally found his Bible. It showed that he had a son. Devin. I was just curious to learn more about him."

Ruby's brows furrowed. "I never knew that. The folks who knew Grady were Mamaw and Jimmy. They used to go to his church. I guess Jimmy took over when Grady went missing. But Jimmy and Mamaw both died back in August."

"I'm so sorry." I took a few more bites. Something put a tickle in the back of my head, and I sat up straighter. "Both died, did you say? How, if you don't mind my asking?"

Ruby placed her plate on the blanket next to her. "Well . . ." She glanced around, then scooted closer to me. "I don't think of this as gossip. It's what I was told. My nephew's friend's dad works for the sheriff's department." Another check for anyone paying us any attention. "They were both found in the garage."

"Uh-huh." I nodded encouragement. They had to be the two people in their sixties on the list the sheriff gave me.

"It was always kept locked. Always."

This time I made sure no one overheard us. "The garage?" I whispered.

"Yes. They have to stay warm, you know. That's why you keep them in a garage, basement, or room of the house."

"Them?"

"The serpents. But you always keep it locked."

I shoved my bowl away, the sight of food no longer appealing.

"The serpents were all loose. Must have been ten or more of 'em. And Mamaw and Jimmy were both bitten. Many times. It was awful."

Jason turned those snakes loose. And killed that couple.

"I'm going to get a slice of pie before the service begins." Ruby stood. "Can I bring you a piece?"

"No thanks."

People were slowly cleaning up and moving away.

A beautiful, dark-haired woman with mahogany skin and wearing a long khaki skirt took Ruby's place. "Hi. I'm Lindsay." She offered a soft hand smelling faintly of lavender skin cream.

"Hi, Lindsay." I shook her hand. "I thought we didn't use names."

She shrugged. "It's not as if it's a big secret. I heard you're a forensic artist and wanted to meet you."

"You don't—"

"Look like the other folks around here?"

"I was going to say 'sound like you're from this area.'"

Dimples bracketed her smile. "I'm from California. I'm here visiting my cousins."

I looked around for other people of color.

This time she laughed out loud and pointed to a redheaded man. "Over there. The Scottish side of the family."

I made a wry face. "Got me there. So you're a snake handler?"

"I think they prefer 'serpent handler,' and no, I'm not. I'm

196

here because these are simply good people and I like being around them. I come every fall."

"I see."

She crossed her legs and leaned back onto her elbows. "I wonder if you do." She watched the people sitting around the different campfires talking and laughing, then getting up and wandering toward the outdoor church area. "I've checked out their history."

Nodding, I raised my eyebrows.

She shrugged. "Just making sure they weren't a Jim Jones–like cult. Their background is quite interesting. Back in the 1890s, there was an average of three lynchings a week of African-Americans. But in the Pentecostal churches, even in the deep South, we were accepted, treated as equals, and given leadership positions." She looked at me. "With the Azusa Street revival—"

"I'm sorry, the what?"

"A lot of folks point to an event, a revival, in the spring of 1906. People think the Pentecostal movement started in the South by whites, but it started in California with an African-American minister in a mission on Azusa Street in Los Angeles."

A man walked by and called out, "Folks, time to start."

"Anyway," Lindsay said, "I didn't mean to ramble on—"

"I found it fascinating. Thank you. Let's stay in touch, or should I say, I'll give you a buzz?" I held out my hand for another handshake.

"A buzz it is. I'd like that." She shook my hand, then gave me her cell number.

"I'm sorry." I stood. "I don't have any way to write it down—"

She giggled and rose, brushing off her skirt. "It's easy to remember." She gave me the area code. "The next seven letters spell out my name. I'm terrible with numbers, so I always try to come up with a way to remember." She headed to the gathering.

"We'll be startin' soon," called out a man in his forties with a shaved head, blunt features, and mustache and beard.

I glanced around for Aynslee in the approaching dark, finally spotting her with Sarah in tow like an eager puppy.

Standing, I dropped my dishes into the garbage bag. Ruby joined me, shoving the last of a piece of pie into her mouth. She stopped, dropped the plate, and reached for her neck.

"Ruby?"

Her eyes opened wide and she clutched her throat with both hands.

"Ohmigosh!" I leaped behind her, reached around her abdomen, and made a fist with my right hand. "Hang on, Ruby. I've got you." Wrapping my left hand over my right, I yanked backward and up as hard as I could.

Ruby started to slump against me. No one was around. No shouts of discovery.

I gave the Heimlich maneuver a second time. Then a third. The world retreated, my harsh breath the only sound.

Ruby grew limp.

Struggling to hold her weight, I jerked on her abdomen again.

The woman coughed, then took a deep breath.

Releasing my grip around her middle, I steadied her until she was more solidly on her feet.

She panted a moment, then finally said, "Girl, you saved my life."

"I'm just glad I was here. Please, Ruby, don't say anything." I let go.

She turned and looked at me, placed her hand on my cheek, glanced over my shoulder, then moved toward the gathering.

I glanced behind me to see what had drawn her attention. Blake charged up and stared at me. "She okay?"

I nodded.

He turned and followed Ruby to the gathering.

I waited until my pulse came back to normal, then trailed after Blake.

For the first time I noticed one end of the field had a natural rise where a card table had been placed. A Bible, a glass soda pop bottle with a rag stuffed in the top, and a jar of clear liquid rested on the surface. On either side of the table were portable speakers.

Speakers? My gaze followed the cables leading to the speakers. On the far right side of the clearing, all the four-wheelers, most with off-road trailers, were parked. The speaker cables led to a generator still resting on a trailer. *Apparently primitive only goes so far.*

The worshipers were grabbing folding chairs and creating rows in front of the rise, leaving a large area between the front row and the "pulpit."

Four men strolled to the front, each carrying a variety of hinged boxes, and placed them behind the table.

The snakes had arrived.

CHAPTER TWENTY-SEVEN

AYNSLEE HAD FOUND TWO FOLDING LAWN CHAIRS and was watching the throng. "What took you so long?" she asked.

"Um, a bit of a problem with . . . a piece of pie." I needed to be able to see faces for my later drawings, so we sat to the side where I had a clear view of the participants. Sarah joined us, dragging a chair as close to Aynslee as possible.

I stared at Sarah for a moment, then stood and looked at the worshipers.

My stomach did a quick flutter. Professor Wellington said they believed the children attending this homecoming revival would be forced to drink poison, handle fire, and hold snakes.

With the exception of Sarah and Aynslee, there were no children. Maybe they were together in one of the larger tents?

That didn't seem likely. I bent over and whispered, "Aynslee, when you were with Sarah, did you see any other children?"

"No," she said slowly. "Sarah took me around the camp,

showed me the tent they set up for us, and then we ate dinner. I didn't see any kids at all."

Before I could formulate what to do next, the bearded man moved to the front. From the restless movements of the group, this appeared to be the preacher. A gray-haired woman with a tambourine and three men with guitars joined the preacher.

I sat down and leaned forward.

The preacher gave a signal and the generator coughed to life. Four bare lightbulbs dangling from a wire stretched overhead cast a wan light over the preacher and worship team. He picked up a wireless mic, tapped it a few times, then covered it with a white handkerchief. "Are ya ready to worship?"

The congregation leaped to its feet, shouting, "Hallelujah" and "Praise God!" The woman with the tambourine took the mic and began singing, enthusiastically accompanied by the guitarists. People joined in, clapping in time or raising their arms.

I didn't have a clue what they were singing, so I just clapped along.

After the first song ended, a second started. A man raced to the open space between the chairs and pulpit area and started dancing with steps vaguely like Irish clogging. A second, younger man quickly joined him in the front and spun in circles.

Smoke from the campfires drifted around the worshipers like streamers of chiffon. The electric lights turned the smoke into a swirling, jaundiced fog.

Almost everyone was standing. Two women on my right jerked, spun, and shouted words I couldn't understand. Another man moved to the front and ran from side to side. Ruby looked like she was crying, hands overhead, mouth moving.

The preacher grabbed the mic. "Hallelujah! God's not dead, He's still alive! Do you feel it?"

I could see the need for the handkerchief over the mic. He didn't just shout, he sprayed his words. The music tempo increased. More men rushed to the front, jumping, spinning, running. Most of the women were to the side, locking arms or waving hands overhead.

The preacher handed the mic to the tambourine woman and joined the cloggers.

The smoke stung my eyes and burned my nose. I blinked rapidly, focusing on faces.

The music slowed, but the frantic movement didn't. Now more people were talking in tongues than singing with the worship team. Gradually the pastor made his way to the raised pulpit and retrieved the mic. "Aaaaah, thank Ya, Jesus!"

A chorus of "thank Yous" echoed his sentiments.

"Let us pray," the preacher said. The congregants found their way to their seats but remained standing for the prayer. I took my cue and stood as well.

Once finished, everyone sat. For the first time since I arrived, I could hear the frogs and crickets of the forest. The moon rose behind the trees, turning the branches into fingers reaching for the sky. The falling leaves whispered to each other in a chilly breeze. I snuggled into Blake's jacket, inhaling the hint of hay and aftershave.

The pastor opened the Bible on the table and began reading one line at a time. He'd then pause and the congregation would repeat the words. "For we are the circumcision, ha! Which worship God in the spirit, ha! And rejoice in Christ Jesus, ha! And have no confidence in the flesh, ha!"

Like a verbal exclamation mark, the "ha" was a burst of air at the end of each statement, lending a cadence to his sermon. His voice rose. "God is Spirit, ha. Do you know that, brothers? Do you know that, sisters? Do I hear an amen on that?"

Various people rose to their feet shouting, "Amen!"

"Those who worship Him, ha. Do you worship *Him*?"

Once again the congregation stood, arms waving, lips moving.

"Do you worship in spirit and truth, ha?" The pastor charged to the open area between the congregation and the pulpit. "Do you feel the Spirit? Ha!" he yelled into the mic. "The Spirit *moves*, ha! Hallelujah, praise God, ha!" He ran back and forth, jabbing his finger at the crowd, punctuating his words. "We're in revival, ha. God's Word says He'll pour out His Spirit upon all flesh, ha." He spun and clogged, joined by several other men. "Now the Spirit is here, ha. Do you feel His Spirit, ha?"

The pastor stopped his clogging and glided to the snake boxes.

My toes curled and creeping ripples crossed my shoulders.

He reached into the box and grabbed two rattlers with one meaty hand, then hoisted them overhead. Easily over four feet long, they stretched forward and upward, their tongues flicking in and out.

I drew my knees to my chest and wrapped my arms around my legs. Aynslee had her hands in front of her eyes but peeked through her fingers. Sarah imitated Aynslee but peered through her fingers at my daughter.

He wrapped one snake around his neck and began clogging again, the second rattler dangling like a limp scarf from his hand. A younger man stopped twirling and reached for the snake. The pastor passed him the one in his hand, then removed the one around his neck and continued to dance.

The tempo increased. Another man pulled more snakes out of a box and held them up. Dust joined the campfire smoke and swirled around the dancing worshipers. A woman lit the rag stuffed in the Coke bottle. The tang of kerosene touched the air. She passed the flame under her chin and outstretched arm. She didn't flinch, nor did the flame seem to burn her.

Again the music changed, slowing down. One by one, the handlers returned the snakes to their boxes. The woman extinguished the flame and placed the bottle on the card table. The pastor returned to the earthen pulpit, sweat pouring down his face and dampening his shirt under his arms.

"Praise God." He wiped his face with a handkerchief. "Do I have an amen?"

The congregation shouted enthusiastically as they returned to their seats.

I lowered my feet to the ground and rolled my head from side to side to relax my neck muscles.

"My brothers and sisters in Christ." The pastor waved his arms, urging the congregation forward. "Are ya hurtin'? Do you have Christ?"

This was the altar call. As people went forward and gathered in groups for prayer or dropped to their knees in front of the rise of earth, I studied their faces. I identified six who were the primary snake handlers. Itching for a pencil, I concentrated on the individual features. My gaze then shifted to the rest of the congregation. I spotted Blake in the last row.

He was staring at me.

Quickly I turned to the front and slid down in my chair.

I could still feel his gaze burrowing into the back of my head.

Jumping to my feet, I whispered to Aynslee, "I'll be right back." I strolled over to the group praying closest to me, making sure they were between Blake and myself, and put my hand on the nearest shoulder. It wasn't until Ruby reached up and took my arm that I realized it was her. A woman near the center led the prayer, while other voices murmured agreement or spoke in tongues. I peeked through the bowed heads but couldn't see Blake.

The prayer continued, this time with Ruby speaking. "Lord, I ask You to cleanse Sister Gwen."

My head shot up. They were now praying over me.

Ruby gently propelled me forward until the prayer group surrounded me. Hands touched my arm, head, and back. "Touch her, O Lord. Free her . . ."

My face burned, my eyes spilled over. *God already knows the outcome. Why are you praying for me?*

A large hand slid across my back and cupped my neck. *Blake.* I knew without looking.

Breathing became difficult. Was he praying over me or giving me a warning?

After an eternity, the prayer ended.

I turned. No one stood behind me, but I could still feel the heat of Blake's hand on my neck.

The tambourine woman had the mic and belted out a heartfelt rendition of "Amazing Grace." I rejoined Aynslee and Sarah on the lawn chairs.

"What's wrong with your face?" Aynslee asked.

"You mean, besides having on no makeup, being dirty, and getting some horsehair smeared down the side?"

"You look funny."

I felt funny, but now wasn't the time to analyze my emotions. Being married to Robert and with our turbulent divorce, I'd become very good at stuffing down feelings. I shrugged, hoping she'd drop the subject.

The evening's service wound down. A few believers were in front of the pulpit, some on their knees, but the bulk of the folks were moving off into the dark toward the tents. "Come on, Mom, I know where we're sleeping."

She wove around the chairs, tents, campfires, and attendees to a blue-and-white tent near the stream. Blake stood by the opening, a propane lantern in his hand.

My steps faltered for a moment. "Um, did you want your coat back?"

"Eventually. For now, you need a light." He handed me the lantern.

I took it. Our fingers barely touched. Heat flooded my face and I looked away.

"Would you, ah, would you like to go for a walk?" he asked. The lantern glinted on his sun-bleached hair, and his lip twitched with the tiniest smile. A hint of a five-o'clock shadow edged his strong jaw.

My rear end and thighs ached from riding, eyes burned from campfire smoke, and stomach churned from digesting squirrel stew. "Sure." I handed the light to Aynslee and gave her my most devastating mom stare. *Don't you dare say a word . . .*

She smirked at me. "Don't stay out too late."

I gritted my teeth. *This has to be Robert's influence on my daughter.*

He nodded to the right. I stuffed my hands in the coat

pockets and moved in that direction. The different tents lit up as the worshipers settled in for the night, and the full moon offered a blue tint to the landscape. We didn't speak until we reached a place where the stream pooled, forming a medium-sized pond.

My hands became sweaty, and I pulled them out and wiped them on my skirt. Why did I walk out here? Blake didn't trust me. He probably just wanted me alone to grill me on my purpose for being here.

The stream burbled pleasantly, and the fragrance of some flower perfumed the air. The moonlight glinted on the watery surface, and an occasional splash told me fish were seeking a bug dinner. Cool air fluttered through my hair.

Glancing at Blake, I found him studying me. "Do I have something on my face?" I reached up and checked.

"No. No."

It just figured. Finally, here I was under a romantic moon with the best-looking man in the state, if not the East Coast, rich as King Solomon, and I was dressed in a puke-green blouse, long dirt-brown skirt safety-pinned at the waist, no makeup, and smelling like a horse.

"Did you just snort?"

Oh yeah, the icing on the cake. I just snorted. "I . . . uh . . . had something in my throat." *Smooth, Gwen.*

"Well, Gwen—"

"Yes?"

"I'm just wondering what your story is."

"My . . . story?"

"You have a daughter, but no wedding ring. You're not a member of this group, but here you are."

"I told you why I'm here."

"Where did you learn to ride a horse like that?"

"A long time ago I rode green broke horses. As rusty as I was, I was just happy to stay on. Now my turn. Did you put me on Rowdy to keep me from coming here? Hoping I'd get bucked off?"

He moved closer. Heat radiated off his body. He smelled of a blend of aftershave and campfire smoke.

I didn't care if he answered my question.

"And you saved Ruby's life." He reached up to touch my hair, then let his hand drop.

"A pleasant good evening to you, is it . . . Blake? Yes. Blake." The pastor's teeth gleamed in the dim light as he approached. "And you must be the new one."

"Ah, yes, I'm—"

"No names, please." The pastor looked over the pond. "Baptism here tomorrow. I wouldn't stay out late."

"We were just leaving." Blake motioned toward the tents and said to me, "Let me walk you back to your daughter."

I didn't want to walk back to my daughter. I wanted more time to see what was next with him.

Careful not to touch me, he waved his hand toward the tents. "Evening, Pastor."

"God bless you, son."

The moonlight-on-the-water-in-autumn moment was gone, and I didn't know how to get it back.

Aynslee sat cross-legged on the ground outside the tent. She stood when she saw us. Blake gave a small salute with his fingers, then merged into the night.

"I like him." Aynslee's eyes crinkled with delight. "Even if you do think he's a Neanderthal."

A short laugh came from the direction of his retreating footsteps.

I dove into the tent. A cot with a sleeping bag sat on my left, a second sleeping bag on the ground to the right, both with pillows. A paper sack resting on the cot contained two toothbrushes, a comb, a travel-sized tube of toothpaste, a sliver of soap obviously lifted from a motel, and a hand towel. Also included in my travel inventory were two very worn but clean flannel nightgowns. From the generous size I guessed they belonged to Ruby.

Missing was some industrial-strength deodorant. "I don't suppose in your wandering around camp that you overheard how long this revival lasts?"

Aynslee's mouth was open in horror at the nightgowns. "Am I supposed to sleep in *that*?"

"Yes, and be grateful we're not sleeping in our clothes. We smell like horse and smoke. And soon we'll reek of sweat. Now, to answer my question?"

"Morning baptism. Singing and praying and stuff after lunch. Another service tomorrow night, this time with communion and foot washing."

"Maybe I can opt in for whole body washing. In the meantime, I'll just have to stay downwind of everyone." Starting with the sleeping bag, I inspected it for spiders, snakes, and other critters. I did the same for Aynslee's bag, then moved on to examining the tent from top to bottom. Satisfied the area was clear, I turned off the lantern.

"What did you do that for?" Aynslee asked.

"I'm getting into my nightie. I don't need to give anyone a silhouetted show." And if anyone were watching, they'd see my silhouette was that of a boy once I took off my bra. What would Blake, or any man, think about that?

Tugging off my crumpled blouse and skirt, I draped them as flat as possible on the webbed floor of the tent. Cool air chilled my skin, and the nightgown, smelling of sunshine and fresh air, felt soft and warm. I slipped inside the sleeping bag and fluffed up the pillow. I thought about Blake and snuggled deeper into the bed.

"Why can't Sarah talk?" Aynslee asked.

"What?"

"Sarah. Why can't she talk?"

I made an effort to shift gears. "I don't know exactly. As I understand it, she stopped speaking when her sister died several months ago."

Aynslee was silent for a few moments. I thought she'd fallen asleep when she spoke again. "I think she wants me to be her sister."

"That's very perceptive of you."

Again Aynslee was silent. Finally she said, "That's the first time in . . . like, forever . . . that you've given me a compliment."

"Oh, sweetheart, that's not true! I think the world of you and I love you more than you'll ever know. I tell everybody what a great person you are."

"Ya gotta say it to me, Mom. I need to hear you say it."

I lay in bed a long time, staring into the dark.

CHAPTER TWENTY-EIGHT

THE RICH AROMA OF FRESHLY BREWED COFFEE pulled me from my restless sleep. The gray light in the tent spoke of early morning, but Aynslee's sleeping bag was already empty. I dressed, shivering in the cool, damp air, and wrapped Blake's coat around me.

Aynslee, with her Sarah shadow, was sitting beside Ruby at a campfire. Ruby nodded at a blue enamel coffeepot perched on a rock next to the fire. I found a cup and helped myself before sitting down.

"Did you sleep well?" Ruby asked.

"Well enough, thank you. Thank you for the nightgowns and toiletries." Coffee grounds filled the steaming brew.

"It's camp coffee," Ruby said, noting my expression. "Add a bit of cold water to the top and the grounds will settle."

I found the water and did as she suggested. It worked. "Aynslee told me you would be baptizing this morning, with worship throughout the day. Maybe we could work on the drawing of Samuel before all that begins."

"Yes." She smiled at me. "First have some breakfast, then we'll start. And, once again, thank you."

Soon all of us were again seated beside the fire while we consumed overflowing platefuls of eggs, bacon, and grits. I was growing quite fond of grits. They seemed to be an excuse for eating massive amounts of butter.

"Ruby," I said, noticing one of the men who'd handled snakes the night before. "I heard somewhere that . . . well . . . you might force someone . . . or say a child . . . to follow the Mark 16 signs."

"Oh my heavens, no." Ruby put her plate down and ran her hand down her daughter's hair. "Children are not allowed to be near the serpents until they're eighteen. And you need God's anointing to do any of the signs. I've handled serpents, but unless I'm anointed, I'm terrified of them."

"Really?" Her comments were completely opposite of what I'd been told. "So that's why there aren't any children here?"

"Just Sarah. After what happened to, well, you know, I don't want her out of my sight."

Had I been lied to about the practices here, or was it an honest mistake? I itched for my sketchbook and a chance to write down my thoughts, but Blake wandered over, smiled, and waved at Aynslee before looking at me.

My hand flew to my hair, checking for tangles or cowlicks. Blake's grin grew wider.

I stood up abruptly. "I need to use the restroom. I'll be back."

"I'll be here when you're ready to start the drawing."

Thinking about spiders and snakes in the woods, I debated

testing my bladder's capacity, but Aynslee was already giggling at my hesitation.

Straightening my shoulders, I marched toward the toilet paper marker.

Ruby had pulled two webbed lawn chairs together near the stream by the time I returned. The low murmur of conversation around the campfires formed a pleasant backdrop. Birds called each other from the trees, and the smell of smoke from the fires drifted on the crisp October air. The sun warmed me, and I slipped off the jacket, then settled next to her with my Bristol paper and HB pencil. I handed her the first sketch I'd done of Samuel. "What changes should I do to make this drawing look more like your son?" While Ruby studied the drawing, I roughed in the face on a fresh piece of paper.

"His eyes," Ruby said. "They looked more sleepy. And his lips were fuller."

I gave the sketch heavy lids and changed the mouth. "What else?"

"He had such a sparkle about him. He loved the Lord."

The sparkle would be a larger highlight in the eyes. I wasn't sure how to draw "loving the Lord," so I tried a hint of a smile. "Okay." I continued sketching.

"I miss him so." Ruby was staring at the burbling stream. "I miss all of them."

I paused in midstroke. "All of them?"

"Folks who were here last year from our church family. Most of them went to Jimmy and Mamaw's church. Pretty Twyla Fay . . ."

I sat up straighter. "What happened to Twyla Fay?"

"Oh, I just go on some. Never mind me."

I'd never heard of Twyla Fay, but I wanted to follow up on

her comments. I continued to sketch until the hum of voices along with the clatter of chairs indicated breakfast was over and baptisms were soon to start.

Ruby nodded slightly downstream to where the creek formed a small pool. "The baptism will be there. You can watch from here . . . unless . . ." She gave me a slight smile.

"Unless what?"

"You'd like to be baptized?"

"Thank you for the offer. I'm covered."

"Many of our members get rebaptized. Like a rededication to the Lord."

"Thank you, but I'll just use the time to work on Samuel's drawing."

She patted my knee, stood, and strolled toward where people were gathering.

I recognized the six snake handlers from the night before. No one seemed to be paying me any attention, so I turned to a clean sheet of paper and sketched thumbnails of each person. Under each thumbnail I jotted notes on hair and eye color, clothing, mannerism, and anything else to help with the identification.

Someone touched my shoulder.

I jumped and snapped my sketchbook closed.

Aynslee grinned at me. "Scared ya, didn't I?"

"A bit." Glancing around to be sure no one was watching, I tore out the thumbnail sketches and placed them in the back of the pad.

She took Ruby's chair. "Can I ask you something?"

"Sure."

"What would you think if I got baptized?" She twisted her fingers together.

"Well, depending on whether snakes are involved—"

"They're not. I asked. It's just water and stuff."

I touched her shiny ginger hair. "I'd be very proud of you."

She smiled. "You're getting better at it."

"What?"

"Saying nice things to me." She stood and raced toward the gathering.

I made an effort to shut my mouth. Had I really stopped telling my only child how much I cared? How proud I was of the young woman she was becoming? I put the drawing pad down and slowly followed.

Blake was sitting on the opposite shore, watching. I pretended not to see him. I was way too aware of his presence.

The pastor and another man were standing in the middle of the pond in waist-deep water. A line of seven people, of all ages, dressed in white robes, waited their turn. One by one they would wade into the chilly water.

A sudden memory assaulted my brain: another cold stream, the acrid odor of skunk cabbage, the howl of wolves.

I couldn't catch my breath. My legs grew rubbery. I sank to the dewy ground and put my head between my knees. *It's okay. I'm safe. Get control.*

After a moment, I sucked in air and stood. From across the creek, Blake looked at me strangely. Shoving down all my thoughts, I focused on the baptism ceremony.

Once the white-robed candidates reached the center of the pool, they would turn to the people on shore and give a short testimony of a changed life or recite a Bible verse. They would then pinch their nose with one hand, grab their wrist with the other, and be gently submerged backward by the two men.

"I baptize you in the name of the Lord Jesus," the pastor recited each time.

Aynslee took her place at the end of the line. The woman in front of her hugged her, and a man standing nearby gave her a high five.

Although I was delighted Aynslee made this decision, I wanted to ask her, *Why here?* Our church had baptisms every month. She'd never shown an interest.

Soon it was her turn. She waded to the center, turned, and nodded toward me. "My mom," she said clearly, "has a favorite verse. She posted it at home, and when things were really bad . . ." She swallowed hard. "You know, she'd say it. I think it's something to live by."

I blinked rapidly.

"It comes from Hebrews 12:1, 'Therefore we also, since we are surrounded by so great a cloud of witnesses, let us lay aside every weight, and the sin which so easily ensnares us, and let us run with endurance the race that is set before us.'"

My vision was too blurry to see the actual baptism.

As Aynslee left the water, the preacher offered a prayer, then led the congregation in song. The newly baptized retired to change from their wet clothing.

I headed to our tent to find my daughter. I had so much to share with her. I found her partially dressed, still trying to dry off with the hand towel. I hugged her tight.

"S'okay, Mom. I can't breathe."

I let go.

"Is it time to eat yet? I'm starving." She raced from the tent, swinging her black socks in one hand and shoes in the other.

So much for a long, meaningful conversation.

Lunch appeared to be a mountain of sandwiches and fresh fruit. I snagged something on whole wheat, a banana, a large slice of pie, and a paper cup full of water, then returned to my chair beside the stream. The voices around the campfires behind me were muted, and the aroma of fresh coffee mingled with the scent of apple pie.

I wished Blake would come over and sit with me. Maybe I could explain . . . what? *Maybe I'm more damaged than even Robert thinks.*

The sandwich was now a lump in my stomach. I set the paper plate and cup aside and picked up the sketchbook from the chair where I'd left it. Opening it, I evaluated the drawing of Samuel. Almost done. I just needed to tweak the values. I looked for the thumbnails of the snake handlers.

The page was missing.

CHAPTER TWENTY-NINE

I JUMPED UP AND SPUN IN A CIRCLE, CHECKING for anyone nearby. No one paid me any attention. Everyone seemed to have divided into small groups around the dying campfires and were enjoying a leisurely lunch.

Had the sketch blown out of the pad? *Impossible.*

Anyone finding that sketch would know I was recording the snake handlers. What would they do? No one knew where this revival was . . . or that I was here. Something could happen to me and no one would even know where to look.

Was Aynslee in danger?

Ruby and several other women had stopped chatting and were staring at me. I realized I was pacing along the creek bank. I stopped and made an effort to smile and wave. They waved back.

Sweat beaded on my upper lip. Clearly Ruby hadn't taken the thumbnails. It must have been Blake. He was suspicious of me from the start. I must have misjudged last night.

And I just gave him proof that he was right.

The campers, at some unseen signal, again moved their lawn chairs to the outdoor church. I could see the raised podium area and the first row of chairs. They would be occupied for some time. Maybe I could find Aynslee, saddle up the horses, and get out of here during the service.

Right. I had no idea where to go.

What if I made something up about the thumbnails? I could say I was practicing my drawing.

Not with the descriptions under each thumbnail. Okay, what about researching for a book?

The pastor's voice carried clearly, as did the guitars and tambourine. This was my chance to escape if I was going to try. But I needed to find my daughter. If she was sitting with the congregation, I couldn't see her from here.

The preacher exhorted, prodded, and encouraged his flock. It wasn't long before people were dancing, running, twirling, and speaking in tongues.

One of the men reached for a snake box.

Sucking in a breath, I moved closer to the gathering, seeking Aynslee. This time I spotted her in the back row, Sarah on one side and Blake on the other.

The pastor held up two handfuls of snakes before handing them to several other men. He kept one, which he draped across his head.

I tried to get Aynslee's attention.

The same woman from the night before again lit the rag in the bottle and ran it under her chin, then waved her hand over the open flame. The odors of burning kerosene, sweating bodies, and dust drifted on the light breeze.

A heavyset man in a blue T-shirt and gray dress pants,

hands waving over his head, moved to the card table on the podium, lifted a mason jar of clear liquid, and drank. The music drummed on, verse after verse sounding the same. The snakes, passed from hand to hand, would curl, stretch, and weave their heads in the air, tongues flicking.

My heart thudded rapidly with the music, my mouth dry. I couldn't stop watching.

The man in the blue T-shirt now spun in dizzying circles.

Ruby joined the men, taking a snake from the pastor. She danced in a small circle, snake dangling, then returned it to the preacher. Her face was expressionless.

The spinning man staggered, and two other men caught his arms and helped him to a chair. The pastor snatched up the mic, pounded the card table in time with the music, and joined in singing. Sweat stains dampened his shirt around his armpits and down his back. He wiped his face with his sleeve and continued to pound. Dust rose as more and more worshipers moved into the open area between chairs and podium, weaving, bobbing, twirling. The music blared from the speakers while a cacophony of voices intensified.

Then, as if all sound were snatched away by the hand of God, silence.

The crowd parted. The man in the blue T-shirt lay on the ground, convulsing.

I found myself pushing through the gathered worshipers. A circle of praying men and women surrounded the prone man. The worshipers nearest him were kneeling. Convulsing on his back with only his head and heels touching the ground, the man's face was bluish, with lips pulled from teeth covered in foam. His eyes bulged.

"He needs a doctor!" I screamed. "Someone get a doctor!"

No one looked at me. The praying increased, now with many speaking in tongues.

Someone grabbed my arm and yanked. I tripped and almost fell. Tearing my gaze from the stricken man, I found Blake hauling me away. "Let go of me! That man needs help." His grip grew stronger. My feet barely touched the ground.

Blake continued to drag me until we were a distance from the crowd, then spun me toward him and grabbed my other arm. "Stay out of it, Gwen."

"He's dying!"

"It's his choice."

"He's choosing to die? Did you ask him?" My face burned.

"He's not choosing to die—he's choosing prayer."

"Prayer?" I tried to jerk away from him. "D-don . . . don't you get it?" I swiped at the tears on my face. "Prayer doesn't work!"

He pulled me close and whispered in my ear, "What does work, Gwen? The law? Jail time?" He let go of one arm, reached into his pocket, and pulled out a torn-up sheet of paper. A portion of one of my thumbnail sketches was on top. "How much are you being paid?"

A collective moan came from the congregation, then a woman's voice rose in song.

I grabbed at the torn paper, missed, and again tried to get away.

Blake, jaw clenched and lips thin, tightened his grip on my arm.

I punched him in the chest and felt something break.

Keeping hold of me with one hand, he reached in his shirt pocket and pulled out a broken pair of gold, wire-rimmed glasses.

He glared at me before dropping them back into his pocket and dragging me toward my tent.

Once there, he shoved me inside. "Those people who put you up to this, they lied to you. They're not the protectors you think they are. Now stay put until I come back."

Waiting until his footsteps receded, I dashed for the opening. Another man stood just outside. When he spotted me, he shook his head.

Retreating inside, I sank to the cot.

Aynslee appeared, face flushed. "Now look what you've done! You got caught, didn't you?"

"I—"

"I like these people. They're nice. They listen to me. They make me feel like I belong."

"But—"

"I'm glad they found out. You need to leave them alone." She charged outside.

My head pounded and stomach ached. I remembered Blanche's words: *Who knows what they'll do if they find out why you're really there.*

But Blake was right. Whether I'd been deliberately lied to, or Blanche and Arless were misinformed, the only ones needing protection were the members themselves.

And now me. Blake saw me as the enemy.

Calling voices, the clanking of metal, and the roar of ATVs surrounded me. Every few minutes I'd peek outside to see if the guard was still there. He always was. The sun warmed up the tent, increasing the smell of musty canvas and my own unwashed body.

After an eternity, Blake returned. He wouldn't look at me. He motioned for me to follow him.

Once outside, I jerked to a stop. Most of the camp and people were gone. A few folks were still packing their ATVs. Blake marched over to where he'd saddled the horses. Aynslee held the bridle of her mount, impatiently shifting from foot to foot, not looking at me.

I kept my head down. Blake wordlessly helped me mount. The bay decided not to challenge me with another rodeo bucking session and calmly followed the other horses. Someone, probably Blake, had gathered my art supplies and purse contents into the bag now hanging from the saddle horn.

We rode in silence, leaving me with my grim thoughts.

Even though Blake had torn up my sketches, I could draw all the faces of the serpent handlers. But did I want to?

Wellington's voice played in my head. "*. . . the children will be forced . . . burned, poisoned, and bitten by snakes.*"

Ruby's words countered him: "*Children are not allowed to be near the serpents until they're eighteen. And you need God's anointing to do any of the signs.*"

"Just because you were wrong, Wellington, that doesn't mean they shouldn't be stopped," I muttered.

What about the First Amendment? Beth joined in the mental argument. *The free exercise of religion?*

"But people are dying, Beth. I saw one die today!"

"*It was his choice,*" Blake had said.

He was following the Bible, I heard Beth's voice say. *The very words of Jesus.*

"Drinking poison isn't safe." I slowed my horse so Aynslee, riding just ahead of me, couldn't hear. "Nor is handling a bunch of poisonous snakes!" The horse's ears flickered at my soft words.

Then should we pass laws, Blake muttered in my brain,

outlawing everything that isn't safe? Where there's a risk? Car racing? Mountain climbing? Skiing—

"Stop it! All of you. I need the reward money."

Blood money, Blake murmured. *Your thirty pieces of silver—*

"People. Are. Dying," I whispered fiercely.

The voices had no response to that, but something in that mental argument bothered me. People *had* died. I had the list back at the cabin. Before I redrew the serpent handlers, I should review the police reports.

I relaxed and urged my mount to catch up. I would suspend making a decision on the drawings until I could look into it more.

We were almost in sight of the corral when Aynslee finally spoke. "Ruby and Elijah invited us to dinner tonight."

Blake looked over his shoulder. "I haven't told Ruby and Elijah about the drawings." His voice was hard. "I think you should be the one to tell them."

We walked the horses next to the corral to unsaddle. I slid off, then held Aynslee's mount while she did the same. We tied the horses to the top rail, and I walked over to where Blake was unsaddling his horse. "Blake."

The look he gave me made me step backward. "Look, I'm sorry." I reached out my hand.

He turned his back on me.

How much bigger a mess could you make your life right now? I unsaddled our horses, fumbling through blurred vision.

Blake moved the tack to the front of the two-horse trailer, then pulled out a fresh bale of hay. After pulling off the baling twine, he broke up the bale and distributed it to the corner horse feeders.

He didn't bother with blindfolds on the drive to Ruby and Elijah's house, which turned out to be only a few miles from the corral. Blake must have driven around the day before to throw us off.

It was close to four when we arrived. Sarah had to have been sitting by a window. She flew out the front door when we pulled up, followed by her parents. Sarah grabbed Aynslee's hand and led her to the porch.

Blake gave Ruby a swift hug, then drove off without a backward glance toward me.

Ruby came over to me. "Looks like you two had a bit of a spat." She patted me on the arm. "Come on in and have some supper."

"Ruby, Elijah, um, I need to be alone right now."

Ruby's eyebrows furrowed. "Oh dear, this sounds serious."

"It's okay. It's a . . . case I'm working on." I hated to lie, but this was *almost* the truth. "I need to look at something . . . um, read a case file. Could I leave Aynslee here? Just for an hour? I won't be long."

"Certainly. We'll hold dinner for you."

"No. Don't do that. I'm not hungry. I just need to check something out. I'll be back shortly."

"Of course." She patted me again on the arm.

Jumping into the cab, I started the engine, put it in gear, and drove off without looking back. I didn't want, or need, to talk about anything with Ruby. Not yet.

I drove to the cabin. The first thing I did was check the phone. Still dead, but Aynslee's cell was where she left it on the table. I took a long shower, washing away the last traces of dirt, campfire smoke, and horse. Now feeling human, or at least not a stink monster, I pulled on a pair of loose-fitting gray sweats, a baggy off-white fisherman's knit sweater, and fuzzy slippers. I'd dress formally, as in put on shoes, when I went back for Aynslee.

The long skirt and blouse reeked. Without laundry facilities or even a dirty clothes hamper, I hung them over a chair on the porch to air out.

Something rustled in the woods nearby. I stepped into the cabin and searched for the flashlight, then reached into my purse and grabbed my key-ring flashlight. My tiny beam illuminated a startled raccoon grubbing under a tree. It scampered off. Grinning, I put the key ring into my pocket and went back inside.

I picked up the stack of files and the book on Pentecostals, then sat at the kitchen table. I looked again at the list Clay had made for me of recent deaths. I opened the file. The first name on the list was twelve-year-old Mary Adkins, Sarah's sister, and the oldest daughter of Elijah and Ruby. She was poisoned. *But how?* I read the report. According to her mom, she couldn't have been poisoned during a church service.

The autopsy report stated the cause of death was strychnine.

I grimaced. That was a horrible way to die. Her parents and older brother were ruled out as suspects. They'd been visiting family in West Virginia, leaving the two younger girls with their grandmother. Was this an accident? Maybe she'd found her parents' stash of poison.

I read further. She'd been at her grandmother's house in Pikeville. According to the report, Grandma was Catholic. She'd cooperated and allowed the police to search her home and grounds. No sign of strychnine.

Kids don't usually find a stash of strychnine while playing and decide to drink it. Someone had to have given it to her. And that made Mary's death murder.

According to the reports and notes, the investigation was stalled. The signature at the bottom of the last page was Junior Reed.

I stared at the name. So Sheriff Reed turned the investigation over to his son. No wonder the murder inquiry stalled. I pictured Junior plunging over the side of the road, mucking up any hope of finding out more about Trish's death.

Twyla Fay was next, less than a month later. Hit-and-run. Ruby mentioned her name. Ruby said she was a member of Jimmy and Mamaw's church.

I stood and paced, rubbing my arms. Mamaw and Jimmy, the elderly couple who died in their garage. Surrounded by snakes that Jason confessed to have turned loose after being paid. Add the five people who died in the accident, again that Jason probably caused.

Mamaw and Jimmy knew Grady Maynard.

That linked eleven people together. A murder, four "accidents," and Grady's disappearance. At least two other deaths, a poison and a burned body, could have ties to a serpent-handling congregation. Plus Samuel, dying from a snakebite, making far too many coincidences, and I didn't believe in coincidences. What had Trish said? She couldn't get photographs, but she did learn some first names. Mamaw and Jimmy were pretty unusual names, as was Twyla Fay. Did Trish tell someone those names, resulting in their deaths?

I dry-washed my face, then ran my fingers through my hair. "It's ridiculous." My voice sounded loud in the empty cabin. "To think someone is killing off members of a church just because they handle snakes. Ha! Their very practice puts them at risk of dying." I saw the dangers of their form of worship today when the man drank strychnine. If someone wanted to wipe out the practice, all they had to do was wait.

I poured a glass of water and checked the time. I still had a few minutes before I needed to leave and pick up Aynslee. I placed her cell phone in my purse. I could probably get cell reception closer to Ruby's place. I needed to call Beth and find out if she'd discovered anything more.

Someone else had to have made the obvious connection between the deaths and the church they went to. I checked for Junior's name and found it as the investigating officer on not one but three of the cases.

Was the sheriff involved somehow? Did he put his inept son in charge of the investigation to make sure nothing was ever solved? Was this related to the rape cases?

Who could I trust? According to Jason, no one. Sheriff Clayton Reed could be enmeshed in these deaths up to his eyeballs.

I could call Dave. He could get the ball rolling with the state police.

Something else nudged at me, but the more I focused, the more it eluded me.

I replaced the information on the deaths in the folder, laying it neatly on the drawing pad. Underneath was Professor Wellington's map to the cabin and a folder with an article on snake handling. Retrieving the glass of water I poured earlier, I took a long drink.

Something caught my attention.

I slowly lowered the glass. The red light of the fire alarm

was on. Had someone been in the cabin while I was gone? I stood quickly. The room whirled.

Holding on to the chair, then the sofa, I made my way to the phone and picked up the receiver. Still dead.

The room spun faster.

I grabbed for the chair, missed, landed on the floor.

The room went black.

CHAPTER THIRTY

THE SHIP ROCKED BENEATH ME. NO. I WASN'T on a ship. I was in the cabin, under the bed. My pencil was there. More rolling motion. Earthquake? I was going to be sick. Again darkness.

The ground scratched my back. My face was wet. Cold. The earth moved under me. I was . . . I was being dragged. My arms over my head. My legs in the air, tugging, someone tugging my ankles, pulling me toward . . .

Falling. I grabbed for something. Earth tumbled under my fingers. Sliding faster, I frantically grabbed at anything, nothing, more sliding earth, moving faster, faster. A rope. Clinging to it, my downward motion slowed.

The rope jerked. I almost lost my grip as it skated through my hands, tearing flesh. The rope loosened again. I skidded down. Now my legs were over open space. The rope dropped again. My whole body dangled free. The rope broke. I dropped.

The ground slammed into me. Pain shot from my right

ankle. I rolled, then stopped. I remained curled up, waiting for the world to stop spinning. Darkness.

The throbbing from my ankle insisted I pay attention. I opened my eyes, but nothing changed. Inky blackness cloaked me.

Gauzy thoughts filled my brain, but the pain in my ankle helped me focus. The ground under me was solid enough, smelling of freshly disturbed earth and stale air. A few small rocks tumbled around me and on me, dropping from the unseen heights I'd fallen from. I'd lost my fuzzy slippers and my feet were cold. My hands were raw and abraded from gripping the rope still under me—

Not a rope. It had smaller extensions growing from it. A root, one that broke with my weight. Rotating my foot, I winced at the sensation. Probably a sprain. Painful, but at least not broken.

Still lying on my side, I carefully groped around in a semicircle. More freshly disturbed earth and rocks. I found one slipper near my shoulder and put it on. No edge leading to still deeper depths of the earth.

I wanted to cry out for help, but whoever threw me down here could be waiting to see if I survived. I felt for the tiny keyring flashlight and found it in my pocket, but held off on turning it on for the same reason.

Straining my ears, I listened for any voices or sound of movement above. I heard nothing, not even sliding dirt from my earlier fall.

I remained still and tried to reconstruct the past few . . . hours? Minutes? How long had I been drugged? And how? I'd taken a shower, read the files, caught a raccoon sneaking about, drunk a glass of bottled water.

The water. I'd opened it before we went to the memorial service for Samuel.

They . . . he? . . . must have had a key. I'd locked the door. Hadn't I?

Had someone been waiting all that time for me to drink a glass of water?

Nothing made sense. Only that I was someplace cold, dirty, moldy, and dark. I stretched my hand above my head, exploring with my fingers this world I'd been thrust into.

This time I felt fabric.

My heart hammered in my chest. I forced my trembling hand forward, tracing the material, finding a seam. And under that, a leg.

I wanted to scream, but no sound came out. I snatched my hand back and scooted away.

Outside of my pounding heart, I heard no other sounds. No breathing, no movement. Sweat broke out on my forehead and chilled rapidly. Fumbling in my pockets, I found the key-ring flashlight. It took me two attempts before I could switch it on.

A man, a very dead, mummified man, was propped up against a boulder in front of me.

I dropped the flashlight. The light remained on, now shining on a rock wall behind the man. Picking it up, I took a deep breath, then returned the light to his face. My forensic artist brain recorded the details: skin stretched tightly over high cheekbones, prominent nose, square jaw, level eyebrows. I knew this face. "Hello, Grady Maynard."

Grady was well beyond answering.

Playing the light down his body, I stopped at his legs. Both angled off in impossible directions. I shined the light overhead.

The ceiling had to be fifteen feet high, with an opening outside of the reach of my light. Various-sized roots dangled down, but none were closer than ten feet above me.

If I hadn't caught the root and slowed my progress, I'd have a lot more wrong with my body than a sprained ankle.

My second slipper rested against Grady's foot. I put it on, relishing the feeling of warmth.

The flashlight flickered, then went out. I tapped it in my palm to no avail. My ragged breathing sounded loud in the small chamber. *Settle down. Morning will come soon. Then you can see your way out . . .*

Like Grady did? When did the missing person's report say he disappeared—1996?

But Grady had two broken legs.

"Okay, Gwen, here are your options." Hearing my own voice helped slow my breathing. "Unless you want to search Grady's body for matches in the pitch dark, you need to wait until morning."

It figured the first time I'd sleep in a room with a man since my divorce, it would be with a mummified corpse.

Curling up to conserve heat, I tried to rest. A collection of strange thoughts kept intruding on my brain. *The murdered woman. The scratches on the floor. Aynslee didn't know how to start a fire. How did someone know when I'd drink that water?*

I opened my eyes. I must have finally drifted off. In the gray light of morning I could clearly see my prison. The cave was about twenty feet across at its widest by about ten feet, oval in shape, with yellowish rock walls curving inward to the access point overhead. Stones and debris littered the floor and piled up against the walls on the bottom. Grady sprawled close to the back wall, roughly in the middle of the oval, probably where he landed so many years ago.

Tugging off my slipper, I examined my ankle. Swollen, with impressive purple bruising. I rotated it, wincing at the feel.

During my sleep, my subconscious mind had worked on an answer to the puzzling pieces. The scratches on the floor, light on the fire alarm, laced drinking water.

I'd obviously been drugged, but someone had been watching me in order to know when I'd drink that water. No one was outside. They would have sent that raccoon flying. They watched me from *inside* the cabin.

My stomach rolled.

A camera, hidden so no casual visitor would notice. Most cameras had telltale lights when they were on.

Aynslee started the fire on the first morning and failed to open the flue. When the room filled with smoke, the alarm didn't go off, but I'd seen a light on it the night before.

So the camera was in the smoke alarm, and the light came on when the camera was in use.

I gingerly put my slipper back on and looked at Grady. "That camera wasn't set up to watch Aynslee and me."

Somehow it was less creepy talking to the body.

As long as he didn't answer back.

"Sheriff Reed said the Hillbilly Rapist had to have a remote location. The Campbell cabin, your old home, was perfect. But the rapist couldn't just disappear for five-day stretches every time a girl was abducted. Of course, he could have kept her in the snake room, with no outside entrance, assuming he'd found it."

Thinking about getting thrown into that black hole filled with spiders made my skin crawl.

"A camera would both keep an eye on the girl and record his conquests so he could play them back. That's the kind of thing this pervert would like to do, and it fits his profile."

Grady didn't comment.

"There were scratches on the floor under the bed. He moved the bed so it would be directly under the camera."

I rubbed my eyes, trying to get the visual out of my mind. As long as the cabin was ignored or unoccupied, the monster was free to practice his perversions. But Aynslee and I had moved in. He didn't have time to brainwash the victim into leaving town. He had to get rid of her quickly. So he killed her and threw her into the river.

I was still missing something. That kind of rapist wasn't opposed to murder, so what prevented him from killing before?

And he'd been watching me, which meant the man the sheriff arrested, Jason Morrow, was the wrong person. The Hillbilly Rapist was still on the loose.

And he was accelerating. Now that I was out of the picture, his favorite torture location was available.

At least Aynslee is safe. Ruby and Elijah will protect her. And when I didn't return within the hour like I told them, they must have come looking for me.

Various aches and pains, plus the jab of my twisted ankle, protested my standing. I hobbled over to the body. Covered by a sifting of dirt, Grady wore jeans held up by suspenders, a red plaid shirt, and high lace-up boots. A blaze-orange baseball hat was slightly behind him. I couldn't remember if the file I read said what month he'd disappeared, but I'd bet hunting season.

Should Grady have been located, his death would have looked like an accident. Poor ole Grady fell down an old mining

235

shaft, or hole, or whatever this place was. But someone knew he was down here. Someone wanted me to share in his same fate.

Unless I found a way out, Grady's killer would be my killer.

In the light of day, I could more clearly see his features. His skin looked like yellowish leather stretched across his face, pulling his lips slightly open and revealing a chipped front tooth. He had a prominent nose, heavy brow ridge, and high cheekbones. His thick, chestnut-brown hair tumbled across his forehead. The cave must have been just the right combination of cool and dry to have preserved his body so well. He looked vaguely familiar, but I couldn't figure out if that was because of the photo I'd viewed or someone I'd met.

His left hand was on his lap, index finger slightly raised, the rest of his hand making a loose fist holding the stump of a pencil. A gold wedding band with three engraved crosses had slid to the end of his ring finger. His right hand rested on the dusty floor of the cave. A piece of paper lay under his fingers.

I moved closer.

Grady had written something on the paper. Gingerly I retrieved the note. One side was a grocery list, written in ink, now faded. I could barely make out the words on the opposite side. The writing was sprawled across the paper as if done in the dark.

I glanced upward. If someone had sealed this cave after shoving Grady down here, it would have been inky black. No bugs, air, water, or anything else could get in, forming the perfect conditions for creating a mummified body.

I shivered.

When I could hold the paper steady enough to read, I held the note to the light. The first line read, *Devin killed me.*

Grady identified his own son as his killer.

The second line read, *The boy was strange. I sent him away...* The rest was illegible.

Early behavior of serial rapists included Peeping Tomism and fetish burglaries. If Grady had been aware of Devin's actions, he might have sent him away.

Grady's cabin was the key. The Hillbilly Rapist knew of its existence, used it, abducted me from it, and knew where Grady's body lay undiscovered. The Hillbilly Rapist could only be Devin.

CHAPTER THIRTY-ONE

THE THIRD LINE HAD JUST ONE WORD. *COLD* WITH a triangle and a line. "I bet you were cold. You went out during the day. No jacket. And it is cold down here, which is why, I have to say, you're looking mahvalous, dahling."

I knew why I was being flippant. I was going to have to touch his remains. He might have something on him that I could use. "I hope you're not ticklish . . ."

Slipping the note into my pocket, I kneeled next to him and reached for his shirt, hesitated, then patted the pocket. A hollow noise greeted my tapping.

My skin crawled at touching his mummified chest.

Nothing in the pocket. Next came touching his jeans. "Come on, girl, it's just a body. You've seen lots of bodies." I wiped my hand on my pants anyway.

I checked the jean pockets. The leg underneath felt like a cold log. The left one held a stainless steel pocket watch. Engraved on the outside was *To Grady, Love Miriam*. The right one held a small pocketknife.

Moving away from the corpse, I sat down and inspected

my treasures. The watch had long since stopped, but the knife could be useful. I slipped the watch into my pocket and opened the knife. Maybe I could carve steps into the stone to reach the roots . . .

What then, Tarzan? Swing from root to root to reach the opening?

Okay, dumb idea. Ruby and Elijah would be looking for me. When they didn't find me at the cabin, they'd worry, knowing I wouldn't leave my daughter and not return. Maybe they'd start one of their famous "buzz" phone trees to alert others. For sure someone would call in the sheriff.

Even if Clay was convinced he arrested the right man, he'd see the same evidence I saw. He'd process the cabin, if for no other reason than to gather forensic evidence.

And Blanche and Arless were expecting me to show up with the thumbnails and finished drawings of the serpent handlers. Arless, with all his money, would offer a big reward for someone to find me.

I just had to wait it out.

I didn't want to think about the alternative. What if the rapist, or whoever threw me down here, cleaned all my things out of the cabin? Made it look like I left town?

No. No one would believe I'd leave my daughter.

"So if Devin is the rapist, and threw me down here, why didn't he take advantage of me?" I asked Grady's body.

You know why, Robert's voice whispered in my brain. *You're damaged goods. Not even a sex-crazed rapist wants you.*

"Nobody asked you, Robert, and quite frankly, you're wrong. Rape is about power and control. I suspect he didn't have time, and probably wouldn't 'enjoy' himself unless he was hurting someone." It felt good to lecture Robert for a change.

Why didn't he just kill you? Robert asked.

"Because . . . because of the same reason: power and control. Now, I'd appreciate it if you'd vacate my brain."

To ward off more inky thoughts, I hobbled to the nearest wall to inspect my prison. High overhead, an opening provided diffused light. I couldn't see the sky. The angle of the gap had allowed me to slide and grab the roots, slowing my fall.

If I couldn't see the sky, then chances were that someone on the surface couldn't see down here.

I touched the stone. Using the pocketknife, I tested the hardness, ending up with a broken knife tip.

Turning my attention to the dirt and rocks piled against the walls, mentally I added up the distance to the opening above me, then compared it to the quantity of material available to pile up. Too far to go, too little to work with.

The boulder Grady leaned against was good-sized and about three feet from the back wall. I limped behind him, then crawled on top of it, wincing when my hand accidentally brushed against his hair. When I stood on the rock, some of the roots were just above my reach. I jumped up slightly, grabbing for the nearest root. I caught it. It held me for a moment, then broke loose, pelting me with rocks and dirt. I fell, attempted to roll upon landing, and ended up sprawled across Grady's body.

I screamed and shoved away from the corpse.

Grady's left arm had flopped off his lap and now lay beside him, his index finger pointing at me. "Hey, I didn't put you here, so don't point an accusing finger at me." My feeble attempt at humor didn't seem to impress him. He continued to point. I shifted until it was no longer aimed in my direction.

I rubbed my sore ankle and studied the walls and ceiling,

then crawled to my feet. Once again I circled the cave, this time with my hands feeling the surface, looking for a way to scale them. The inward curve and smooth sides gave me no handholds to try climbing.

The taproot that broke my fall lay on the floor. Could I throw it up and . . . what? I needed a grappling hook at the end. I found a rock with a slight indent around the middle, then tried to tie the root to it. The first upward toss wasn't high enough to reach the opening. I tried again. And again. Each time my toss would come up short. Hobbling to the boulder behind Grady, I climbed on top and tried throwing the rock again. This time it landed at the opening and stuck. I gave a slight tug, then put a bit of weight on it.

The root snapped apart in the middle.

I threw the section left in my hands at the stone wall. "Doggone it! Doggone it!" My voice echoed loudly in the space. "Can anybody hear me?" How far would sound carry to the surface? "Hello? Can you hear me? Help!"

No sound came from outside.

"Help! Help! I'm down here!" Once I started, I couldn't seem to stop. I screamed until my throat was raw and my face burned with exertion.

Slowly I lowered myself from the boulder and sat on it. "Anyone?" I croaked. My mouth was dry. Rolling my tongue around inside my mouth, I tried to find a tiny bit of spit. I ached for a drink of cold water.

Rising from the boulder, I limped to the nearest wall and pulled out the knife. Using the metal end, I tapped the stone, listening for a change in the sound. I made a complete circuit of the space, tapping. No hollow *thump*.

I threw the folded knife across the cave. Reaching down, I picked up a rock and threw it as hard as I could in the same direction. "Get. Me. Out of here!" Then another. And another. I hurled stones until my arm ached and I was out of ammunition. I moved over and started flinging the next small pile of rocks.

The stones got heavier, my arm weaker, my aim wilder. I sank to the floor.

Gasping for breath, a hot flash raced up my neck and to my face, bathing it in sweat. My gaze darted around the cave before ending up at Grady. The man seemed to be grinning at me. "I suppose you think this is funny? Were you lonely and in need of a second stiff to keep you company?"

Grady's empty eye sockets stared at nothing.

My sweat dried and the heat leached from my body, leaving me shivering. I wrapped my arms around my legs. "So, Grady, did you and God come up with a way to break me?"

Grady smirked.

"Cancer isn't enough? This is faster? Dehydration, starvation?" I rubbed my arms in the fisherman's knit sweater. "Exposure maybe?"

Shoving up from the floor, I grabbed another stone, this time hurtling it at the ceiling. "Talk to me, God! Answer me!" I threw another rock upward. "Do You hear me?"

I limped to Grady's body and pointed to him. "Grady was a man of God. One of Yours." I shook my fist at the ceiling. "He handled snakes, for Pete's sake, just because You said so. I bet if You told him to jump off a cliff, he wouldn't have hesitated. And You let him die here!"

My voice caught on the word *die*. I sank to the floor and

stared at the dirt walls. How long had I been down here? Less than a day? And how long to die of dehydration?

Calm down. They'll find you.

But they never found Grady.

I couldn't sit still. Standing, I paced the length of the cave. Eighteen hobbling steps. Turn. Eighteen steps. Turn. "I've been captive before. And someone wanted me dead. But I made it out. I used my head. The Lord helps those who help themselves. Right?"

Wrong, Beth whispered in my brain. *Remember what happened?*

Eighteen steps. Turn. Eighteen steps. Turn. "Okay. I got it. I know." I swallowed hard. Eighteen steps. "Everything happens for a reason." Turn. "And You're not obligated to reveal the reason." Five steps. My ankle screamed at the partial weight I was placing on it. "Is all this because I stopped talking to You? Well, I'm talking to You now." My voice rose. Three steps. "If You get me out of this, I'll talk to You all the time." I was in the center of the cave. "I won't shut up. And I'll pray about other people, not just whine about my own lot in life. How about that, God?" I dropped to my knees, thought for a moment, then said a quick prayer. "Okay. I've done my part. Do we have a deal?"

I listened carefully for that still, small voice. I heard only my own ragged breathing.

"Fine, God . . ." Burying my head in my hands, I cried. Not with Blanche's delicate, hankie-dabbing tears, but loud, gut-wrenching sobs.

After a time, the sobs gave way to hiccups, then to a throbbing headache.

Nothing changed. I was still in an earthen mausoleum with a corpse, but now my head hurt and stomach ached.

I slowly rolled off my knees and wrapped my arms around my legs. I had no strength. Only a miracle would get me out of this grave. A miracle that didn't occur for Grady. I thought of my daughter, bringing her face into focus in my mind. Then Dave, then Beth. They would never know what happened to me. Like many of the families that had no closure on a missing loved one.

Would they have a funeral for me?

Would people say as many nice things about me as they did for Samuel? Blake wouldn't. He hated me. I tried to bring down his family and the faith they practiced.

It felt like a knife twisted in my gut. I didn't want Blake to hate me forever.

I wanted him to like me. *Maybe even love me.*

That would be asking too much.

You're a hypocrite, Gwen. Robert poked at me with his words.

I sat up. "What do you mean?"

There you are, thinking about Blake as someone to love, to marry even.

"So what?"

So you had no such thoughts when you believed he was a minimum-wage chauffeur. Are you so sure you're looking for love and marriage? Or just a trophy? Someone to parade around to prove you still have it? That you're desirable?

"I told you to leave me alone, Robert." Maybe I needed to be wanted and loved by a man just one more time before I died. But there wasn't time now. Death was drawing so near. So near I could feel its breath on my neck.

In the silence, I heard a soft *tap-tap-tap.*

Water was dripping from the opening overhead. Standing,

I shuffled to the spot and put my hand under the drip, then moved so the water would land in my mouth.

Liquid dirt.

I spit it out, but the mud coated the inside of my mouth. I coughed and spit, trying to clear the muck.

Wanting to cry again, I sat opposite Grady.

The drips continued to tap on the floor, pooling slightly.

"In the dark, could you hear the rain above you? Imagine the rain wetting your tongue?"

The liquid formed a tiny stream that drifted toward the body.

Pushing off the floor, I hobbled closer to Grady, tracking the tiny rivulet. It brushed against his shoe, then disappeared under his leg. I moved still closer to the body. The water appeared to be absorbed by the denim of his pants.

"How terrible your death was, Grady. In agony with two broken legs. Thirsty, but with no way to get water. Alone, betrayed by your son."

Except for God. Did Grady have a meltdown? In the end, did he curse God?

The seeping rainwater stopped.

There was something important about what I'd just seen. I looked at the ceiling, then at the point where the drips struck the floor. Water. *What's the message, God? Couldn't You at least give me a hint?*

I was cold, thirsty, hungry, and my brain was fuzzy. The stone walls kept the temperature even cooler than the outside air. "Okay, Gwen, take it slowly. Leaking ceiling?" I wrapped my arms around myself, trying to preserve heat. The air seemed to pierce right through the material.

I stood perfectly still.

Water. Cold. Pierce. I reread Grady's note. *Cold*, then a triangle and line. Could they be connected, forming an arrow? Shuffling behind Grady to the side of the cave the partial arrow pointed to, I bent over and inspected the ground. A tiny channel of disturbed earth disappeared in the rocks and dirt against the wall.

I plucked a hair off my head and held it toward the piled debris.

It moved slightly away from the wall.

CHAPTER THIRTY-TWO

WITH MY ABRADED HANDS, I GRABBED, SHOVED, and pushed the rocks out of my way, exposing more dirt. *It has to be here somewhere.* Finally I found a small opening, undoubtedly created over many years by water seeking an escape from the natural cave. Now I could feel the cool air on my sweaty face. I renewed my efforts, enlarging the hole. The earth gave way to a rocky opening, roughly two feet across and a foot high. *Thank You, God. Thank You!*

I lay on my stomach and peered inside. A pinpoint of light shone at the other end. It appeared to be about eight feet away.

Trying to swallow, I found my spit had long dried like an Arizona summer. I could reach the end, but I'd have to crawl into the tiny space.

I hated small spaces.

Maybe someone could hear me from this opening? "Help! Help me! Can anyone hear me?"

No sound, just that elusive hint of sunlight. A light that would fade as the day progressed.

Are you going to crawl in there in the dark? Wait here for someone who will never come? In the meantime, you're getting weaker and less able to get out, and a sadistic rapist could find your daughter.

Thinking of Aynslee, I could hear her clear voice—was it just one day ago?—when she'd recited my favorite verse. *"Run with endurance the race that is set before us."*

I sucked in a shaky breath. "That's all you have to do, Gwen. Endure."

My body balked at the task ahead. My hands burned from the dirt now embedded in the cuts. My ankle throbbed. Glancing over my shoulder, the still body of the entombed Grady seemed to say, *Don't end up like me. Climb in there or die.*

Returning to Grady's body, I slipped his wedding ring off his finger and into my pocket next to the note and the pocket watch. If I ever got out of here, I wanted evidence to prove Devin killed his father.

Rolling back onto my stomach, I edged forward until my head and shoulders were in the hole. The space ahead narrowed even more. I wiggled ahead.

My bulky sweater caught on the jagged rocks overhead and held tight.

I couldn't move.

I screamed and shoved. After an eternity, I clambered backward and out of the tunnel, leaving the sweater still attached to the rock inside the hole.

Shaking all over, I ended up sitting cross-legged outside the opening. I couldn't take the chance that my clothing would catch on something. I'd be stuck and become permanently enshrined in that stone coffin.

Bile rose in the back of my throat at the thought.

The bottom of the sweater was within arm's reach. I snagged it, jiggled it free, and pulled it out. The thick, knitted fabric felt so warm.

Don't linger or hypothermia will set in.

Retrieving the knife from where I'd thrown it, I had to wait for my hands to stop quaking before I opened it. I cut the top of the sleeve slightly and started unraveling. Once I had a pile of yarn, I placed the knife with Grady's note in the pocket and stepped out of my baggy warm-up pants. After tying a knot in each leg I poked holes in the slippers, sliding them to the end near the knots, followed by my panties. My bra, holding the prosthetic breasts, went next, and finally the sweater, which I evenly distributed. It looked like half a body doing the splits. I tied the yarn to the other pant leg. Once free of the cave, I'd drag my clothes out and get dressed. A dicey move, but I'd risk being naked over being buried alive.

The icy floor radiated up my legs. I shivered. Swiftly I tied the yarn around one ankle, then got on my hands and knees. The opening looked even smaller than before, the light farther away.

With endurance, Lord. Help me do this.

I lay on my stomach. My whole body rebelled at the stone floor's cold hardness. *Go. Now.* I started forward, my gaze firmly on the light ahead of me.

The rough surface scratched and dug at my skin. I used my torn and bloody fingers to pull me ahead. Slowly, so slowly, the tiny tunnel engulfed me.

The space narrowed. The rock sides closed in, the roof pressed down.

I heard whimpering. It was me. *What if there's a cave-in?* I would be buried alive just as surely as the legendary Octavia Hatcher. Only without a monument.

The cave grew smaller yet. I had to turn my head sideways and put my arms straight forward, blocking the light. The stone sarcophagus was inches from my face. *Oh please, oh please.* Wasted tears burned down my frozen face. Goose pimples erupted over my shaking body. My teeth chattered.

No longer able to bend my elbows, my fingers and toes inched me forward. The space grew narrower yet. I panted for air, choking on the dust.

The ragged ceiling caught on my shoulders, halting my creeping movement. I couldn't take a deep breath. I dug with my toes, willing my body to go forward. Another inch.

The rock compressed my lungs. Breathing was difficult. I fought back blind panic. *With endurance, Lord, help me.* Another inch. The stone bit into my skin, tearing gouges. My blood warmed my frozen skin briefly before congealing.

Sharp jabs came from ripped toenails as I shoved harder, snaking another inch. My sprained ankle howled in protest. How far had I covered? How far to the other side, to freedom? My fingers groped desperately for the opening at the end, encountering only more rock.

A final shove and my shoulders were free. I sucked in dusty air, coughed, and sent more dirt into the confined space. My feet and hands were numb from the cold. My fingers fumbled, trying to grip the rocks. *Endure.*

Groveling forward, my hips now caught in the constricted space. I gave a mighty shove with my feet, jamming myself firmly in its grip.

I was stuck.

My fingers grappled for something to pull me free. The ground was smooth. I cried, pounded the earth, and finally screamed. The sound deafened me. Earth filled my mouth. I didn't have any saliva to spit it out.

There wasn't enough air. I couldn't breathe. I couldn't . . .

I was having a dream. A nightmare. I'd open my eyes—

Nothing happened. I was still horizontal, on my stomach, in the rock casket. Dirt clogged my nose and mouth. My hips were firmly caught in the cave. My face pressed against my arm, stretched ahead of me. The stone leached the last of my body heat.

I was going to die.

But I didn't want to die. Not like this. I wanted to see my daughter graduate from college. Get married and start a family. I wanted to hold my grandbabies.

"God. If You get me out of this, I'll fight the cancer. I'll live as long as possible, until You call me home."

No miracle, bright light, angel, or savior appeared. The words of Job came to me, and I whispered them. "Naked I came from my mother's womb, and naked shall I return . . ." *And no one will ever find my naked body.* Moving my arms slightly, I folded my hands together and prayed. *Oh, Lord, forgive my sins. Make my death swift. Watch over my daughter and keep her safe.*

The cold was so intense I could barely feel my fingers. They felt wet and slippery.

Maybe my hands were crying. That was okay. I was getting warm. So warm . . .

"Mom."

251

I heard my daughter's voice.

"Mommy."

She needed me. I had to wake up. Fight. Endure. Focus. Hands don't cry.

Feeling the rough tunnel floor, I slid my hands sideways. A sharp edge.

I puzzled over that for a moment, my brain fuzzy. A sharp edge on the side . . . I could grip it . . . but what about the hand tears . . . Rotating my other hand, I found a corresponding sharp rock. Rocks with edges. The edge. The outside opening of the cave.

With renewed strength, I grabbed the rocks at the opening and pulled forward. Skin tore from my bottom and hips. I shoved with my feet, ignoring the pain of my sprained ankle. The jagged stone encasing my hips dug deeper into my flesh.

Pausing, I sucked in ragged dirty air. One last try. One . . . two . . . three. I heaved forward, arm straining, feet thrusting, skin flaying.

The rock I was gripping broke, starting a slide of stones bouncing off my exposed hands. Cold air washed over me. My bloody hips and bottom slid free. I could turn my head and look forward. Glorious gray sky appeared in the enlarged opening. I wiggled onward. More rocks tumbled and slid over the widened hole. *Thank You—*

A freed boulder crashed down on my left hand.

Pain exploded up my arm. I screamed in agony.

The rockslide slowed, then stopped. I advanced using my elbows until I could cradle my broken hand. Misty rain joined my tears. The icy rain increased and I shivered uncontrollably.

"Mom." Aynslee's voice in my head pulled me from my cocoon

of misery. I didn't want to move. Crawling meant more pain. Fire burned my shoulders, hips, bottom. My ankle throbbed, my hand pounded.

"Mom, move." Aynslee's insistent urging reverberated in my brain.

I advanced, still using my elbows, until my shoulders were free of the cave. Ahead of me was a mountainside, misty with low-lying clouds. Below was a narrow rocky ledge, now covered with rocks and dirt from the slide. Below that, far below, were the tops of trees. With a sheer cliff in between.

CHAPTER THIRTY-THREE

WRIGGLING MY LEGS FREE, I CAREFULLY SAT ON the widened opening and pulled on the yarn attached to my ankle, praying the material wouldn't break. Slowly, slowly my pants emerged. I fumbled the sweater out first and tugged it on, moaning as it passed over my injured hand. Rather than exposing my left arm where I'd had to unravel the yarn, I left it inside the sweater, bunching it inward to form a slight sling. The rain quickly dampened the sweater, but the wool maintained what little body heat I had.

The knots in the yarn and pant legs resisted my one-handed attempts to undo them. I used my teeth and emptied out the slippers, bra, and panties. I pulled on the pants, then slipped my icy, bluish feet into the slippers.

Never had anything felt so good.

I drew my right arm through the sleeve so it was next to my body, tucked my broken hand in my lap, and curled up my legs. I smelled of wet wool, sweat, and dirt. Tilting my head back, I let the rainwater drop into my mouth, then spit it out to rinse out the dust.

I'd move as soon as I got warmer. Or maybe I could just stay here until someone found me.

A big dollop of rain plopped on my neck and slithered down my back.

On the other hand, movement would warm me. So would getting out of the rain.

My bra and panties lay beside me. Putting on the bra one-handed was out of the question, and I didn't need the extra weight. I could chuck the bra over the cliff, a fitting end to the prosthetics I'd named Thelma and Louise . . . but if I left it here, it could help me find Grady and give him a proper burial.

The panties were another matter. I didn't want anyone to find my industrial-strength, sold-six-to-a-package, white cotton briefs. A swift kick and they went sailing over the ledge.

Lowering my legs, I tested the ledge. It seemed sturdy enough. Gradually I eased more and more of my weight until I stood on the narrow surface. Below me was a sheer cliff, ending in a pile of rocks. Above me was more rock, but not as steep. The ledge continued on either side before petering out.

I'd have to climb up. With a broken hand and sprained ankle.

Reluctantly I drew my good arm out of the sweater, leaving my broken hand inside. My slippers were loose-fitting with a smooth bottom. I wouldn't be able to climb in them, but would need them when I reached level ground. I wound the yarn around the slippers, then wrapped the ends around my waist, creating a shoe fanny pack.

The yarn was tight enough that it cinched my sweater at the

bottom. After I pulled the sweater looser in the front, my broken hand rested in the knitted sling.

I patted my pockets to be sure the watch, ring, note, and knife were all accounted for.

Turning toward the hillside, I mapped my route. Although rather steep, a number of shrubs and small trees had taken hold. The real problem could be the wet stone and loose gravel. I stepped to the cave opening, then reached up and grabbed a sturdy shrub. A few test pulls assured me it would hold. I took a deep breath and climbed to the bush. Above that and to my left was a smaller tree. I could reach it, but would have to reach across my body or use my left wrist. Reluctantly I pulled my arm from the sweater sling. My hand was swollen to double its size and my fingers were turning into purple sausages.

I searched for a foothold with my foot, finally hooking a thin outcropping. Stretching sideways, I reached for the tree and hooked my wrist over it.

The stone broke under my foot. I let go of the shrub and lunged for the tree. I caught it just as my wrist slipped. I clung there for a moment, breathing quickly. I'd barely climbed a foot above the cave opening.

The rain slowed to a drizzle. It seemed darker. If night came before I could climb this slope . . .

The next tree was larger, a pine, and almost directly overhead. I pulled myself up onto the tree I was clinging to, then carefully stood, holding on to a tiny ridge. The tree bent but held my weight. Wrapping my left arm around the pine, I moved upward.

Another shrub, this one big enough that I risked a glance behind me.

I clutched the bush harder, not willing to move. I'd traversed the hill far enough that the ledge was no longer under me. If I slipped, I'd drop directly down the cliff to the woods far below. Burying my face in my arm, I closed my eyes. I could smell the tang of the pine and odor of wet earth. "Endure. Just . . . endure." I stayed motionless for a few moments, until the damp chill started to replace the heat of my exertion.

"Come on, Gwen, get tough." I found the next small tree to grab, but loathed letting go of the bush.

The rocks grew more jagged, providing hand- and foot-holds, but tearing at my clothing and flesh. I tested each one before committing my weight to it. One outcropping caught my sweater at the shoulder, ripping a hole and stabbing into my skin.

I gasped at the new assault of pain but didn't stop to see the damage.

Slowly, painfully, I scrabbled up the slope until my burning muscles gave out. I'd reached a good-sized maple and I hugged it like a life raft. I couldn't feel my bare feet, my hand pounded with every heartbeat, and I was soaking wet and freezing. If I just closed my eyes for a moment and rested . . . I was so sleepy . . .

A stream of images passed through my mind. The sketches I'd done of the snake handlers. Aynslee getting baptized. Blake's piercing gaze. Ruby and Elijah outside the police station. Blanche telling the story of Octavia Hatcher being buried alive. Junior's fluttering hands. Clay appearing in my hotel room. Samuel's ravaged face. Grady's Bible. Trish's body. Aynslee at Ruby and Elijah's—

A thought slammed into my brain like a steamroller. Devin believed he'd taken care of me, that I was as good as dead. What if, after dumping me into that cave, he'd gone back to the cabin? Sooner or later, Aynslee would show up looking for me.

"What if Devin is someone she knows?" My voice shook as much as I did. Grady's Bible didn't show a birth date for Devin. His mother married in 1978 and died five years later. Devin would be somewhere in his midthirties. That eliminated Clay. Too old. But not his son. Junior was adopted. And that fit Grady's words *The boy was strange*. Clay could be protecting his son, maybe even helping. And Clay would be more likely to send the victims away rather than let his son kill them. He had money, or at least acted like he did, according to Beth.

But Arless had money. Scads of it. And a reputation he needed to protect. He owned the cabin, so that part was easy. And women would find him handsome, so it wouldn't take much to get them to go with him. Initially. The FBI profile commented on how easily he found his victims, mentioning homeless shelters. Didn't Trish say the Campbells helped fund a homeless shelter?

But why would he put up the money to bring me out as a forensic artist?

Wellington was also in the right age range. He'd arrived at about the same time as the rapes started. But he'd needed a map to find the cabin, a map I'd found under the groceries. Trish was usually with him. But I didn't cross him off my list.

You're forgetting someone. I didn't want to consider it, but Blake could be added to my list. He had the money, grew up in the area, and was wildly handsome.

And he wears gold, wire-rimmed glasses. Just like my composite from the surveillance still. And he had a black pickup.

I didn't want it to be Blake.

Let's face it, Aynslee would easily trust any of them. He'd just tell her he was going to drive her to me. I had to find her.

I shoved against the maple to sit up. The day was rapidly drawing to a close, and daylight was fading fast. *Get to the next tree or bush.*

An oak stood about five feet away. There was something strange about it. I bit my lip and tried to work it out. My brain was full of cotton batting. *Let's see. The oak is . . . slightly above me and . . .*

Slightly above.

I'd reached the top of the hill.

Instead of climbing with hands and feet, I could stand and walk. Or hobble. I made it to the oak, then leaned against its bark. The slippers were still fastened around my waist with the yarn. I pulled out the knife to cut the wool, but the blade was folded into the handle. It would take two hands to open it. I stuffed the knife back into my pocket, then pulled on one strand of the yarn. It tightened and squeezed my waist, but didn't break.

I sat and leaned against the tree. *Just give up.*

No. I had to get to Aynslee. I pulled on the slippers until the yarn was loose around them and tight around my stomach. Working one slipper back and forth, I tugged it out, followed by the second. I dropped them to the ground and jammed my frozen feet into place.

The drizzle stopped and I stood and looked around. I had no idea where I was. The mountains rolled around me in endless uniformity. No sounds carried in the breeze beyond the *shuuusssss* of tossing trees and soft plops as rain-drenched leaves dropped. The light was fading, turning the dusky sky to dreary gray.

Go downhill. *Right.* I was at the top of the mountain. The

only downhill that wasn't an option was the direction from which I just came. *Think about it. Reason it out.* The opening to Grady's tomb was fifteen feet overhead. The tunnel I'd just climbed out was level with the floor. I climbed up a cliff more than fifteen feet to get here. Therefore the way into the cave would be around here somewhere.

That meant something. I couldn't concentrate; instead, my brain seemed focused on all the throbbing injuries.

You are out of time.

Okay, okay. The opening . . . the opening you were thrown down. Someone had to have brought you up here. Someone dragged you from a car or truck. A car needs a road.

I scanned the area around me again, this time paying attention to the ground. A grove of trees with an outcropping of limestone boulders stood to my right. I hobbled over to them. At first I didn't see anything. Circling the area, I discovered what I was looking for: a narrow track where the fallen leaves were thinner. Someone pulled my marginally conscious body through here.

There wasn't time to look for the cave entrance. I followed the barely discernible path made by my dragged body into the rising mist of the evening.

CHAPTER THIRTY-FOUR

THE ROAD—WIDE DIRT TRACK, REALLY—WAS just out of sight of the top of the hill. I slid down the last few feet, raising new shrieks of protest from my gouged bottom. The lane crested the hill at this point, then disappeared downhill in both directions. I kicked four rocks into a line to mark the spot, then listened for any sound of human habitation. An owl hooted somewhere behind me. Who knew how deep in the rolling Appalachian mountains I'd been driven or how far it was to civilization? Squinting in the gathering dusk, I checked for lights. Nothing appeared in either direction. "Lord, anytime now You can send a sign."

The faintest whistle of a train blew in the distance to my right. I turned to that route. Even though the road was downhill, I soon panted with the exertion. I tried to put as little weight as possible on my sprained ankle, which meant I walked with a half-hopping step. The jarring motion reverberated up to my broken hand. The minutes crawled by, the last of the rain clouds passed, the temperature dropped, and the daylight faded.

I tried to get my mind off my situation by thinking about the mummified face of Grady. I'd seen that face before. Or was I just remembering the photograph? Devin might resemble his father. I superimposed the faces of all of my suspects over his image. Nothing.

Devin grew up in Pikeville, at least until he was in his midteens. Wouldn't he have been easily identified when he returned home? Unless some plastic surgery was involved, which would take money. Surgery plus time. Grady had been in that cave for close to twenty years. A lot could change in twenty years.

All the murders and rapes began about six months ago. There had to be a trigger that set Devin off. Wellington arrived then. Blake's fiancée left him. I didn't know about Junior or Arless, but I'd find out.

I tried not to think about the time passing as I walked— make that hobbled—off the mountain. I needed transportation.

The road leveled somewhat, but I found it harder and harder to see. I increased my pace but still seemed to move at a crawl. The moon came out, casting blue light over the landscape.

A waft of air brought the scent of fresh hay and manure.

I stopped and listened.

A horse snorted.

The road took a sharp left turn. I hurried as fast as I could, then slowed just before the turn. If I found a house, the logical thing to do would be to ask to use their phone and call the sheriff. In this case, though, I wasn't sure who I could trust.

Even if no one was home, I'd probably find dogs on guard duty. Fortunately I was downwind of the farm, which bought me time to get the layout of the land.

I peered around the turn. Instead of a barn, a small clearing with a makeshift corral held two horses. I knew this spot. Those were Blake's horses.

The black pickup and two-horse trailer were missing.

Approaching the corral, my heart sank.

Blake's and Aynslee's horses were gone. Remaining were the packhorse and the high-spirited bay who'd tried to buck me off. Both horses eyed me as I drew near.

There you go, Gwen. Transportation.

Blake must have had the saddles and bridles in the horse trailer. How would I ride without a bridle? On an ornery, crow-hopping horse? With a broken hand?

I could just wait. Blake would return for the remaining two steeds.

But the amount of hay on the ground looked like the horses could be here for the night. I had to get to my daughter. And Blake would still be mad enough at me that he may simply refuse to help.

You think he's angry with you now, just wait until more serpent handlers die, like Ruby and Elijah. His own family members.

My breath caught at the thought. I couldn't let that happen.

The bay wore a halter, but no lead ropes hung conveniently from a fence post. Crossing to where the trailer had been parked, I searched the ground, moving back to the corral. I found what I was looking for: two loops of orange twine that had originally held the bales of hay together. Tied to the halter, the loops were too short to work as reins, but if I cut them open, they'd be long enough.

Pulling out the pocket knife, I placed it in my broken hand. My sausage fingers refused to close over it. *Come on, time's wasting.* I placed the knife on the ground and braced it under my foot. When I tried to pry the blade open, my slippers were too loose and floppy to hold it. I kicked off my slippers, shivering at the feel of the cold earth, and braced the knife with my toes. The blade remained stubbornly closed.

Grunting with exertion, I tried a different angle. The blade opened partway. I flipped the knife over and used the earth to pry the blade completely open. I sliced the looped baling twine, then entered the corral. The packhorse snorted and moved away, but the bay continued to eat. I quickly caught him and awkwardly tied the twine to his halter.

I'd have to mount the horse outside the corral. I wouldn't be able to control my ride and open the gate with one hand. If I failed, or was bucked off, the horse would run.

"Nice horse, good horse." I patted his shoulder. Blake had helped me mount before, so getting on Rowdy's back would be a challenge. He obligingly followed me outside the corral. Climbing up the side of the fence, I threw my leg over his back and slipped on. I had just enough time to grab a chunk of mane before he bolted.

CHAPTER THIRTY-FIVE

THE HORSE PLUNGED AHEAD AT A DEAD GALLOP. I desperately clung to his back with my legs. My one good hand held a chunk of mane. The twine reins were useless for control.

Night had fallen. I could see nothing and had no idea where we were going except downhill. Cold, damp air whipped past my face and body. *Lord, don't let the horse stumble or fall.* I leaned forward for better balance. My broken hand, still inside my sweater, pounded with the drumbeat of the horse's hooves.

We raced for what seemed like hours. I tried to picture our route from the day before. *Has it just been one day since the revival?* Blake had driven a few miles from the corral until he reached the main highway. How far had the horse run? What would happen when we reached the main road?

The bay's easy breathing became labored. My strength ebbed, hand cramped, legs felt like cooked spaghetti. If the horse swerved, I wouldn't be able to hang on. The horse's sweat warmed my legs, but the salt seeped through my warm-up pants and burned the skin torn in my escape from the cave.

The headlong gallop became a canter. Car headlights danced through the trees ahead and the sound of engines grew and faded. The scent of wet pavement joined that of woodsmoke.

The canter became a walk.

I took a deep, shuddering breath. *You're almost there. Turn right at the highway. Elijah and Ruby's house is just another mile or so.*

The what-ifs loomed in my brain. What if Junior or Clay were patrolling the highway? Or anyone on my list of suspects? What if the horse bolted again when he saw cars?

What if it was too late and Devin already had Aynslee? He'd had the time. I'd been gone for over a day.

Clenching my teeth at the last thought, I urged the bay to a slow trot. The bouncing gait jarred my hand and foot, but it took my mind off useless speculation.

I stopped the horse behind a line of trees just before the road and watched for a few moments. Only a couple of cars buzzed past.

Once again I urged the horse forward, crossed the road, and turned toward the oncoming traffic. The dark horse would be hard to see in the inky night. Two trucks drove by, slowed beside me, then sped on. A car also reduced speed when its headlights picked us out. As they drew abreast, they rolled down the windows. Spider-Man and a pirate stuck their heads out.

I blinked rapidly. Neither Spider-Man nor the pirate disappeared. I was hallucinating.

"Nice costume," Spider-Man called out before the car picked up speed.

Of course. Halloween. People dressed up. I probably looked like the living dead.

We encountered only one other vehicle, an SUV, before I

saw the small turnoff to Ruby and Elijah's house. I kicked my tired mount to a slow canter to cross the road and go up the driveway.

No lights showed in the windows.

My heart sank.

Were they gone? A white Toyota Camry sat in front of the house.

Maybe everyone had gone to bed. I had no idea what time it was.

Sliding off the horse, I ended up on the ground, my legs too rubbery to hold me up. The bay sniffed my hair, then lightly bumped my head with his muzzle. I stroked his velvety nose. "Yeah, I know. Give me a minute."

Finally I pushed off the ground, then held on to the horse's withers until I could stand. I limped to the nearby gate that led to the cow pasture and turned Rowdy loose, then hobbled to the house.

I knocked on the front door. "Hello? Ruby? Elijah? I'm sorry to be so late. It's me, Gwen."

No lights turned on. The house was as still as a tomb. I knocked again, harder. Still no sign of life. I grabbed the doorknob and turned it. Unlocked. Slowly I pushed the door open, encountering slight resistance. The smell of something burning assailed me.

Directly in front of me I heard a distinctive sound. A slow *chchch*, then speeding to a continuous *cheeeeeeeeeeheeeeeeeeeeeeeeee*.

I groped for a light switch on the wall beside me, found it, and flipped it on, illuminating the space like a stage.

The room was crawling with snakes.

Lying in the middle of the floor were two bodies. Ruby and

Elijah. I recognized them more from the clothing than appearance. The june bug–blue, bloated flesh distorted their faces and exposed skin. Ruby had clutched the rug under her in agony. Elijah had his arm thrown across her body. A large rattlesnake glided across Ruby's back. A smaller snake, with a flat, triangular head and dark banded body, curled under Elijah's leg.

My heart raced. My feet seemed rooted to the floor, my hand frozen on the light switch.

Where is Aynslee?

I searched every inch of the room. Snakes, big, oxide-brown rattlers and darker snakes with white mouths, slithered or coiled under furniture. The warning rattle came from the canebrake rattler in front of me. Another snake, raw sienna and burnt umber in color, raised its large, flat head and was flicking the air with a split tongue. Burnt-sienna copperheads wound around the walls.

The open door to my left proved to be the snake room. Empty cages and upturned Plexiglas containers filled the space. A pile of laundry lay tossed on the table that had earlier held Samuel's memorial display. Car keys rested next to a battered black purse and beige sweater on the coffee table. The stench of burning food grew even stronger.

Prying my hand from the switch I'd flipped, I stepped away from the front door, leaving it open. I didn't know much about snakes, but I did know they were cold-blooded and liked warmth. Maybe the cooler outside air coming through the open door would drive them into the warmer snake room.

I hobbled across the porch to the window on the side of the house and peered in. The room was too dark to see clearly. The next window was high and frosted. The bathroom. I stumbled forward in the darkness, now trailing my hand against the house, until I found another window. No scrap of light helped me see in. Turning the corner, a glow came from a door at the back of the house. I paused, picturing the layout. This would be the kitchen. The snakes were in the living room with the doors shut to the other rooms. The kitchen should be safe. Aynslee had to be in there. I opened the door. Rancid smoke billowed past me. The glow came from a burning pot on the stove.

Rushing across the room as fast as my swollen ankle would allow, I turned off the burner. A wooden spoon sat in a spoon rest next to the stove. I used it to shove the pot off the burner. It looked like the remnants of dinner left on low. Probably keeping it warm for me.

I'd been gone for over twenty-four hours. This must have happened within hours of my leaving for the cabin.

Fire still licked upward from the contents of the pan. I spun around, looking for a fire extinguisher. No extinguisher, but the lid to the pot was by the sink. I grabbed the lid with a pot holder and shoved it into place.

More smoke filled the room, this time from the white-painted cabinet over the stove. Using the wooden spoon, I nudged the door open.

Several boxes of cereal puffed into flame.

I spun and turned on the kitchen faucet. A thin stream of water came out, not enough to make a dent in the inferno. The fire grew, lapping around the cabinet's wooden edges.

Turning my back on the flames, I forced my brain to analyze the scene.

The table held a single place setting. The rest of the room was tidy. Elijah and Ruby had expected me to return. But when a car drove up, it wasn't me returning for Aynslee. It was Devin. He must have tied everyone up, then forced Aynslee into the car before returning to turn all the snakes loose.

I clutched the counter to keep from crumpling to the floor. I *had* to be calm. *Focus.*

The heat grew, pushing me from the room. I limped outside. The stale odor of my own sweat replaced the smell of burning wood. Bile rose in my throat.

This was designed as another "accident." *Oh dear, the snakes got loose, bit both Ruby and Elijah as they tried to catch them. In her hurry to catch the serpents, Ruby forgot to turn off the burner under dinner.*

Sarah was missing along with Aynslee. He'd probably taken them to the cabin. I couldn't get back on Blake's bay and gallop after them. That was too far and I was too injured.

Elijah's car was parked next to the house.

But I'd have to go into the living room to retrieve the car keys. What would smoke and fire do to the snakes? Would they want to get away, or would it make them angry and aggressive? I limped to the front of the house, up the stairs, and to the open door where I could see into the living room.

The snakes were still there, restlessly slithering around each other. A few had crawled into the snake room, the room off the living room that Blake had prevented me from entering during Samuel's memorial service. A thick cloud of smoke poured in from around the kitchen door toward the open front door. The car keys were in the middle of the room on the coffee table.

A long black snake with faint, light yellow markings glided across the bare floor, stopping beneath the table. It looked different from the other snakes.

I shuddered. Something about that serpent made me want to run.

The pile of laundry on the table moved.

The hairs on my neck stood on end.

Sarah uncovered her face. Her eyes were unfocused and glazed.

The black snake whipped its head in her direction and raised its upper body. Its neck widened and flattened, forming a hood.

King cobra.

CHAPTER THIRTY-SIX

I DIDN'T HAVE TIME TO WAIT. SARAH LOOKED like she'd been bitten. Her parents must have shoved her to the table before they succumbed to their bites. She had to get to a hospital. And I had to get to her.

The smoke increased, burning my eyes, filling my lungs. I coughed. The kitchen door glowed around the edges. I should have found a scarf or something to cover my mouth.

My legs and feet had no protection from snake venom, just the thin material of the warm-up pants and slippers. I didn't have time to find something to protect myself. I wouldn't even be able to sneak through with this sprained ankle. The snakes would feel the vibration of my thumping step and see me clearly.

"Okay, God, I said I'd talk, so here's the deal. I don't know what anointing feels like, but I could use some of that now." I waited for something to change, a tingling, or warmth, or prickly feeling. I felt only my racing heart, the sweat under my arms, my dry mouth.

Sarah moaned.

Painstakingly I tugged my broken hand from the sweater sling. My fingers were bigger than before, the bruising more spectacular, the pain more intense. *How are you going to pick up that little girl?*

Shoving the question away, I took a step into the room. The angry rattler shook his tail. *Cheeeeeeeeeeheeeeeeeeeeeeeee.*

I moved sideways, away from its coiled body. Its head, with the vertical, catlike pupils, watched me. I put my hurt foot down.

A snake twisted under my slipper.

I screamed, jerked my foot upward, then clamped my hand over my mouth. *Quiet!*

Snakes are deaf. The rational thought didn't help. I coughed again.

Sarah shifted restlessly. She could easily roll off the table. And the cobra was just below.

Carefully I looked for a clear place to step. The snakes were everywhere, moving away from the fire and the freezing air from the open door, making the floor look like it was undulating.

Taking a shuddering breath, I took another step. A slithering body skated past my ankle. Just two more steps and I'd be at the coffee table where the car keys lay. Another three and I'd be next to Sarah. And the cobra.

Step-hop. A smaller rattler let me know I was too close. "Oh, Lord. Anytime now. Anoint away." Step-hop. Just a little farther. Step-hop.

I snatched the keys and put them in my pocket. On impulse, I picked up the sweater.

Sarah rolled slightly. Her body now teetered just on the edge of the table. The cobra reared up, fanning its hood, and hissed.

I threw the sweater. It landed near the snake.

With lightning speed, the cobra struck the fabric.

I froze.

A rattler coiled and shook its tail to my left.

The cobra turned away from the sweater and slithered under a nearby chair.

Sarah rolled off the table and hit the floor with a thud. Several more snakes coiled and shook their tails.

I limped forward, coughing, and ignored the warning rattles. Kneeling by the prone girl, the air was clearer, but I couldn't stop coughing. Her breathing was rapid and shallow. Her left leg had swollen and turned reddish.

Lifting her gently with my right hand, I slipped my left under her shoulders. I couldn't grip with my hand. I'd just have to pray she wouldn't struggle. I got my other arm under her knees. Now all I had to do was stand up.

Although the child was only six and small, she was over forty pounds of deadweight. My strength was running on empty. I tried to stand. My legs refused to work.

Another snake joined in the rattling, adding to the soft hissing sound. The cobra slithered from under the chair.

I grabbed Sarah's arm and pulled her away from the cobra. Glancing over my shoulder, I blinked rapidly to clear my burning eyes. I located the open front door, then the path I would need to take. Taking a limping step backward, I dragged the child.

"Endure, endure," I softly whispered.

Sarah moaned and her face looked worse. I didn't have time to worry about avoiding the snakes, I had to get her to a hospital. I stopped looking where I put my feet. I staggered backward as quickly as I could.

Something caught on the back of my slipper. I fell, landing on my already injured backside on the front porch. I'd tripped over the doorjamb. Swiftly I tugged Sarah outside the living room, then crawled back to the door and slammed it shut. Returning to Sarah, I pulled her the remaining distance to the edge of the porch. I didn't want to pull her down the steps. Maybe I could lift her by kneeling on a step and—

A truck roared around the corner, spotlighting me with its headlights. It skidded to a stop, showering me with dust. The door slammed and Blake charged into the light.

I wanted to dive into his arms.

Grabbing Sarah with one arm and me with the other, he hauled us away from the burning house and to his truck. He let go of me and placed Sarah on the ground. "Elijah and Ruby?"

I shook my head.

Blake sprinted to the house. Just as he reached the porch, the fire blew out the front windows.

He threw up his arms and retreated to the truck. "Get in. I need to drive you both to the hospital."

"No. Take Sarah. She's been bitten."

"Don't argue with me. Get in!"

At that moment I wanted so badly to have someone take care of me. "No." I shook my head. "I need to find my daughter." I held up the car keys.

"We can take Sarah to the hospital and find her together."

"There's no time."

"I can't leave you like this."

His voice nearly melted my resolve. "You need to go. Save Sarah. I'll get Aynslee and meet you at the hospital."

He spun, jumped in the truck, then careened off. The

taillights blurred and hot tears slid down my face. At least Sarah had a chance.

I bit my lip and lowered my chin to my chest. *No time for this.* I moved to Elijah's car, got in, and started the engine. There was only one place my daughter could be. I just hoped I wasn't too late.

Even though I drove as fast as I could, it still took forever to get to the cabin. I drove past the driveway and parked the car around a corner and out of sight. I didn't want to be greeted by a rapist who had time to find a rifle. As I limped between the trees as quietly as possible, the cabin soon came into sight. No vehicles were parked in front, but the lights were on inside.

I paused and listened for any sound. Tonight even the crickets were silent. I'd gone up and down the porch steps enough times that I knew which ones squeaked. Light spilled from the partially curtained windows, creating golden rectangles on either side of the front door.

On the far side of the porch, away from the light, someone sat in one of the chairs.

My hand flew to my mouth to stifle the scream. I gripped the railing to keep from falling.

He didn't move.

I strained my eyes, trying to see who was sitting and waiting. Gradually the shape formed.

My clothes from the revival were still slung over the chair.

Taking a deep breath, I sidled to the window nearest the bed. The room was empty. All of my things—clothes, books, purse—everything was gone. The bed had been moved from the wall and now squatted in the middle of the open space, with the sofa pushed into the kitchen area. The bathroom door stood open. The camera inside the smoke alarm glowed red. Someone was watching—or recording.

Was Aynslee in the cellar snake room?

I grasped the window ledge. *Calm, calm.* I took several deep breaths.

I tried the door. Unlocked. Easing it open, I slipped through and listened.

If she were in the cellar, she might be unconscious, or hurt, or . . .

I didn't know how wide the camera lens would be, but I had to take a chance. Pressing up against the wall, I made my way until I reached the drawer that held the kitchen knives. I found one and slid around the room until I was standing near the trapdoor. With only one good hand, getting to the floor was a slow and painful task. I couldn't hold the knife and crawl with one hand, so I put it in my mouth and crawled slowly forward. Wedging the knife into the edge of the trapdoor, I pried it up until I could get my arm under the lip, then flipped it open. Even without much light, I could tell no one was down there, and the snake room hadn't been disturbed.

So where was my daughter?

I'd assumed Devin had her and had taken her here. But what if . . . what if Aynslee had gotten worried when I didn't return? What if, instead of getting Ruby to drive her to the cabin, she called Blanche and Arless looking for me? Arless was on my suspect list. He could have simply told her I was detained, picked her up, and taken her to his house. She'd have gone willingly. Tonight was the big Halloween party. Arless wouldn't have time to do anything to her. She was probably at the party right now, in costume, having the time of her life.

In fact, with the exception of Blake, all my suspects were probably at that party. Blake was at the hospital with Sarah. Probably.

I could just drive right up and retrieve her. No one had any idea where I was for the past day. Only Devin would be in shock that I was alive. He probably figured I was dead by now or at least suffering horribly.

There was only one problem with my plan. I didn't know who Devin was. Everyone at the party would be in costume and wearing masks. And Devin wore at least two masks.

Not knowing his identity meant that anyone I asked for help could be Devin. And my attempted murderer.

Trust no one.

I'd have to flush him out, lure the killer away from the party, and put him out of commission.

Studying the cabin space, I groped for ideas. If I had a gun, I'd be tempted to shoot him. Except I'd never shot anyone.

A small ax still rested by the stove.

A plan formed in my battered brain. It might work. *Lord, it had better work.*

It took me a few moments to climb to my feet. Still pressing against the wall, I limped to the corner of the room, snatched up the ax, and placed it near the front door.

Moving to the bed, I pulled Grady's note, ring, and watch from my pocket and placed them on the bedspread underneath the smoke-alarm camera. I flattened the note, looked again at the crosses on the ring, and reread the inscription on the watch. I held up each item long enough for anyone viewing through the recorder to see what I held.

I looked around the room, then into the open trapdoor in the floor. Picking up the items, I stashed them back in my pocket, then limped to the opening.

Gossamer spiderwebs crisscrossed below, and the bottom was shrouded in darkness.

I thought of my daughter.

Taking a deep breath, I got on my hands and knees and started down the rope ladder to the snake room cellar.

CHAPTER THIRTY-SEVEN

THE WEBS CLUNG TO ME, DRAPING OVER MY clothing. I tried to keep from whimpering, but a few escaped.

I waited long enough for the watcher to believe I'd hidden Grady's possessions in the cellar. The seconds ticked off in my brain.

Something plopped on my shoulder.

I screamed and tore back up the ladder, not stopping until I was free of the opening. Batting at my clothing and hair, I spun in a circle, ignoring the pain.

Stop it. Get a grip. I looked one last time into the cellar, then shut the trapdoor. Kicking the rug into place, I hobbled out the front door.

Devin had probably been the one to reset the cabin. He'd missed my clothes on the porch once. I hoped he'd miss them again. I crouched behind them, clutching the ax, just as a car raced up to the front of the cabin. I caught a glimpse of him as he jumped from the car.

I wasn't surprised at the identity of Devin, only the pistol in his hand.

That complicated things.

Breathing heavily, he charged up the steps and slammed the front door open.

I gripped the ax and pushed farther behind the chair and into the corner.

He cocked his head and quieted his breathing, then entered the room.

I stood, moved to the door, and peeked in.

He dropped to his knees and set the pistol on the floor, then pulled something out of his pocket and flicked it open. A switchblade.

I clamped my jaw shut.

Shoving the rug aside, he used the switchblade to pry open the trapdoor.

Swiftly folding the knife and tucking it into his pocket, he picked up the gun. Grasping the rope ladder with one hand, he started climbing down to the cellar.

I wiped my sweaty palms on my pants. Gripping the ax tighter, I crept forward. The tension on the ladder loosened.

Racing the last few feet, I brought the ax down on one side of the rope ladder. The rope split.

The man cursed.

Bang! The bullet smashed into the ceiling above the open trapdoor.

I ducked.

The remaining side of rope tightened as the man started climbing up. *Bang!* Another shot hit the ceiling.

I bit my lip and tasted blood. Swinging the ax as hard as I could, I struck the rope.

Bam! The bullet ricocheted off the ax blade.

The rope split but held.

His face appeared out of the gloomy depths, lips pulled from clenched teeth, glaring eyes showing white at the top. One hand gripped the rope, the other swung the pistol, taking aim at my head.

He couldn't miss at this distance.

I kicked his hand with my injured foot. He lost his balance and clutched at the rope ladder.

I swung the ax again, splitting the rope.

He dropped.

I slammed the trapdoor shut.

Bam, bam, bam! Bullets split the floorboards. I jumped away from the hail of shots and leaned against the wall. A second barrage of fire came from the cellar, blowing holes through the floor.

Gauging the distance I'd have to cover, I did some quick calculations. About twelve feet. Five or so jumps, assuming my sprained ankle would hold.

A lot of bullets.

I tossed the ax to my right. It smashed into the floor and skidded. Immediately the floorboards around it erupted in gunshot. A pause while he reloaded.

I ran.

Bullet holes punctuated my path to the door. I didn't stop until I crossed onto the porch. I caught myself on the railing and held on, afraid if I let go I'd not be able to stand again. My ears continued to ring from the sound of gunfire.

Now I just had to drive over to the Campbells' Halloween party and pick up Aynslee. Just as soon as my legs and hands stopped quivering.

All my things were missing, including my purse. Without a driver's license, I'd have to be careful not to get pulled over.

Devin's muted screams came from the cellar.

"See how you like being in a hole in the ground." My voice shook.

What had he told the others about my whereabouts? Had I solved all my problems by putting him out of business? Did he have allies?

I thought about the two men in Halloween costumes who commented on my appearance earlier in the evening. A costume at a costume party. My long skirt and blouse still hung over the chair where I'd left them. Snatching them up, I wrinkled my nose at the still-strong horse and campfire smell, then turned and hobbled across the porch and down the stairs. I already looked like Octavia Hatcher, with shredded nails and a broken hand. *If anyone sees me at the party, hopefully they'll think I'm wearing a costume with stage makeup, and not in need of serious medical attention.*

Pulling on the stinky long skirt and ugly blouse, I continued to shiver in the chilly night air, all my injuries protesting the movement. Clouds moved in, blanketing the night sky, and the only illumination was from a few stars. An owl hooted somewhere in the distance. The Stygian night was dense with unseen eyes and malevolent forces. Halloween night.

Devin's car blocked the driveway. I opened the door and the dome light came on, but no keys conveniently dangled from the ignition.

If he escaped, his car was far too handy. I looked around the yard, straining my eyes in the dark.

A snake coiled by the front steps.

CHAPTER THIRTY-EIGHT

I GASPED. IT TOOK ME A MOMENT TO PROCESS that the snake wasn't moving. I wiped the sweat off my face, then limped over to the coiled garden hose. Once I turned the hose on, I dragged it to the car, unscrewed the gas cap, and shoved in the hose.

I found my way to Ruby and Elijah's car and started it. Putting the car into gear, I turned around, heading toward Pikeville. Driving with one hand wasn't hard, but using my left foot on the brake and accelerator was. Total exhaustion threatened to take over, and I had to use every ounce of energy to focus and drive. And to pray no police officer pulled me over.

Most of the houses I passed had turned off their porch lights, and many were dark. The trick-or-treaters were long since finished going door to door. The car's digital clock showed 11:15.

Maybe crashing the Halloween party to rescue a daughter who didn't know she needed rescuing wasn't a great idea. I could call the state police.

Yeah, right. I could hear that conversation.

"911, what's your emergency?"

"Hi, I just caught Devin, a murderer and probably the Hillbilly Rapist and—"

"That person is dead. Shot by police."

"No. Not really. I mean, he's actually in the cellar, well, make that the snake room—"

"Where is this . . . snake room?"

"Oh, gosh, I don't know the address. He's shooting holes up through the floor, but to him it would be the ceiling—"

"Someone is shooting a gun?"

"Well, yes, but he's not the problem, at least not right now because he can't get out. It's my daughter, who's attending a Halloween party, but she thinks it's just a party—"

No, it would take too much time to convince someone that I wasn't a nutjob.

I could call Blake. I wanted, *needed* to hear his voice. He would have delivered Sarah to the hospital by now and she would be getting treatment. Maybe he could get away and help us. I'd just have to apologize for stealing his horse and putting his family and friends into mortal danger. And indirectly killing his cousins, Ruby and Elijah.

Ruby and Elijah were both dead because of their religious practices. As were a bunch of other folks. Everyone who'd been identified as belonging to that church had been systematically killed by Devin, starting with his own father.

If Blake hadn't found my sketches, all of the serpent handlers would be identified and murdered.

I tried not to go through a series of what-ifs on the way to the party.

A patrol car came toward me, driving slowly.

Here's your chance to get help, get someone to go in with you and get Aynslee. And what? I had no identification. I looked like the walking dead. And this officer could work for Clay.

I waited until the car was closer, then leaned forward and looked down as if adjusting something on the dashboard. From this angle I couldn't see the driver.

As soon as the patrol car drove by, I checked the rearview mirror. No lights or siren.

I found the correct street and turned, then coasted slowly past the Campbell house. Cars lined the street and all the windows glowed with light. Rock-and-roll music pounded the air. A fake cemetery, complete with a skeleton crawling out of the ground, decorated the front yard. It reminded me of Octavia Hatcher and my own clambering from the bowels of the earth.

I shivered, then turned the car heater up.

The pavement ended at a cul-de-sac. The parking for the Campbell party had spilled up the street, and I didn't spot any open spaces. Taking a chance that the owner wasn't going out this late, I turned off the headlights and coasted into the driveway of the neighboring Tudor house.

I got out of the car, locked it, and stumbled up the street.

The wind stirring the leaves sounded like voices whispering around me. My footsteps echoed off the trees pressing in and surrounding the glowing Campbell house. The scent of caramel and popcorn reminded me I hadn't eaten for over twenty-four hours.

Devin was contained, but did he have allies? Should I march into the party and look for Aynslee?

Trust no one.

Ducking slightly and keeping the parked cars between the

well-lit house and myself, I aimed for the large rocks that I remembered marked the path through the grounds. I walked past the rocks twice before finally locating them. Under the trees, the track was almost invisible. I moved ahead slowly, feeling for the stone walkway with each step. Up ahead, the trail had tiny solar spotlights illuminating the trees and casting a dappled light on the gazebo to my right.

A soft cough came from the gazebo.

I froze.

A man muttered something, and a woman replied.

I remained stationary, still hidden by the dense foliage.

The murmured conversation continued along with shuffling sounds.

Licking my dry lips, I continued forward as quickly as I dared, listening for partygoers out for a late-night stroll. Finding the patio leading to Arless's office, I waited, hidden, to be sure it was empty. I doubted Aynslee would be in Arless's private office, but I could get into the house more easily, or at least more unnoticed. Light glowed through the closed French doors, and I could see no movement inside.

Creeping across the patio, I reached the multipaned doors. They were locked.

My shoulders slumped and eyes blurred. I wanted to just sit down and give in to a good old-fashioned meltdown. *Why can't anything be easy? Just once, God, couldn't You cut me some slack?*

God didn't answer. And the door remained locked.

Straightening, I pictured the interior layout. I knew of four entrances to the house. The garage door was the farthest from me. The front door was out. That left the patio where I'd had lunch the first day I'd stayed here.

Climbing up the path until I reached the corner of the house, I paused and visualized the next section of the trail. The window to the room I'd stayed in would be coming up on my left. The landscaping would give way to the patio. If I were very, very lucky, everyone would have moved into the den for late-night drinks.

My teeth chattered in the cold, damp air and my hand pounded with each beat of my heart. Maybe I could wait until morning and just boldly go to the Campbell house and ask for my daughter. *Ha. That's the pain and cold talking.*

What if Devin got out? Morning would be too late. How many people were dead because of that horrible man? My own life was almost forfeited, and Aynslee's fate would be unimaginable.

I moved forward, rounding the corner. Voices, laughter, and music greeted me.

My heart sank. Going slower as the foliage thinned near the patio, I halted by a large maple tree.

Skull-shaped, LED string lights dangled over the inebriated crowd. Witches, devils, ghosts, and superheroes, all wearing Venetian masks, clustered around propane patio heaters. A woman in a much-abbreviated nurse's outfit wobbled over to a man in a Grim Reaper costume, knocked against him, and sloshed his drink. Several characters broke into drunken laughter. Mrs. Fields, dressed like a maid and carrying a serving tray, poked through the crowd, making sure everyone's drinks were replenished. A white hankie poked from her sleeve, and she paused by the door to dab her eyes.

Blanche, dressed in a burgundy-and-gold Renaissance dress, joined a group of partygoers standing by the doors. A gangster handed her a folded check. She smiled, peeked at the amount, then kissed him on the cheek. He said something to her and she shrugged and shook her head. No sign of Aynslee, or at least someone Aynslee's size.

I'd forgotten this was more than a party. This was Arless's political fund-raiser. No wonder the alcohol flowed freely.

I'd never be able to sneak in unnoticed.

Turning, I started down the path to the street, but stopped outside the window to my old room. I'd opened it when I first arrived, then closed it without locking it. Maybe no one had checked.

Reaching over with my good hand, I gave the sash a tug.

It didn't budge.

"Saaay, missy, you mushh be Octavia."

I spun around.

A drunken cowboy tottered closer from the direction of the patio. His breath could have locked up a Breathalyzer.

"Yeah, sure. How'd you guess?" I sidled away from him.

"Your hands. Look like they clawed out of the ground. Great job, but . . ." He wagged a finger at me. "But you took off your mask. You're not schupposed to do that till midnight." He pulled off the black-and-red mask he wore and slipped it over my head, then rested his clammy hand on my shoulder.

I wanted to slap it off and run, but he could raise an alarm and bring attention to my presence. "Well now—"

"That's better." He let go of my shoulder and took my arm in a surprisingly tight grip. "Let's go join the party." He pulled me toward the patio.

CHAPTER THIRTY-NINE

I DUCKED MY HEAD AS WE APPROACHED THE raucous crowd, risking quick glances to see if anyone recognized me. I gathered a few curious looks, but most were making the most of the free booze. Still no Aynslee.

The cowboy let go of my arm long enough to grab up a drink on a nearby table. I used the moment to slide through the crowd to the door and into the house.

The living room had directional lighting behind spiky artificial plants, casting eerie, stippled light. I remained motionless, staring at each costumed body, searching for Aynslee's tiny frame. She wasn't here.

Pressing against the wall in the shadows, I sidled toward the hall, my leg muscles tightening, ready to bolt should anyone look my way.

Fake spiderwebs draped the plants and waved with the movement of air and people, and fat plastic spiders clung to a few of the larger webs.

A decayed ghoul with glowing eyes spewed fog from its

open mouth. Guests appeared to glide on legless bodies as they floated through the low-lying fog swirling around the floor. Boisterous conversations rose over the blaring sound system as the theme from *Ghost Busters* ended to be replaced by Michael Jackson's "Thriller."

Blanche drifted out of the side of the room, moving in my direction.

Shrinking farther into the shadows, I glanced from side to side, searching for a better hiding place. She was coming directly toward me but was looking over her shoulder. All she had to do was turn her head and she'd see me.

A heavyset man dressed in a Greek toga passed by, aiming toward the hall. Darting from my hiding spot, I stuck my arm into his and gave a quick squeeze.

He jerked his head and looked at me, then leered. "Why not? The bedrooms are this way."

Smiling back through gritted teeth, I used his body to shield me from the rest of the room. My skin crawled at the coarse, matted hair on his sweaty arm. I peeked around him, checking one last time for Aynslee.

A jolt raced through me.

Clay, dressed as Sherlock Holmes with a deerstalker hat and pipe, was talking with a lady dressed as Wonder Woman. Standing nearby in a semicircle were Wellington and Arless. The men leaned forward in intense conversation. Occasionally one of them would glance around.

Devin was free.

Where's Aynslee?

When we reached the hall, I raced away before Toga man had a chance to react.

"Oh, so that's how it's to be," he said. "Ready or not, here I come." He lumbered after me.

I limped as fast as I could to the short hallway leading to the stairs going down. I hadn't been to the lower floor and prayed that I wouldn't get lost.

The stairs emptied into a game room with foosball and pool tables. Which way? I needed help. A phone. Hallways led in both directions. I dashed left, dodged into the first room I came to, and locked the door. The lights were off. Leaning against the door, I waited until my eyes adjusted to the inky blackness. The light fragrance of vanilla perfumed the air.

Nothing changed. The room remained totally dark.

The doorknob rattled behind me. "Found ya! Okay, open up and see what I have for you."

Slinking about in the dark was ridiculous. He already knew where I was. I flipped on the light.

A bathroom. No windows, but a door on the left.

I hobbled over, glancing in the mirror as I passed.

A character from *Night of the Living Dead* stared back.

I started to scream but slapped my hand over my mouth to hold it in. Dirt coated my skin, broken only by tear streaks. The clothing was equally filthy. My short blonde hair stood out in brown, spiky disarray, and the red-and-black mask over my eyes added a garish, almost demonic look. My shattered hand was a purple, swollen claw, and the nails of my other hand ended in shredded, bloody tips.

Toga man had really bad taste in women.

Cautiously opening the door on the left, I peeked in. Arless's office. There had to be a phone in here. One call for help and I could leave by the patio doors. Aynslee could be on the other side of the house. The partner desk had a framed photo of Arless, Blanche, and a prominent political figure as well as a few files under a map of Kentucky. I stared at the small array. *Of course!* How stupid I was to have missed it!

Clay's office was a cheap imitation of Arless's setup.

Opening the top drawer, I found a tray holding neatly separated office items: paper clips, pencils, and rubber bands. More elusive memories floated to the surface.

I turned to the bookshelves but stopped short and stared at the wall. Professionally framed photographs covered almost every inch, many of them signed. Most were of Blanche, or Arless and Blanche, with A-list actors, politicians, even a former president. Some were formally posed, but many of them were casual: on what must be Arless's sailboat, skiing, in front of a private jet. A potpourri of the rich, powerful, and famous.

This was Devin's world.

When they find him, do you really think anyone is going to take the word of a broke forensic artist from Montana over the word of these people?

They might, if all the evidence isn't destroyed.

I tried to shrug off the weight that settled on my shoulders. I would never win a head-on confrontation. I could only slow him down. For now.

The bookshelves opened, revealing not a secret room as I'd believed, but the work area of the office: phone, fax machine, oversize copier, file cabinets, shipping supplies, and a worktable. Phone.

Walking forward, I snatched it up and turned.

Toga man blocked the exit.

CHAPTER FORTY

"WELL, WELL, WELL." HE SWAYED IN THE OPENING, reeking of alcohol and failed deodorant.

"You know I was just kidding." I licked my dry lips. "My . . . my husband's upstairs. I need to get back to him or he'll get nervous. He is very jealous and has a terrible temper."

"You're a tease. And you know what happens to a tease." He smirked.

I prepared to slam my foot into his crotch.

He moved faster than I believed possible for a man so big and drunk, wrapping his arms around me in a foul, sweaty embrace. My broken hand was caught between us and crushed against his chest.

The agony shot through me. I couldn't breathe. My vision narrowed as blackness rolled into my brain. My legs buckled.

He pinched my jaw and tilted it upward, licking his wet, rubbery lips.

I clenched my teeth. *My first kiss since my divorce is not going to be by a man in a dress.*

I slammed my knee up between his legs.

He let go with an *oof* and bent forward.

Bringing the palm of my hand upward, I smashed it under his chin. Blood appeared on his lips as he bit his tongue. He dropped to the floor and writhed.

I picked up the phone. I needed help, and it couldn't come from law enforcement. I only knew one phone number here. I dialed. A recording of Lindsay's voice, the Californian woman I'd met at the revival, came on.

"What are you doing?" Professor Wellington stood at the opening, looking between Toga man and me. He'd pulled on a *Phantom of the Opera* mask but otherwise was in street clothes.

Toga man groaned and cradled his injured parts as he continued to thrash on the floor.

A man in a doctor's coat and a woman in a mime outfit pushed in behind him. "Is this where all the action is?" the woman slurred.

Wellington glared at the drunk couple.

One chance. My daughter's life was at stake. I smiled at all of them, my jaw clenched. "Just let me finish this phone call. Yes, hi, Lindsay, this is Gwen. I just wanted you to buzz Blake for me. Tell him thanks for the comment on Aynslee's Scripture. No. No." The phone continued to record. "Just say I'm not very protected here." I hung up.

Wellington smiled without showing his teeth. "You must be here for your daughter. Let me take you to her."

The two partygoers staggered away.

I assessed the situation. Wellington was out of kicking distance and blocked the only exit from the room. Backing up, I collided with the printer. I risked taking my eyes off the man to search for a weapon. Nothing was nearby but a ream of paper.

When I looked back at Wellington, he had a smirk on his face. His gaze started at my spiky hair, then moved past my broken hand to the long skirt. He cautiously approached.

Keeping the table between us, I matched him step for step. He dodged left.

I dashed for the door. My sprained ankle slowed me too much.

Wellington grabbed my broken hand.

Liquid fire ran up my arm. I tried to scream. He yanked me close and whispered in my ear, "One sound out of you and your daughter's dead. Do you understand?"

Clamping down a scream from the pain, I nodded. Tears burned my cheeks.

Shifting his grip to my wrist, he grasped the waistband of my skirt with his other hand and propelled me forward. "Come with me."

My feet barely touched the ground as we headed to the patio doors. Letting go of my skirt, he reached out and turned the knob. Locked. He rattled it for a moment, then cursed.

Grabbing my clothing again, he turned and headed into the hall. *If he takes me upstairs, I can break free. Even if they're drunk, someone would help. Aynslee must be nearby.*

He hauled me up the stairs, yanking when I stumbled. Not stopping when we reached the living room, he plowed through the partygoers. Voices were louder, laughter more frantic, and "Highway to Hell" pounded from the sound system.

I sucked in a deep breath to scream.

He jerked me close and whispered, "If you yell or say one word, you'll never see your daughter again."

My body was freezing. The room swirled around me.

"How did you get out of the basement snake room, Devin?" I asked the professor.

He waved in Junior's direction. "A most accommodating deputy was performing his door-to-door search when he found me. He was shocked that you'd attacked me. And ruined my car. I said you might have gone nuts and would show up here. They're going to arrest you."

"I'll tell them the truth, Devin."

"Why are you calling me that name? Just another reason to think you're crazy."

We'd almost reached the patio when the music abruptly ceased and the lights came up. The guests on the patio headed inside in a steady stream of costumed bodies, forcing us backward into the room.

Arless, looking like Errol Flynn in a dashing Robin Hood outfit, called out, "It's midnight. Everyone, remove your masks!" The partygoers slowly took off their masks as Arless grinned, showing his perfect teeth. "Now I have an announcement." He put his arm out to Blanche, who'd glided up next to him. "I'll be stepping down from the state senate, and stepping up to the race for the White House." The revelers applauded wildly. He gazed around the room and waved. He spotted me. His eyes widened, mouth dropped, and face grew pale.

Blanche clapped while smiling at the room. She looked over at Arless and paused, then followed his stare. Her hand flew to her chest and her expression dropped. After a moment, she approached. "Oh, my dear, oh my," she whispered. "What happened to you? Wellington, take her to my car in the garage. She needs a hospital. Don't make a fuss. We don't want others to get upset and leave."

Wellington slid his arm around my waist and moved through the guests, who were now loading up on another round of drinks. None of them turned around as we passed. Whiffs of expensive perfume fought against late-night body odor and spilled drinks.

Someone, please notice me. Call the police. Help.

I spotted Junior by the window. I stared hard at him, willing him to look my way. He started to turn just as we reached the kitchen.

The catering staff was busily scrubbing down the already-immaculate surfaces. Disinfectant cleaner replaced the smell of fried food and spices. None looked up, even when Wellington dropped his Phantom mask on the counter. He forced me through to the garage beyond. The three parked cars blazed with showroom polish. Brassy fluorescent lights bounced off the stark white walls and illuminated every corner. I could easily see the entire room from the raised concrete platform. "Where's my daughter?"

"Ah, Aynslee's had quite the party. She enjoyed several Long Island iced teas. I told her they were a special, nonalcoholic recipe. The last one had a special addition to it. My own special blend of GHB."

"What! The date-rape drug?"

"Yes, and so tricky, especially mixed with alcohol. She's passed out in one of the bedrooms. Or by now, she could be—"

Wrenching free, I dashed down the three steps to the spotless garage floor and raced toward the door on the far side.

"Stop!"

Risking a glance over my shoulder, I froze.

Wellington had a pistol pointed at my head.

CHAPTER FORTY-ONE

THOUGH MY HEART POUNDED LIKE A DRUM, I turned to face him.

The kitchen door opened and Blanche and Arless poured onto the raised concrete area, looking like actors entering a stage, complete with costumes. Wellington slipped the pistol into his pocket.

I spun and raced for the garage door. Before I could reach it, Clay and Junior stepped in.

Backing away, I studied the assembled group. Blanche looked surprised; Arless, stunned; Clay, dazed; and Junior, confused.

I stared at each of their faces. The truth stared back at me. I'd been wrong.

My mind whirled, putting the new information together. It fit. It all fit. I turned to Junior. "Junior, arrest Professor Wellington as the Hillbilly Rapist and for the murders of Ina Jo Cummings, Trish Garlock, and Elijah and Ruby Adkins. He may be responsible for other murders as well."

Junior's head jerked back and eyes opened wide. He reached for his sidearm.

"That's ridiculous," Blanche said. "Dr. Wellington's a highly respected, tenured professor at the university. From the look of your injuries, you've probably hurt your head. You don't even make sense."

My face grew warm. "My head's fine. I suspect you'll find a lot of similar cases of rape and torture at or around that very university. Using date-rape drugs." I took a step toward Junior and Clay. I had to get Aynslee to a hospital.

"You're right, Blanche," Sheriff Reed said. "She does need to get help." He looked at me and said in a condescending tone, "Jason Morrow's dead, shot while trying to escape being arrested for the rapes and murder, and Trish was an accident. She fell. You were there. You found her body."

I shook my head violently. "No! Trish was murdered. She didn't have an accident on the way to the cabin. She arrived there just fine. Then Wellington killed her."

"Really, Gwen," Arless said. "Blanche is right. You must have a head injury. Why would you say something like that?"

"Wellington got careless." I slid my foot back another step. "Everyone headed to the cabin was given a map for how to get there. But on the first morning here, Trish told me Wellington grew up in Pikeville. He's also been driving around the countryside to do his research. He wouldn't have needed a map to get to the cabin, yet there was a map on the table—"

Wellington actually laughed. "That's it? Pretty thin evidence—"

I worked some spit into my mouth. "That's just the start. There's tons of evidence. Trish was going to give me a magazine article about the serpent handlers. You were out of the room, Wellington, when she said that. If Trish were killed before she arrived at the cabin, why was her article in the cabin, *under* the map Blanche gave her?" I looked at Junior.

Wellington leaped forward, flying over the three steps, and grabbed my arm before I could run. "I think you need to . . ." His gaze darted to the people on the platform, then to Clay and Junior. "Um, get to that doctor as soon as possible. Get in the car. I'll drive you."

I can't get in that car. I'll disappear and Aynslee will die. I ignored Wellington and continued to press Junior. "Arless suggested I stay at the cabin with my daughter, a place that Wellington had been using for his perverted attacks. Big oops. He'd just kidnapped his next victim, Ina Jo Cummings. He didn't have time to complete his ritual—"

Wellington grabbed my injured arm and pinched hard.

Pain shot up my arm. Tears sprang to my eyes, but I continued. "With us arriving, Wellington needed to get rid of her and hide the evidence of his work. So he killed her and threw her in the river. He returned to the cabin to clean up, but Trish appeared and caught him at it. He murdered Trish and made it look like an accident."

Wellington shifted his grip closer to my broken hand and squeezed again. "You're raving. You need medical attention."

The pain was so intense I could barely draw a breath. "Junior. It's up to you. Have your crime-scene technicians go over the Campbell cabin, especially the stain on the underside of the mattress," I gasped out. "Remember Locard's exchange principle. The transference of evidence occurs—"

I ran out of air.

"No one's buying this, Gwen," Wellington whispered in my ear. "Junior is incapable of doing anything useful. But you know what I'm capable of. And I have your daughter. Just wait—"

Adrenaline surged through my veins. "You'll also find," I continued in a louder voice, "a camera that has been hidden in the smoke alarm. I bet, with a subpoena, you'd find a collection of very interesting tapes in Wellington's possession."

Wellington squeezed harder.

The sheriff's gaze moved from me to Wellington. Beads of sweat stood out on his forehead and upper lip.

The pistol quivered in Junior's hand. He looked at Clay. "Dad?"

I spoke even faster to Junior. "Your dad loves you, but he was afraid *you* were the rapist. He has a DNA report under the tray in his desk. He's had the evidence of who gave twelve-year-old Mary Adkins poison since April, but he's been terrified of comparing your DNA because it would confirm who the killer was. So he did nothing. And more people died." I looked at Clay. "But that DNA won't match Junior."

Clay swiped at the sweat on his face and held out his hand toward Wellington. "Son, I'd appreciate it if you'd let go of Gwen and let me take her to the hospital."

"No." Wellington pulled the pistol from his pocket and aimed it at the sheriff. "First of all, I'm not your son. But speaking of sons, let me remind you you're in this mess up to your neck. You have political ambitions, which would be dashed by having a rapist son. He's a mental midget—"

"He's not." I had to keep the sheriff on my side, even though he'd made some foolish mistakes. "Junior has Asperger's syndrome. High-functioning autism. I finally recognized the—"

Wellington squeezed harder.

"You might want to shut up about my boy," Clay said. "Before I—"

"Before you what?" Wellington swung his pistol, now aiming it at Junior. "Both of you, move to the platform and drop your weapons."

Both men remained motionless.

"Or shall we talk about"—Wellington wiggled the gun—"how a backwoods, small-town sheriff can afford a Rolex Daytona watch, worth, what is it? Ten, fifteen thousand? And there's that gold cigarette lighter. You've been well paid to look the other way."

Clay stared at him. "They were gifts. I was going to be Arless's campaign manager."

"Really?" Wellington said. "Did Arless tell you that? Or were you led to believe that lie? Think about it. You failed at your own attempts at getting elected for anything but sheriff. Why would Arless hire you when, with his money, he could have anyone?"

"Clay, please, do the right thing." I reached out my good hand toward him. "Too many people are dead. Too much pain and suffering. It has to end."

"And end it will," Wellington whispered in my ear.

Clay, with Junior trailing, moved to the platform. Reluctantly, he pulled a snub-nosed .38 from his back holster and placed it on the concrete floor of the garage. He turned to Junior. "Put your gun down, son."

Junior's hands fluttered for a moment, then he unbuckled his service belt and set it on the platform next to his father's weapon.

"See?" Wellington whispered.

"What is going on here?" Arless asked.

"Blanche," Wellington said. "Pick up the guns."

Blanche scooped them up. The modern weapons looked incongruous with her Renaissance dress. "Now what are you going to do?" she asked Wellington.

"Take her someplace where she can get the help she needs."

"Good," Blanche said. "I have no idea what's going on, but we can sort this out in the morning. Darling"—she touched her husband's cheek—"please go back to our guests."

Arless shook his head.

Wellington dragged me toward the car and said under his breath, "I'm going to get rid of you. And your daughter."

My blood ran cold. Wellington once again gripped my arm. "Move."

I squeezed my eyes shut in pain. Once in that car, I would be dead. And Devin would win.

I jerked my arm as hard as I could, breaking free of the professor's grasp. The pain made me stagger for a moment. Sucking in air that smelled of gasoline, tires, and wax, I leaned against the car, then turned toward Arless. "You said it was time for the masks to come off. I agree. I think it's high time for Devin Maynard to unmask."

All the expressions around me looked confused. All but two.

"I know the truth, Devin." I looked straight at the killer.

"I have no idea what you're talking about," Arless said. "Oh, wait. Are you referring to the name in that old Bible?"

"I'm talking about your wife, Arless. Blanche Campbell, or should I say, Devin Maynard Campbell. The daughter of Grady Maynard. And a cold-blooded killer."

CHAPTER FORTY-TWO

ARLESS STIFFENED. "YOU ARE TALKING ABOUT my wife."

"Yes."

Blanche's eyes were black, stone-cold pools of fury. "Very theatrical, Gwen."

"Impossible," Clay snapped. "I grew up around here. Everyone would have recognized a looker like her the moment she returned to Pikeville, even married with a different name."

"But she wasn't a 'looker,' as you so tactfully put it, Clay. Twenty years ago she would have left town as a holiness woman, with long hair, no makeup, and old-fashioned, frumpy clothes. No one would have looked twice at her. I'm guessing, after viewing her dad, that she had a nose job." I looked at Blanche. "How long did you save up for that, I wonder."

Blanche gripped the gun tighter.

"Elocution lessons, new hair, makeup, and voilà! A new woman. But your ears, Blanche. I noticed your ears at dinner the first night I was here. One ear smaller than the other and ever so slightly deformed. I figured you had grade one microtia. In a very small percentage of people, that malformation can be inherited. When I saw your dad in that rock grave where you shoved him all those many years ago, he was well preserved. Every feature: nose, lips, and ears. He had grade three microtia. I put it all together—"

"I don't know what's going on here." Arless looked from one person to the other. "But I think it's gone on long enough. Blanche, dear, give the sheriff back his guns. Wellington, I have no idea what Gwen is talking about, but I'm going to look into it. Someone needs to get Gwen to a doctor—"

"Arless, listen to me." I spoke fast, not knowing how long I had to make my case. "Blanche hated her father, hated his church, and hated the practice of snake handling. I'd bet her early life was one of being different, ostracized by her classmates."

Air hissed between Blanche's clenched teeth.

"Ridiculous." Arless made a dismissive wave with his hand. "She's always been beautiful and popular."

"I bet she's the one who pressed you to increase the punishment for serpent handling in Kentucky."

Arless didn't answer, but his eyebrows rose.

"She threw her own father into a cave to die, but before he did, he wrote a message. I have that note. I used it as bait to hopefully identify Grady's killer. I'd bet when Wellington told you I was at the cabin and what I had, you sent him up there to kill me."

Blanche's mask slipped further. "Shut up, Gwen. You're delusional."

Arless looked at his wife and frowned. "Don't be upset, dear. Gwen is obviously ill."

"I marked his grave," I said.

"Wellington, drive her to the hospital," Blanche said through tight lips. "Clay, Junior, please rejoin the party."

Clay stared at her, his hands forming fists.

That reminded me of something. "Clay, the body you found in the river so many years ago, the unidentified one . . ."

He grew still.

"It was a woman, wasn't it? And her face was mutilated. I'd bet her fingerprints were missing as well. I'm sure if you did a little background checking, you'd find out you'd had the real Blanche all along."

Clay didn't say a word. He jerked his head at Junior, and both men left through the kitchen door.

My shoulders slumped. *Please don't leave me with the killers.* I'd have to convince Arless.

"Hear me out, Arless." I looked at the man and spoke even faster. "After Blanche murdered her father, she re-created herself, saying her parents died in a car crash."

"How dare you bring up that horrible event," Arless said. "I saw the newspapers."

"With no photos, and I'd bet Blanche was the one who showed you."

"No!" Arless shook his head violently, as if he could stop my words.

"Instead, she killed a young woman, destroyed her face, and threw her body in the river. She now wasn't some poor, hillbilly daughter of a snake handler. She was the cultural beauty looking for the right vehicle to propel her to her ambitious goals. That was you, Arless."

"Please go back inside to the guests, darling." Her smile

didn't reach her eyes. "They all should be properly lubricated with alcohol by now. Sometimes they forget they've already donated to your campaign and they'll write a second check."

Arless blinked at her. "It isn't true. It can't be. I won't accept it." He fumbled for the doorknob to the kitchen.

Wellington stepped closer to me. I pushed off the car and moved away, trying to put the car between us. "Arless, wait!"

Arless turned his head and looked at me.

"About eight to ten months ago, did Blanche start acting strange? Phone calls coming in with no one on the line when you answered? Trips without good reason?"

Arless dropped his hand and turned slightly.

"Didn't you wonder why she invited her old buddy, Professor Wellington, to visit out of the blue? An instructor she'd never mentioned before?" The smell of my sweat, along with horse, dirt, and blood, made me ill, but I pressed on. "He arrived six months ago and took over. Suddenly there are bodies, rapes, 'accidents.' I'd bet Blanche just as suddenly had need of more money for pressing cultural issues—"

"The orphanage in Haiti." Arless now leaned against the wall.

"And didn't anyone wonder how poor women could just up and move on? That takes money. Money she *claimed* was going to that orphanage. Did you ever actually go there and see it?"

"Photos," Arless said faintly.

"Probably downloaded off the Internet. Wellington saw the glamorous Blanche on, what, television? Newspapers? In spite of the changes in her appearance, the professor, growing up here in Pikeville, recognized her—" A thought popped into my brain. "Of course." I glanced at Blanche. "Your father, Grady, wrote that he 'sent the boy.' Tom Wellington was your boyfriend, wasn't he, Blanche?"

A vein throbbed in Blanche's temple.

"Grady sent Wellington away, told you never to see him again. He was an agnostic or atheist, right? Hardly the right choice of marriage material for a devout girl like you. So you killed your father in anger and revenge. Or shame."

Arless glared at Wellington. "If you've touched my wife—"

"Enough of this fantasy." Wellington moved toward me again. I dodged around the car.

"No!" Arless shouted. Wellington stopped. Arless stepped forward and spoke with authority. "Go on, Gwen."

"So Devin and Wellington struck a deal. Wellington wouldn't give Devin's past away. And in return, he could prey upon the young women in Pikeville, girls he met when Devin had her open houses or visited the shelters for the less fortunate in the community. I'd bet that event started six months ago."

Arless's steely gaze answered me.

"In return, Blanche would fund the exit route for the family to leave town, just so not too many bodies of dead women started showing up. And a large percent of rape victims don't even report the crime. But she extracted one extra benefit from Wellington. He'd help her get rid of the embarrassing, and potentially revealing, members of the snake-handling church. The perfect relationship. You enlisted the help of Jason Morrow, until he realized what he was doing and refused."

Arless looked at his wife. Blanche put her hand to her chest and stepped backward. "It's true?" he asked. "All of it?"

I wanted to pump my arms and cheer, but I was afraid to call attention to myself. All eyes were on Blanche. The only sound was the distant pounding of music from the party still going on in the house.

"Not so fast, my darling." Blanche stepped closer to him. "You're in this thing deeper than I am. Who do you think signed the checks to send those families out of town? Who put up the reward for Gwen to do the drawings that would have identified the snake handlers? Who do you think ordered that lovely, and terribly expensive, watch your buddy Clay wears? And"—she moved closer still—"whose blue-and-white sailing rope do you think was used to strangle that woman? Only your fingerprints will be found on the box the rope came in."

Arless's face drained of color. "You wouldn't—"

"Try me. You told me once"—Blanche pulled stiff lips back over her teeth in a parody of a smile—"that you'd sell your soul to reach your goal. Well, darling, you're almost there. You're on your way up. The next stop is the White House."

Arless seemed frozen, staring at his wife.

"You think you're the only politician with a closetful of skeletons?" Blanche asked. "Only in your case, they're real bodies."

Wellington snorted.

Blanche reached around Arless and took hold of the doorknob. "Now, be a dear and return to the party. Tom and I have work to do." She pushed open the kitchen door. "Oh, and turn up the music." "Superstition" boomed from the speakers inside, and a hubbub of voices and laughter echoed off the walls.

Arless's shoulders slumped. Woodenly he left the garage. Blanche shut the door behind him. A moment later, the pounding music grew louder.

I was alone. With Blanche and Wellington.

CHAPTER FORTY-THREE

I STARED AT THE PISTOL BLANCHE HELD. IF I died, well, with cancer I was going to die anyway. But I wasn't giving up on my daughter's life. Every moment without medical help pushed her closer to death, and the seconds were ticking away.

My call for help had failed. So now it was up to me.

Blanche raised the pistol she'd collected from Clay. I didn't wait to see where she aimed it. I dove to the floor, attempting to protect my broken hand by curling around it. The gunshot resounded in the enclosed space. The bullet grazed my hip, burning a line across my skin.

My pulse raced. I flattened out and rolled under the car.

"Shall I just shoot her?" Wellington asked. I could see his dirty shoes from my hiding position. The underside of the car was inches from my head. Frantically I raced through escape possibilities. If I used the element of surprise—

"Run over her," Blanche said. "Then dump both their bodies."

"Open the garage door."

The car could easily snag my generous clothing if he backed up, dragging me to death.

Wellington's feet approached, then disappeared as he got in. The undercarriage dipped with his weight. He started the car and revved the engine. I wanted to cover my ears from the assault of noise.

Time crawled. Sweat beaded on my face. The stench of gasoline and fumes burned my nose. Tensing my muscles, I strained to hear the sound of the garage door. The steadily revving engine overwhelmed all other sounds. *Please, Lord, don't let me get run over or dragged.* Only the cool air striking my exposed ankles let me know the garage door was opening. At a slight change of vibration, I shot out from under the car.

It sped backward.

Ignoring the ache of my ankle and throbbing hand, I leaped to my feet.

Spittle gathered at the corners of Blanche's lips. Her eyes were glittering slits and her nostrils flared. She raised the pistol and took aim at me, her hands shaking in fury.

Please, Lord. I wanted to close my eyes. I couldn't.

She glared past me. Her eyes widened and face paled. She lowered the gun.

I risked a glance out the open garage door. Wellington had stepped from the car and was facing the crowd. Most of the worshipers from the revival gathered in a semicircle around him. They were taking pictures and movies with their phones. As Wellington moved backward, they followed, forcing him into the garage. Blake, front and center, looked as if he'd personally strangle the other man. Lindsay, on Blake's left, spotted me and waved her phone.

The only local number I could remember: an area code and name. I'd hoped she'd get the message to Blake and he'd understand I needed, as the Scripture said, a cloud of witnesses.

Something changed. It took me a moment to figure out what. The throbbing music from the house had stopped. The door to the kitchen burst open and partygoers flooded the raised concrete platform. Costumed cowboys, superheroes, witches, and historic figures flowed out of the house, down the stairs, and into the garage. A drunken woman in a poodle skirt, being held upright by an equally drunken sailor, burst into laughter when she spotted the gun in Blanche's hand. Her laugh slowed, then stopped. She looked at me, then out the door at the gathered members of the church.

One by one, the party guests' loud talking and laughter ceased as they caught sight of the long dresses and simple garb of the holiness people, then the pistol-wielding Blanche.

The last three to enter the garage were Arless, Clay, and Junior.

I faced Devin. "You're finished, Blanche." I waved at all the people. "This time there are just too many witnesses. You can no longer kill everyone who might know who you were."

Blanche opened her eyes wide. "That's not why at all. We tried to make the snake handlers go away. But they wouldn't leave."

All the attention was focused on Blanche.

"They were an embarrassment."

Slight movement from my periphery caught my attention. Wellington had slipped sideways, toward the edge of the crowd.

"We had to make a point," Blanche continued in a chillingly normal voice. "Arless was on his way to the White House.

313

We couldn't have such a backward group of people in our state. What would people think?"

My mouth dropped.

Wellington moved again. This time Blanche saw him. "Oh no, darling, this time you're not leaving me." She raised the pistol and pulled the trigger. Wellington, a surprised look on his face, dropped to the concrete floor.

All the partygoers in the garage froze. Most of the holiness women ducked away from the garage opening, while several of the men grabbed Wellington and pulled him out of sight.

Blanche aimed the pistol at me.

Sweat slid down my back. "You're lying to yourself, Devin."

"Don't call me that!"

"Why not? That's your name. Your pedigree. Your background. Nothing you did changed that. No one you killed affected your DNA."

Blanche's attention was focused totally on me. Her finger tightened on the trigger.

Junior moved closer to her.

I gauged the distance between them. Too far. Too far. "You need to get rid of Devin once and for all." I held my breath.

Blanche blinked.

Junior lunged for her weapon. They spun, twisted, then fell off the concrete platform, with Junior on the bottom. He let out a loud *umph*.

The gun went off.

Someone screamed. Clay leaped off the platform at the prone pair. Kneeling beside them, he gently rolled Blanche off his son. The front of her gown was bloodstained. Her sightless eyes stared at the ceiling.

Junior sat up, trying to regain the air that had been knocked out of him.

Arless, his face the color of parchment, glanced at his wife, then he panned the faces in the room. Without a word, he left, closing the door quietly behind him.

The only sound was the click and whirl of digital cameras and phones recording the scene.

My legs started to buckle. Leaning against the nearest car, I yelled, "My daughter's been given GHB and alcohol. She's in a guest room. Please find her. She needs to get to a hospital."

Several of the holiness men and two of the partygoers raced into the house.

Before the blackness completely filled my brain and my legs gave way, a strong arm slipped around my waist and I was lifted up. "*Now* can I drive you to the hospital?" Blake whispered before he kissed my cheek.

CHAPTER FORTY-FOUR

I OPENED MY EYES. THE ROOM LOOKED, SOUNDED, and smelled familiar. An infusion pump above my head *click-click-click*ed away and cool, antiseptic-smelling air wheezed from a wall vent. In a moment, the memory nudged my consciousness. I was in Shelby Lee's room, or one like it, at . . . Pikeville Community Hospital.

In a rush, the rest of my memories returned. *Aynslee.*

A series of chirps and pings came from my right.

Turning my head, I peered through the bed railing. Aynslee lay hooked to an array of devices in the bed next to me. She was partially upright, cell phone in hand, thumbs flying. Beyond her, late-afternoon amber sunlight spilled between the blinds on the window.

From the open door to the room came a creak of turning wheels, squeak of shoes, and murmuring of voices. Someone gently snored.

I pushed up enough to see a sleeping Blake sprawled in a chair at the foot of the bed.

"The nurses told me he's been here all day," Aynslee whispered.

"How do you feel?" I asked her.

"Like I've been run over by a cement truck."

I winced at the expression as more memories of the previous night flooded back. Blanche, lying dead on the floor of her garage. Aynslee's almost-lifeless body next to me racing to the hospital in Blake's truck. The emergency room where a detective took down my babbling account of the events.

A nurse marched in. "Good. You're awake. We have you scheduled for X-rays on that hand." She fiddled with the IV line threaded into my wrist.

Blake opened his eyes and smiled at me.

The stupid heart monitor beside me gave away my thoughts.

He stood and moved closer.

"You, go." The nurse shooed him away.

I contemplated throwing something at her head. Before I could figure out a weapon, an orderly arrived with a wheelchair. "Ready?" he asked the nurse. For the next several hours I spent quality time in that wheelchair, gliding from hallways to X-rays, then on to various tests devised in the Middle Ages by medieval monks.

When I was finally wheeled back to my room, night had fallen and Blake was gone. The room had sprouted flowers ranging from exquisite bouquets to plastic-wrapped grocery store bundles. Lindsay and the woman who'd first spoken to me at the revival were talking to Aynslee.

"Lindsay, thank you." I gave her hand a squeeze as I was wheeled past. "You saved my daughter's life. And mine."

The orderly helped me into bed and plugged me back into the infusion pump.

"What did you say when you called her?" Aynslee held up her phone. "Mattie wants to know."

"I told her to buzz Blake, that is, use the phone tree." I straightened the covers and tugged at the ugly hospital gown. "I mentioned the verse from Hebrews that tells us 'since we are surrounded by so great a cloud of witnesses.' I finished by mentioning not being protected, which told him I was with people he said were 'not the protectors I thought.'"

Aynslee texted away, grinning.

"You know the weird thing?" Lindsay said to me. "I didn't get it. I just called Blake and said you were in trouble. He told me to call everybody and meet him at the Campbells' house. He'd figured out that only someone with a lot of money or clout could be behind all this. But he thought it was Arless."

"He was on my short list of suspects."

"Actually," Lindsay said, "I came by to give you the latest news. The sheriff's department—"

"What!" I said.

"Minus Clay, who's under investigation for obstruction of justice," she amended, "followed your directions and found Grady's body. It's been recovered and the church will be having a memorial for him along with Elijah and Ruby tomorrow at four o'clock."

"How did you find out about Grady's body?" I asked.

"My cousin, the one I was visiting, is with search and rescue. She told me about the cave." She cleared her throat. "She also said they saw a bra sitting on a ledge below the cave. She said it was too risky to try to recover . . ."

"So Thelma and Louise are gone for good." I bit my lip. "They didn't, by any chance, um, recover some underwear . . . ?"

"No." Lindsay raised her eyebrows at me.

"Good."

Blake entered the room pushing a wheelchair with one hand and an IV pole with the other. Sarah sat bundled in a white blanket. She grinned and waved when she saw my daughter.

A short, tawny-skinned, black-haired doctor strolled in. The name badge said Dr. Kumar. He paused when he saw all the visitors. "If you could all please step outside for a moment?"

The room emptied. He moved between my bed and Aynslee's. "Good news for both of you. I want to keep you one more night, but if all goes well, I'll release you tomorrow. Gwen"—he nodded at my bandaged left hand—"you have three fractures and I've stabilized the bones with that splint. You'll need to have it looked at when you return to Montana. I've been in touch with your doctor and there are a few more tests I want to review."

"Which doctor?" I asked.

"Dr. West."

My oncologist. My stomach twisted.

"Young lady." He turned to Aynslee. "You were very, very lucky. Another few minutes and . . . well, like I said, you were lucky." He patted her foot and left.

Blake returned, this time without Sarah. "She was getting tired, but she wanted to say hi to Aynslee."

"What's going to happen to her?" I asked.

"She's my niece. I'll take care of her."

Before I could respond, Arless stepped in.

I stiffened.

Blake moved close to the bed. "What do you want, Arless?"

Arless hesitated, then placed an envelope on the tray next

319

to my bed. "I can't apologize enough for all the damage Blanche did. I would like to ask you to forgive me and take this as your earned fee."

"I forgive you, Arless." I waved at the envelope. "You don't need to do that."

"Yes, I do." He just as quickly turned and left.

I reached for the envelope to tear it up, but Blake caught my hand. "Don't. You did earn it. And you might just need some money. None of your clothes, art supplies, identification, or possessions have shown up."

"Just Thelma and Louise."

"What?"

"Nothing." Thinking about cancer treatments or my daughter's education, I slowly nodded.

Blake continued to hold my hand until I fell asleep.

The next morning Aynslee was already dressed by the time I woke up. "There's stuff for you on that chair," she said.

"Have you seen—"

"Nope. Blake hasn't shown up."

I had to wait until the nurse arrived and removed my IV line before I could check out the white bag Aynslee had indicated. Inside were jeans, a sweater, slip-on shoes, and underclothes along with a note from Lindsay. *Thought you could use these.*

I tried not to feel disappointed it wasn't from Blake. With Aynslee's help, I got dressed.

A nurse showed up with a mess of paperwork requiring signatures, scrawled prescriptions, and last-minute instructions. I thought about the bill for our treatment. *Oh, Lord, how will*

I ever pay for this too? After she left, I gathered up the cards from the flowers and peeked at the envelope Arless left the day before.

My legs became rubber. I sat on the bed.

"What?" Aynslee asked.

I couldn't answer. I just looked at her. Arless had given me enough money for Aynslee's college. Or my cancer treatment. Or to let me finish the house.

When my mouth worked again, I cleared my throat. "Shall we go?"

Before I could get out of my room, an orderly with a wheelchair appeared and insisted I sit in it. He pushed me onto the elevator and out the main doors.

I felt like an idiot, so I gave queenly waves to arriving visitors until we reached the street. I tried not to think about the check, focusing on what I'd need to do before I could get home to Montana. I could get Beth to express me my passport so I had some identification, book a flight—

"Mom!" Aynslee pulled on my arm.

I glanced over to the car parked on the curb. Blake was standing beside an open door. "Need a ride?" He caught my swift glance into the car. "They're not releasing Sarah until tomorrow."

My pulse raced. "Sure." He helped me out of the wheelchair and into the passenger's seat, then rounded the car and slid into the driver's side.

He placed a cell phone in my lap. "I told you I'd get you a new one."

"Oh, wow!" Aynslee said over my shoulder. "The latest iPhone. Just out—I mean, *just* out."

"Oh, Blake, I don't even know how to turn this thing on."

Aynslee reached over and snatched it up. "Like this. But it needs a password to work." She handed it back.

I glanced at Blake. He grinned at me. I typed N-e-a-n-d-e-r-t-h-a-l. A new screen came up with a bewildering array of icons. "And, um, how do I find the list of contacts?"

Blake took the cell and tapped the screen, then handed it back to me.

His number was the only one listed.

Heat rose up my neck and I kept my head down to hide the blush.

The phone vibrated in my hand and the name Kumar came up on the screen.

I jerked. "Who gave him this number?"

"I did. The hospital wanted a contact number."

The phone vibrated again. I answered. "Gwen Marcey."

"Ah, Gwen, good. I got hold of you. I mentioned your Dr. West wanted me to run a few more tests."

I tried to get some spit into my mouth.

"He said I should call you."

"Couldn't this wait until I—"

"I don't think so. Your tests came back clear."

"What does that mean?"

"According to Dr. West, every indication showed your cancer had returned. Now"—he cleared his throat—"I went over everything with your oncologist several times. There's no sign of anything out of the ordinary. We need to be cautious and retest in a month. It could be a cycle, or . . ."

"Or a miracle."

He was silent for a moment. "Or a miracle."

I hung up and laid my hand over the phone. I remembered

my thought when viewing Shelby Lee, the first victim. *Oh, Lord, we need to catch this guy.* I could still feel the hands of the holiness people on my back. *Touch her, Lord.* I thought of my petition for an escape from the cave. My whispered hope that the racing horse wouldn't fall, the prayer to walk among the snakes to rescue Sarah, my plea not to get dragged to death or shot by Blanche.

I looked down, my good hand folded over my bandaged one, and smiled. *You made Your point, Lord. Thank You.*

LOOKING FOR YOUR NEXT GREAT NOVEL?

Romantic Times *gives* A Cry from the Dust *four stars and says, ". . . this is an excellent book that is sure to put Carrie Stuart Parks on readers' radars."*

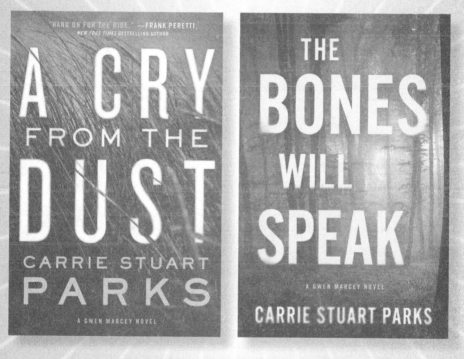

PORTRAIT OF VENGEANCE
— COMING AUGUST 2017!

DISCUSSION QUESTIONS

1. Review Mark 16:17–18. Serpent handlers point to this passage as a sign that they are followers of Christ. Many have the words *signs following* in the name of their church. What do you think about this?

2. Kentucky is the only state in the Union that specifically mentioned religion when they made it illegal to handle snakes. Contrast that with the First and Fourteenth Amendments that prohibit laws created to curtail the free exercise of religion.

3. Gwen struggles with her prayer life throughout this book, reasoning that God, who knows everything, should already know what she will pray for. Reflect on this.

4. Gwen is diagnosed as having cancer again in the beginning of the book, yet is free of the disease at the end. Do any other miracles occur in this story? Do you know someone who has had a miraculous recovery?

5. Aynslee got baptized in the mountains. Gwen wanted to talk with her afterward, but couldn't. What do you think Gwen might have said? What would you have said?

6. Though Gwen thinks of herself as open-minded and fair, she judges Elijah, Ruby, the serpent handlers, and Blake. What does she think of them before knowing more about them? What changed her mind?

7. When Gwen can't find a way out of the cave, she becomes angry, then bargains, then is depressed before finding a solution to her imprisonment. Discuss this.

8. Gwen goes through several changes (character arcs) during the book. What are they and how did she change?

ACKNOWLEDGMENTS

ONCE AGAIN A VARIETY OF FOLKS, BOTH KNOW-ingly and unknowingly, helped me with this book. I'll start with my dear husband of twenty-seven years, Rick, who brought me the idea of looking at the serpent handlers as a possible story line. Sssssssuper idea! A HUGE thank-you to Barbara West (Bobbi), from the Kentucky State Police, who suggested we come to Pikeville, then shared the great history and the beauty of fall in the Eastern Kentucky Appalachian Mountains. To Paul Glodfelter, the author of the play *Sleep in Safety, the story of Octavia Hatcher*, and to the members of the very talented cast, thank you for your inspiration.

To Betty Tackett of Dreamz Stables, thank you for inspiring me with your steep mountain trail ride on your Tennessee Walkers. I was transported back to my teen years of riding on our ranch in Idaho.

My husband, Rick, Bobbi, and I researched the serpent handlers by attending the Apostolic House of Prayer in Lord Jesus' Name, in Bug Hurley Hollow in Jolo, West Virginia. We found the congregation to be warm and caring, and Reverend

Tommy Addair to be most helpful. The five-foot rattler they pulled out to show us, however, still gives me the heebie-jeebies.

Colleen Coble, it was such fun to have our characters meet. I know Gwen loved to visit Folly Shoals and meet Mallory in your suspenseful novel *Mermaid Moon*.

I want to thank my forensic art students for the caring attention to even the smallest detail of the life and times of Gwen Marcey. In this spirit of thanking everyone, I want thank Carrie Doss for suggesting adding peas to Gwen's famous tuna noodle casserole. And a special thanks to Lindsay Moore for suggesting a beautiful, dimple-cheeked, biracial character. Thanks to Kari Seibel and Ernest Oropeza for loaning me their names and suggestions on how to write the police report. To Jason Tapp, my favorite snake expert, thank you for (shudder) snake suggestions. To Trish Hastings and Michelle Garlock, thank you for lending me your names and letting me kill you.

Olivia Garlock, you darling young lady, thank you for sharing your fourteen-year-old perspective on how to annoy your mom. Without you, I would never have had the much-needed, digitally obsessed, *whatever*, eye-rolling charm of Aynslee.

To the beta readers, thank you for all your help in developing this story. I appreciate you taking the time from your busy lives to suggest the holes in the plot.

Frank Peretti, once again you've proved why you were named the dean of Christian fiction. You saw in a heartbeat what was wrong with the story and what would make it better. I'm forever grateful to you and your lovely bride, Barb. Dinner soon? No zucchini.

Finally to my Lord and Savior, Jesus Christ, in whom all things are possible.

ABOUT THE AUTHOR

ANDREA KRAMER, KRAMER
PHOTOGRAPHY

CARRIE STUART PARKS IS AN award-winning fine artist and internationally known forensic artist. She teaches forensic art courses to law enforcement professionals and is the author/illustrator of numerous books on drawing. Carrie began to write fiction while battling breast cancer and was mentored by *New York Times* bestselling author Frank Peretti. Now in remission, she continues to encourage other women struggling with cancer.

Visit her website at www.carriestuartparks.com
Facebook: CarrieStuartParksAuthor
Twitter: @CarrieParks